PRAISE FOR

The Haunting of Alejandra

"V. Castro has written the retelling of La Llorona I've been waiting to read my whole life. *The Haunting of Alejandra* is deeply
rooted in culture and beautifully explores diaspora and generational trauma through the lens of the supernatural horror
genre."

—ZORAIDA CÓRDOVA, author of *The Inheritance of Orquídea Divina*

"Wonderfully heartfelt, relentlessly dark, and superbly written,
The Haunting of Alejandra is folklore-infused horror that goes
deep into the roots of La Llorona while telling a story of
motherhood, fragmented identity, and autonomy. V. Castro is
one of the most exciting voices in contemporary fiction, and
this is her best outing yet. Don't miss it."

—GABINO IGLESIAS, author of *The Devil Takes You Home*

"V. Castro charts a terrifying legacy of tears with *The Haunting of Alejandra,* an empathic epic that maps out the birth of a curse and tethers itself to the very ancestry of its tragic protagonist."

—CLAY MCLEOD CHAPMAN, author of *Ghost Eaters*

"A powerful story about motherhood, trauma, love, and the ways that myths can and should be rewritten . . . If you're a horror fan and you haven't picked up V. Castro, you *need* to fix that."

—SARAH LANGAN, author of *Good Neighbors*

"Sometimes being a woman can be *hell*. In V. Castro's dark, heroic tale, a woman draws on her familial roots to save herself and her children—by facing down a soul-devouring demon."

—ALMA KATSU, author of *The Fervor*

"Using the Mexican folklore of La Llorona as a frame and expertly updating it for a modern audience, Castro writes a story about generational trauma, colonization, systemic oppression, and the horror at the heart of motherhood. Utterly terrifying and wholly immersive, this novel will wow readers with its confident and unflinching tale of a woman reclaiming her power."

—*Library Journal* (starred review)

"Castro returns to her sweet spot—layering folkloric monsters onto private trauma—for this generational ghost story. . . . At a deeper level, Castro's tale of a woman both asking for help and taking possession of her own spirit delivers cheerworthy moments of empowerment. . . . A surprisingly moving, piercingly effective parable about exorcisms of all sorts of demons."

—*Kirkus Reviews*

"The fierce imagination of V. Castro has given us recent genre successes like *Queen of the Cicadas* and *Out of Aztlan*. Now, with her next novel, Castro turns her storytelling powers on the legend of La Llorona. . . . Castro is one of the most exciting genre authors on the scene right now, and this might be her most powerful book yet."

—*Paste Magazine*, "The Most Anticipated Horror Novels of 2023"

"V. Castro's *The Haunting of Alejandra* isn't your typical horror novel. In addition to the rich Mexican folklore laced throughout, it also dives into what it means to be a multi-hyphenate woman: a mother, a wife, and a daughter."

—*People en Español*

"V. Castro's heroine is haunted by the spirit of La Llorona—or, at least, an ancient evil that has found a way to embody a folk legend. She must go to a curandera and process her personal and generational trauma before she can even hope to be free of the demon possessing her, in what also functions as a perfect metaphor for clearing the fog of depression and seeing the societal structures and history that contribute to our present-day malaise."

—*CrimeReads,* "The Most Anticipated Crime Fiction of 2023"

"Speaking of Goddesses, Castro is the goddess of Indigenous Mexican horror."

—*Literary Hub*

"Provocative, haunting, and packed with secrets."

—*Electric Literature*

By V. Castro

The Haunting of Alejandra

Mestiza Blood

Queen of the Cicadas

Goddess of Filth

Hairspray and Switchblades

THE
Haunting
of Alejandra

THE
Haunting
of Alejandra

A NOVEL BY

V. CASTRO

DEL
REY

New York

2024 Del Rey Trade Paperback Edition

Copyright © 2023 by Violet de Neef
Excerpt from *Immortal Pleasures* by V. Castro copyright © 2024 by Violet de Neef

Published in the United States by Del Rey, an imprint of Random House, a division of Penguin Random House LLC, New York.

DEL REY and the CIRCLE colophon are registered trademarks of Penguin Random House LLC.

Originally published in hardcover in the United States by Del Rey, an imprint of Random House, a division of Penguin Random House LLC, in 2023.

This book contains an excerpt from the forthcoming book *Immortal Pleasures* by V. Castro. This excerpt has been set for this edition only and may not reflect the final content of the forthcoming edition.

LIBRARY OF CONGRESS CATALOGING-IN-PUBLICATION DATA
Names: Castro, V., author.
Title: The haunting of Alejandra: a novel / by V. Castro.
Description: First edition. | New York: Del Rey, [2023]
Identifiers: LCCN 2022038895 | ISBN 9780593499719 (paperback; acid- free paper) | ISBN 9780593499702 (ebk)
Subjects: LCSH: Llorona (Legendary character)—Fiction. | LCGFT: Horror fiction. | Novels.
Classification: LCC PS3603.A8885 H38 2023 | DDC 813/.6—dc23/ eng/20220829
LC record available at https://lccn.loc.gov/2022038895

Printed in the United States of America on acid-free paper

randomhousebooks.com

2 4 6 8 9 7 5 3 1

Book design by Debbie Glasserman

Dedicated to my beautiful children
and all the women in my family
who came before me.
Thank you for your love.

THE
Haunting
of Alejandra

We must listen to the women who came before us. We change the future by unloading the sorrow of the past. We sever the cord of generational curses. Some cords are meant to shrivel to blackened dead flesh. They are our blood, but we are not them. We do not have to accept it. None of it.

—FLOR CASTILLO, SOLDADERA AND MOTHER, 1919

Alejandra
Philadelphia—2019

Alejandra sat beneath the square showerhead in their newly refurbished bathroom. Her feet touched the glass, and her head leaned against the tiled wall. The bathroom was the only place in the house where she could lock the door.

She felt numb as she imagined her mind and body crumbling, her every cell fragile as limestone. The image came to her of a skull, like the ones from centuries ago at the bottom of cenotes in Mexico. For the last four years, she had been that skull.

The doorknob jiggled.

"Mom, Mom, hurry up," a small voice called for her over and over.

Just five minutes. One minute.

Please.

One second alone to breathe?

She looked toward the door. Her body trembled with the

overwhelming desire to shrink to the size of the blood clots trailing down her legs.

Her period arrived like clockwork every month—the only thing she could predict after her tubal ligation. No more children. Never again.

She already had three children. Each birth had left an open wound where each of those pieces of flesh had been hacked off from her.

Since then, Alejandra's inner world had felt like the scary part of death: They say nothing exists after the brain short-circuits to darkness and the heart squeezes out its last bloody tears. And that was her. For years she abandoned herself to be a willing sacrifice to please everyone around her, and now nothing existed within her anymore. Even her own hand was not a hand at all, but a blade she used to carve her heart for anyone who asked her for it.

Beyond the beaded veil of water on glass, a white form appeared in front of the towel rack.

Alejandra didn't have her glasses or contact lenses on. It was likely just steam. Or was it her towel? She could have sworn she'd hung it on the hook behind the door. She glanced in that direction. The towel was there. She turned back to the rack, her neck popping from the quick movement.

The form lingered.

What could have been a towel now appeared to be a torn dress. It looked almost like a white mantilla. Her poor vision moved in and out of focus.

From the center of the silhouette rasped a voice so minute it might have come from her own mind.

"You want to end it. Let me help you."

Alejandra whispered back with the sensation of hot water burning her throat, choking her: "No."

The steam billowed with the water. It reminded her of the day she'd tried on wedding dresses.

A loud bang on the door made her head jerk and legs tense as they folded into her body. "Alejandra, it's dinnertime. Are you coming down to cook? The kids are hungry."

Her eyes broke from the amorphous figure to the door then back again.

The figure was gone.

"Give me a minute," she called out as best she could through her tearful confusion.

"All right, but you've been in there over twenty minutes."

Matthew's voice brought her back to the present, the reality she wanted to escape from. His voice had a childish whine. His footsteps down the stairs could be heard through the door. She was relieved he would not be lingering in the hallway to question her further. She rose from the floor to rinse the blood from her legs. Her duties waited, leaving her no time to wallow. Now all she could think about was her hope that the children would actually eat what she cooked. Or would it be another mealtime of watching them spit it out? Every time they did, a feeling of rejection burrowed into her like termites.

Alejandra turned off the water and stepped out of the shower to dry herself quickly before they called to her again from outside her door. She couldn't stand to hear any of them repeat her name. Her anger would flare up—aimed at herself for being weak. Sometimes her knees threatened to buckle when she thought of how she didn't own a single thing in the world. She had no money of her own. No job. Her name was not even on any of the bills. Half her life lived as a shadow.

As she ran the towel down her legs, she noticed a slimy substance on the glass door where the hallucination had appeared. *It's probably from the children,* she told herself. Alejandra put on sweatpants and a T-shirt, then wrapped her hair in the towel.

Before leaving the bathroom, she paused with her hand on the light switch. Something as deep inside her as the lining of her uterus told her what she already knew: What she had seen was not a hallucination. The presence of something or someone lingered in the heat of the room. She could tell by the way the mist parted and shifted.

Alejandra held no illusions of having any value in the world. But her emotional and mental instability felt monumental, like a large wave in the distance. She felt it gaining height and speed before it crashed onto the shore and pulled her into the depths of the unknown.

She switched off the light, then rushed to the kitchen. The staircase creaked beneath her feet with each step. She paused when she reached the bottom. The stained-glass window in the front door caught her eye. Fractured yellow-and-red light splayed across the floor in broken shards. Her maternal instinct told her to sweep them up to prevent anyone getting hurt by them. A darker instinct told her to use one of them on herself to no longer feel the pain.

But even if they had been real glass shards, would she have had the energy to grab one of them and plunge it into her flesh to end it all? She remembered the encounter in the bathroom and the imagined words, *"You want to end it. Let me help you."* She placed both hands over her face as if to block the images and sounds her mind was conjuring that could not possibly be real. Only her pain was real, because it was always sitting on her shoulder.

From the kitchen, the voices of the children bickering and Matthew telling them to stop broke her thoughts of death.

You are still adjusting to the new house. Get a grip, she told herself.

Just three weeks ago, they had moved from Texas to a quiet and leafy suburb of Philadelphia. Matthew had gotten a new job that offered a salary and bonus that they could not turn down, and this large six-bedroom house was one of the many luxuries afforded by his new position.

She had tried to overlook the fact that she didn't much like the neighborhood, the school run commute, or the repairs that would inevitably fall to her to oversee. But the move made sense for Matthew, and the space was more than most people could hope for. *Be grateful. Don't start, Alejandra,* she told herself. It was meant to be a long-term, putting-down-roots kind of home. So why didn't it feel like *home*?

She had brought just two things to remind her of her birthplace. One was the Frida Kahlo coffee-table book she found at a secondhand store before leaving Texas. The cover was the painting of Frida in her white back brace and flowing white skirt against a barren background. Tears streamed from her eyes, yet her face remained stoic. Inside of her was a crumbling Doric pillar.

The second was a photo of Alejandra and her birth mother, Cathy, displayed in the hallway. It had been taken in the coffee shop they regularly met in. They were both smiling. Alejandra wanted to smile like that again. And she wanted to tell Cathy what was going on inside her, but she didn't want to spoil their budding relationship; they had only just met when Alejandra moved away.

The bickering in the kitchen grew louder. Matthew stood in the kitchen with the same curious look as the children as she entered. "What took you so long?"

She inhaled a deep breath. Her impatience with him was something not easily washed away in a shower. "You could have started making dinner."

He gave her a wide smile and furrowed his brow. "But that's your thing. I don't know what you have planned because you buy all the groceries. You always do the cooking."

Her belly sank as she envisioned a snapshot of cooking for him for the next fifteen years. But the children were listening to their conversation, especially nine-year-old Catrina, who was waiting for her mother's response with an expectant stare. Alejandra couldn't deal with this now. The steam from the shower had somehow carried itself into her head in the form of a heavy exhaustion. "Can you at least wipe down the table?" she asked Matthew.

He glanced back at the glass tabletop. "Yeah, sure. It's disgusting from whatever they ate earlier."

Alejandra walked to the fridge to take out something that would expire soon and would make a meal with minimal effort. She used to love to cook, but it had become a chore. The thought of ordering food crossed her mind until she imagined the conversation that would ensue as they tried to decide what to order. They had reached a place in their relationship where they couldn't even agree on Indian or Chinese.

She grabbed a bag of prechopped vegetables and an easy roast-in-the-bag chicken with new potatoes. One pot for the vegetables and the one roasting tray for the chicken to toss in the oven. It would take just over an hour for it to be done. Two episodes of some cartoon on Netflix would keep the kids quiet with Matthew sitting next to them. She hoped that they would remain in the other room because her patience had evaporated like water left to simmer to the bottom of a pot. It wouldn't be long before something inside of her burned.

"Elodia, could you please eat something?" Alejandra was on the verge of tears watching all three children pick at the meal. Her only job in the world was making a mushy pile of food that Elodia would later spit out. Will and Catrina poked around their plates. Alejandra's face felt hot.

Matthew laughed. "They're just kids. What do you expect? By the way, can you take my dry cleaning tomorrow? You don't have anything to do. I have to rush out." She stared at Matthew with an icebox-cold heart as he doted on giggling Elodia.

How happy Matthew had been to have another child. All his many dreams had come true in the last few years. He had a stay-at-home wife with beautiful, healthy children and no money worries. Without knowing it, or appreciating it, he had all the wind to propel him forward as he coasted with the ease of a kitesurfer on a picture-perfect day. Meanwhile she was that tugboat in the back pulling something bigger through deep waters. She listened to Matthew chewing, knowing he didn't have an inkling of how often the thought of death crossed her mind.

The one time she'd told him she'd thought of ending her own life was after a Saturday alone with all three children. He gave her a look of puzzled irritation before saying, "I'm sorry you feel that way. Why do you feel like that? Look at everything you have."

His answer was enough to close her mouth and shut off the valve in her heart that had once been reserved for him.

There was not much she felt sure of in this life, but one thing had become clear: The disintegration of any love she once possessed for Matthew had to be connected with the painful chasms cracking open in her soul. No, Matthew was not solely to blame, because she had chosen him, after all. But Alejandra had to figure out what was happening to her before she let go of the desire to continue breathing.

Matthew's voice pulled her from her somber inner dialogue and back to the dining table. "What's that face for?" Alejandra looked up from her food. *Not again,* she thought.

"I'm just tired."

He made his displeasure known with his raised eyebrows and a cross expression that magnified every wrinkle and gray hair. There was only a two-year age difference between them. But when he made that face, he looked ten years older. It made her feel like she'd married a version of her adoptive father, Jim.

"You're so miserable, Allie. But it's never going to leave you because that is who you choose to be." Her adoptive father would say this to her when she hadn't managed to smile or exhibit enough excitement. In a house of eight adopted siblings, she always felt like an outsider looking in. She was also treated like an extra pair of hands. It was her duty to help with all domestic matters. Her adopted parents never bothered to ask her, *Are you okay?*

Charlie, her adopted sibling who was two years older, was the only one who would give her reassuring glances and a playful wink when their parents were hard on them about how they did chores and how they presented themselves to the outside world. It made her feel less alone.

Unfortunately, his time at the home was cut short, because he left as soon as he turned eighteen. He promised to keep in touch but never did. That was before cellphones or social media.

Not satisfied with her answer, Matthew turned his attention back to the children.

"All right, kids, bath time." The three children ran past them and up the stairs for their bath, which Alejandra was grateful she didn't have to run. She could stay downstairs alone and clean up. God forbid the table have the smallest smudge on it. Matthew rose from the table. The harder he scowled, the deeper the creases in his forehead and around his eyes appeared. "Just be happy," he sniped. "Look how lucky you are to be home all the time, in a nice home with no worries. You want for nothing."

"I just want you to listen, Matthew."

"I am listening, and all I hear is complaining and negativity."

She kept quiet and swallowed his words. They sat in her stomach like little dormant seeds. Later they would bloom into anger.

He left the kitchen without looking at Alejandra. The tension between them remained in the air like a smoldering vapor. In that vapor floated the dust of all the unloving and inharmonious things they had ever said.

A week had passed since Alejandra's breakdown in the shower. Her routine propelled her from hour to hour. Once her third child had begun to walk, the daily task of putting everyone else first had become as difficult as climbing a mountain of felt. No matter how hard she dug her feet in and scratched at the fabric, she was always close to falling to certain death.

And yet, residing in the same space in her heart as her despair was her love for her children. That love was a sweet blossom she held on to tightly until the thorns on its stem made her bleed. Those wounds were the stigmata of motherhood, precious and painful.

The windshield wipers squeaked away the rain, and the shouts from the fighting children in the backseat of the McDonald's-scented car became distracting. Hunger from skipping lunch made her shake. But not eating was the quickest way to get that postbaby "snapback" everyone around her liked to talk about while wearing their athleisure. No hips or belly. Hard and toned said you were in control. Instead, her body felt gross, distorted like overused Silly Putty.

Elodia was wailing.

"Catrina, help your sister . . . *please.*" Alejandra's *please* barely a whisper through the tears she could not hold back. "Catrina . . . *Please.*"

Nine-year-old Catrina was sitting between two car seats with her hands over her ears and eyes squeezed shut. "Make them stop, Mommy! I hate crying babies! Take them away." Eighteen-month-old Elodia shrieked. She'd tried to wiggle out of her car seat to retrieve a toy just out of her reach, and now her little hand was stuck painfully in the strap. Four-year-old Will complained because he was thirsty, and all the drinks were sitting sweating in the passenger seat.

Alejandra's foot pressed harder on the gas, uncontrolled, her fingers trembling on the wheel. Her uterus was seizing. After her three C-sections she sometimes experienced phantom movements. She watched the speedometer approach the limit and then go over. *Maybe I should leave in the middle of the night while they're all sleeping and find a lake to drive into. Their screams and wants and pleas will forever be silenced because I will be silenced. They won't even realize I am gone.*

Why am I so awful? Why can't I be normal? Alejandra's mind fogged like the window. She didn't want to harm her children. Only herself.

A message popped up over the directions on her GPS. She tried to keep her eyes on the road and read what it said. It was from Matthew.

I'll be home late tonight. Expect me around 7.30/8. And save dinner for me.

Her body slumped. She knew she would have no help tonight with the housework and the kids and no close friends or family to call on. And not just for tonight: In the morning Matthew was leaving for a two-week business trip to California. He loved his new job because it put him in charge of a larger team. Before this he'd hated not having a team to direct and not having direct access to a CEO or, at the very least, the board members of a company. Now his bucket list had more check marks than the shopping list she'd written on the back of the last grocery receipt.

When they'd moved, Alejandra had quit her job in data entry and sold what shares she had in the company. Once they'd settled in their new home, the responsibilities of the family had all fallen on her as Matthew devoted all his time and energy to his new position as a director of sales. The space and time for her to find another job had dwindled until it became more convenient and financially sensible for her not to return to work.

Some parents might've loved this. Many friends told her how they envied her, but was it what she really wanted? "We are a family. Your decisions are our decisions," Matthew had said. "This is what we agreed on when we first met. *You* agreed. You can't go back on what we agreed on. Life doesn't work like that. You are a wife and mother first. That was *your* choice. Why do I have to even remind you of that? That's what normal people do."

He'd left no room for changing her mind or heart.

She grumbled as she swiped the phone forcefully to return to the GPS app.

"Fuck!" She slammed on the brakes.

There was a red light and a car ahead. The sound of screeching brakes, and then crashing metal. But the children stopped crying and taunting one another immediately. Thank god they'd recently bought a tank of a seven-seater that could withstand a tornado.

"Mom!" Catrina screamed.

Alejandra looked back to make sure the children were all right. Catrina glared at her.

"Now what am I gonna eat?" A burger and all its sticky contents had spilled on the floor.

Fried bologna sandwiches, like I had to eat when I was a kid, Alejandra thought. These kids had never eaten a slice of bologna in their lives, only nitrite-free organic honey-baked ham—thinly sliced. What would the other mothers at their new neighborhood school say about bologna? "I'll make you fish sticks, or you can finish Elodia's nuggets."

"Whatever," Catrina said under her breath.

Alejandra didn't have the energy to respond because an angry woman with her hazard lights on was shouting at her to get out of the car. Others were yelling at Alejandra to put on her own hazards as they honked and drove around her.

Your existence is a fucking hazard, she told herself. If only she could just sit on the curb with her hands over her ears to stop the noise.

She would have to somehow tell Matthew she'd gotten into a fender bender on the way home from school because she'd been too busy wallowing in her thoughts after his text. She remembered again that for two weeks she would be on her own to do the feeding, washing, school run, bath time, and bedtime for three children. Two hands to love and care for six of theirs.

Alejandra had never told him she often sat in her car in the school parking lot and cried behind her sunglasses to hide her tears. She cried about everything: her inability to effortlessly care for her children, entertain them with activities instead of TV, cook meals from scratch, hold intelligent conversations, be hot in bed (at least be interested in the same person after all these years), and wear the same dress size as she had at twenty-five.

When she was hurting that badly, the only escape seemed to be death. She had no money of her own and no ambition. Matthew was not the kind of man to turn her out on the streets with only the clothing on her back, but he *could*. Anything of worth was in his name. All the money was earned by him. Not a damn thing was in *her* name. She did not even have her own last name. Not the last name of the children.

Reviving her career or starting a new one seemed an impossibility. First, her work experience was so far in the past that no place would hire her now without going back or retraining. And who would take care of the children? Matthew made it clear he couldn't spare the time. And it was his salary that kept them going. The vacations, the house, the restaurants, the nice things on a credit card without limit, the school fees. The odd texts from friends in Texas gave Alejandra the encouragement to go on, but it was not enough to make her feel like she had a community.

The condensation fogging the windows and windshield inside the car took her back to her breakdown in the shower. Her eyes darted to the right and left, as if she was worried something might appear. Something white, like a wedding dress.

Alejandra put on her hazard lights so that she could get out to speak with the lady standing next to the Volkswagen Jetta. The Volkswagen had only minor dents in the bumper. Before exchanging information with this stranger, Alejandra took a deep breath to appear in control. Her face would not betray her turmoil. After all, she had become good at hiding it: Hiding was what she did best, even from herself. No one would ever believe how many times she'd stood at the precipice of taking her own life.

In a matter of minutes, the exchange was over.

But still Catrina whined, "Can we go home now?"

"That is where we are headed. Home." Alejandra signaled to merge and glanced in the rearview before pressing the accelerator.

She jumped and pressed her foot hard on the brake upon seeing an elderly woman wearing a white scarf over her head who was staring directly at her. The long edges of the scarf tied beneath the woman's chin whipped in the wind. Red light illuminated her face, giving the hollows of her sagging skin a skull-like appearance. Alejandra could feel herself shaking as she looked back to the road. She took a deep breath before checking her rearview mirror again. Alejandra looked to her right.

The woman was nowhere in sight.

Alejandra spent the evening in her usual routine of cooking, bath time, and putting Elodia and Will to bed first. This allowed her to give Catrina a little one-on-one attention.

"Tell me a story, Mom."

Catrina was tucked in bed with a small brown bull Matthew had brought her back from a business trip. She had soft toys from his travels all over the world. Alejandra finished putting away Catrina's folded clothing in a half-empty laundry basket before settling next to her to read a story with her. Alejandra touched Catrina's hand. Side by side their café au lait birthmarks on their forearms touched. Will liked to call it her "night sky" because the small brown dots resembled a cluster of stars. Only Catrina shared the mark.

"What kind of story? What book do you want?"

"I don't know. Not a book. It's almost Halloween. Something scary. Different. Something you were told as a kid."

Before Alejandra could open her mouth to say no, she stopped herself. All the bedtime stories she'd been told as a kid were from the Bible. She'd grown up in a devout Evangelical household. Instead of Halloween they'd had a "harvest festival," which turned out to be just a dull church revival.

Some quiet, vague voice nudged her to tell Catrina the story of La Llorona: the crying woman in white drawn to tears and sadness. She thought again of the lingering mist in the shower. It had looked so much like a phantom.

"You want to end it. Let me help you."

She made a decision. The story was a dark one. But one day Catrina would be an adult finding out who she really was. And one day she would choose a partner. The thing that Alejandra wanted most for Catrina was for her not to give those important life decisions away to others because she felt inadequate. Everyone deserved to write their own story.

And maybe this story would help save her.

"I will tell you the story of La Llorona. When I was about your age one of my Chicana friends from school told me this story. She wanted to know why I couldn't celebrate Halloween and if I knew about Día de los Muertos. I told her my parents didn't believe in Halloween. That is when she told me the story her mother told her."

"What's a Chicana?"

This question caught Alejandra off guard. It had never occurred to her to pass down knowledge of their identity to her daughter. She had always suppressed it in herself.

Her adopted family had told her nothing of her heritage. They had not even whispered about Día de los Muertos to her, even though it felt true when she discovered it through her friend. She had always felt drawn to the color and mystery of this holiday. She went to the school library after finishing lunch and browsed the books on Mexican culture and history. There were the images painted by Spanish priests alongside their descriptions of the pagan Aztecs satisfying their deities through blood. Then there were tales about the slaughter of indigenous people by steel and disease before the survivors were forced to convert. Their own rituals changing until Día de los Muertos was birthed to celebrate the old ways while satisfying forced assimilation.

She wanted to cup a small, brightly decorated sugar skull in her hand, perhaps press her tongue against the crown to see if it tasted like normal sugar. The elaborate altars illuminated with candlelight that emitted ghostlike smoke over plates of food for the dead. The dead could be reached on this day when the veil between the material and spiritual worlds melted like sugar in simmering water.

But after she graduated high school and then became a young woman, followed by marriage, she made learning more about her heritage less of a priority.

"A Mexican American woman. We are a blend of many beautiful things."

"Like a unicorn?"

Alejandra couldn't help but smile. "Yes, I suppose. Half horse and half magic."

"That sounds cool. But can you tell me about La Llorona first? Is it a true story?"

"I have no idea. But all stories begin somewhere. I'm warning you, it might scare you, real or not."

Catrina shifted her body upright and pulled the comforter—robin's egg blue with a large unicorn print—closer to her chin. Alejandra looked at her daughter's innocent face. Sometimes she regretted producing that beautiful face, because all her own pain remained stagnant for years.

"There isn't one version of the story of La Llorona. It's told in many countries in many different ways. This is the version my friend told me.

"Once upon a time in Mexico, there was a beautiful unmarried woman with two small children. She had many suitors, but she fell in love with a wealthy man who was older than her. He lived in the largest house and owned most of the land surrounding the town.

"They crossed paths when he saw her selling fruit in the market. For months he visited her and bought more fruit than a single man would ever need. During one of his visits to her market stall he said he didn't want children. He wanted a companion to travel with and share his wealth with. She was tired of working the market stall and wanted to feel beautiful and important. She thought being married to a man like this would make her life perfect.

"And so, in desperation for true love, she drowned her children. She thought his unconditional love would make her happy. When the man found out what she'd done, he said he could never be with her and left. Worse, he'd known she had children all along, and would have accepted her if she'd just told the truth. Filled with regret, she killed herself in the same lake she murdered her children. For her sin, she was destined to roam the land for eternity, wearing a white dress, and crying for her children."

Catrina stared toward the closet with glassy, vacant eyes.

"Why weren't her children enough?"

Caught off guard by the question and by Catrina's distant gaze, Alejandra followed the direction of her child's eyes. The closet had opened at some point during the story. The sequins on a dress hanging inside glittered. At least, she hoped they were sequins and not eyes.

Eyes.

Why would you even think they were eyes? So ridiculous, she told herself then turned back to Catrina.

"Uh, back then women did not have the same opportunities as now. We couldn't dream very big. You couldn't vote, own land, and some never went to school. All that was expected was to get married and raise a family no matter what interests they had. Maybe she did what she was told by her mother and great-grandmother despite having other dreams. But it's just a story. Unfortunately, the story of La Llorona is not told in her own words. If it was true, we still don't know what really happened to her."

"Are we enough for you? Did you have other dreams?"

The pain began in the center of Alejandra's chest. It rose inside her like a geyser.

"Of course you are enough." Alejandra always wondered what harm she did by even entertaining the thought of wanting to run away from her children, even if only for a short spell.

Catrina returned her eyes to the black crack in the closet door. She appeared almost hypnotized. *"No, I hope we live long enough."* The little girl's voice sounded monotonic and hollow. As if it were not her own voice.

Alejandra gently touched the sides of Catrina's arms. "What did you say?"

Catrina blinked and looked back at Alejandra. "Huh? Did I say something?" Then the little girl's expression softened, and she returned to Earth, her voice sweet and childish again. "I love you, Mommy. I'm not scared. Thank you for thinking I'm big enough to understand. It makes me feel special."

Alejandra kissed her daughter on her forehead, feeling an outpouring of love that could've flooded the entire world. She rose from the bed thinking that just maybe she could give her child what she hadn't received enough of.

But then in her peripheral vision she caught a glimpse of the glinting sequins in the closet. She whipped her head to look inside.

"What's wrong, Mommy? Are you afraid of something?"

She didn't want Catrina to sense her fear. "There is nothing. I thought a dress had fallen inside the closet. Sweet dreams, my love."

Alejandra shut the bedroom door, not wanting to walk down the stairs and leave Catrina alone, or spend time with Matthew, who should've been home. She felt trapped by her trepidation. *Stop being so anxious,* she said to herself while closing her eyes and exhaling deeply.

All she wanted to do was get into bed to read a book. But the rest of the clothes had to be put away, and Matthew would expect her to spend time with him. Recently, though, Alejandra had an overwhelming desire to be alone.

As she began to walk down the creaking stairs, she could hear Matthew in the kitchen. A flush of frustration made her muscles ache, her steps fill with lead, and her chest tighten. Matthew was whistling. It made her jaw clench.

Lately his presence felt like a plastic bag over her head. Still on the staircase, she instinctively grabbed her neck with one hand, as if there really were a bag around it, before inhaling deeply though her nose. What if she removed his hands and removed the bag? She didn't want to think about the fuss it would cause. They'd call her selfish, unloving.

"Alejandra, you coming down? Is this plate for me?"

She rolled her eyes. *As helpless as a fucking baby in the body of a forty-four-year-old man.*

It was time to appease and entertain Matthew—usually they'd watch a show on Netflix or Amazon Prime as long as *he* was in the mood for it. After watching a show they'd retire to bed, where he would stay on his side of the mattress playing iPad games while she shifted around trying to get comfortable and quiet her mind.

Many nights Alejandra lay in bed with her sleep mask over her eyes, simply relieved she'd made it through another day before it rolled into another one identical to the last. If she was lucky, there would be no dreams. The dread of her impending dreams made her toss and turn and kick off the blankets.

Of late she'd had two recurring dreams. In the first, she tumbled in sand and fought viciously with an entity she could neither touch nor see. But the blows from her unseen assailant were very real. The assailant would claw at her belly like a snarling beast in the wild emptying a carcass. Picking. Pulling. Slicing. As if it wanted to eviscerate her. She could hear her children crying in the distance even though they were nowhere to be seen. While her body became a bag of organs, she would hear the howls that she was helpless to calm.

It would end with Alejandra no longer sensing the assailant and her children falling silent. As she lay half alive and crying, the sand would transform into water, and then the water would drag her body under in a whirlpool. Just before her eyes closed, the silhouette of a half-creature, half-woman in a white dress would stand over her. Her white dress and the loose skin on her head whipped and twisted in the wind. From the figure's mouth hung viscous strings of blood and saliva. The woman would watch her as if memorizing the moment of Alejandra's demise.

The dream reminded her of the nature shows Catrina loved to watch. She watched them sitting at the edge of the sofa in silent fascination, her full-moon eyes taking in the vicious scenes of predator and prey. No one was allowed to make a sound as she absorbed the narrator's every word. Alejandra had hopes Catrina would become a vet or study biology. She was willing to invest in any way to make it possible for Catrina to pursue the path she chose. Perhaps part of the reason she had picked Matthew was because he could give her children all she had never had: real security in a wild world that resembled a jungle or the Serengeti. She'd seen in her own adopted family what uncertainty with limited resources and so many mouths to feed looked like.

Other times the dream took her to a body of placid water with gauzy steam rising from the surface. A hidden cenote. There, women floated on their backs, eyes wide open, tears streaming from the corners, their clothing, long brown hair, and limbs splayed in the water, their palms up as if to catch the rain or rays from the sun to claim whatever the gods had to offer them. One in particular always stood out to her. She wore a black cotton-and-lace dress with a matching black veil, like the kind of dress a woman would wear in mourning in the early twentieth century. In one hand she carried a rifle, and two bandoliers crossed her chest. The combination intrigued Alejandra, but she didn't know who the woman was. More women stood at the edge of the cenote. A centimeter closer and they would tumble in. Behind them was another row of women, followed by another. This created concentric circles of women like the ripples from a drop of rain hitting a puddle. They all stared at her, not speaking, their lips slightly parted as if ready to shout, muscles in their shoulders and legs tensed as if they were waiting for some action to take place, terra-cotta soldiers lined up just for her. Their silent tears on their cheeks reflected the sunlight. Sometimes the brightness of their tears caught her eyes, and though the light felt blinding, it was not painful. She knew that all she had to do was speak the words to make them move and she'd summon their power, an electric spiritual charge at her disposal. The vibrations of that power were so strong she could feel them rattling her bones. Alejandra wanted to be part of that wreath of energy. Did it even exist in the real world?

That last night before Matthew's trip she had dreamed of the women. They had given her comfort. When she'd woken, she'd thought in the dark, *I want you to be real,* before checking the time on her phone. 4:44 A.M. There were still hours left to sleep. She lay there with her eyes closed, trying to fall back asleep. Instead, she found herself praying to the dark ceiling of her bedroom that she would find her way into the sunlight again.

The stillness of the room alerted her to every sound in the house and every sensation in her body. She got up to pee, and as she walked barefoot the cold bathroom tile sent a chill up her legs. As she sat on the toilet, something brushed the hair on the right side of her head. In her peripheral vision she sensed a dark shadow moving across the white tiles. She slowly reared her head toward the movement. The hair on her left side rose slightly as a soft breath puffed against her earlobe. She jumped off the toilet to look around, urine dripping down her leg. If her heart had lived outside of her body, the hammering would've been louder than a car crash. She sat back down and placed both hands on her head. *What the fuck! What is wrong? You have everything. Everything! Stop being such an ungrateful cunt. Control your mind. You have to get over this.*

After sitting with her eyes closed and experiencing no other sounds or sensations except her breathing, she wiped her leg then flushed the toilet. Before leaving the bathroom to go back to bed, she glanced at the wall, where there was nothing except bath toy–shaped shadows.

The morning arrived to take her only source of help away. They hired a local girl to babysit sometimes, but Alejandra felt guilty using her because taking care of the kids was her only job. The guilt came from that gnawing feeling that she had no right to ask for anything. She reserved the babysitter for the nights she went out with Matthew.

As they waited for Matthew's Uber in the driveway, he inspected the damaged car again with a frown. "It's not that bad. I expected you to wreck it a bit when we bought it. What the hell happened? Were you speeding? Not paying attention?"

"I just . . . I don't know. I didn't notice the car in front of me braking."

He raised both eyebrows and cocked his head, giving it a little shake. "Arrange to get it fixed while I'm away. Remember, you're the adult here. Don't let them run you."

He kissed her on the lips softly, trying to make it feel romantic. "All right, difficult woman. I love you anyway."

He often called her "difficult woman" in jest. She hated it. Was she difficult to love? A difficult woman despite catering to him at every opportunity, even when he gave her a cold shoulder or stormed away like a fourth child? His lips pecked hers, and it didn't strike a loving chord within her. When did she become numb to the slightest show of affection from him? He pulled away from her and grabbed his bags to meet the Uber pulling up to the curb.

"I'll call you and the kids, but I have drinks and dinners most nights. See you in two weeks."

She could feel the agitation rising inside her, just as it had in the car before the accident. Meanwhile, Matthew would soon be sitting in an airline lounge alone with a glass of wine, playing Candy Crush. No small hands slapping the phone away. Then he would sit on an airplane with someone serving him food while he watched a new movie. No small voices demanding that he change it to Peppa Pig so they could watch it for the hundredth time.

At least she would now have a couple of hours of free time after the kids went to bed. Despite the chaos that erupted at times and the sheer exertion of tending to a family without help, there was a freedom in being alone when he was away. It allowed her time to fulfill her wants and needs without his displeasure. He frequently made it obvious he was displeased with her when her needs didn't align with what he wanted in that moment. She could listen to the music she liked but Matthew hated. *The Miseducation of Lauryn Hill* was one of her top albums to play loud. She could also watch the movies she wanted but he hated: *Shudder* would be on every night.

While he was searching for porn in his hotel room, she would masturbate under the covers with one of the three vibrators he'd bought for her as Valentine's Day gifts, thinking about the men and women she found attractive. The women would be far more beautiful than she had felt in a very long time. At times she wondered who he thought of when they fucked, because surely it wasn't her if she wasn't thinking of him. Sex with Matthew wasn't bad: It satisfied her and gave her physical sustenance. He was the only man who had ever made her orgasm from penetration because he'd taken the time in the beginning of the relationship to find out what she liked sexually.

Yet nowadays, her feelings for him got in the way of that thrill of mental and physical attraction that could make sex amazing and soul-binding. She still initiated sex with Matthew regularly because the need to disengage from being a tired mother to just being a woman was still so strong. The release and relief were a necessity for survival. And damn if it didn't feel like she was in survival mode most days.

Whenever "Running Up That Hill" by Kate Bush came on the radio or her playlist on her phone, she turned it all the way up. Sang it out loud, every word. The song made her reflect on the thought that if only God could truly swap her place with Matthew, he could understand her better and reach out a helping hand as she climbed this mountain called motherhood. Music had a way of expressing what she could not articulate. And knowing another woman possibly experienced something similar was a comfort.

These memories screeched in her brain as she stood in the doorway of the world in front of her and her home behind her. A burst of crying from Elodia and the sound of something banging against the floor broke her stupor.

Looking in the window, she saw Elodia and Will fighting over a pile of trains, knocking over a tower of blocks in the process. The small squares reminded her of the decisions she'd made in life. She had always just stacked the blocks without knowing what she was building. Her soul languished within the rusty scaffolding of the tower she'd built.

Catrina was sitting on the sofa with her iPad. Alejandra kept promising Matthew she'd limit the children's screen time, but that meant she would have to spend the next few hours hearing "I'm bored" or trying to entertain one child while the others ran loose. It was all too much. She would never say it out loud, but having her own children made her think perhaps she didn't like small children much at all.

"*You're a sick woman.*" Alejandra looked around, wanting to believe these words came from a logical source, maybe a TV show from an open window, or a random passerby. She didn't want it to be something wrong in her brain.

While she'd only heard her own voice in the bathroom the previous night, this voice was the same as the one she'd heard during her breakdown in the shower. That same voice began whispering "*sick woman, difficult woman*" over and over, like an open-handed slap across each cheek.

She looked around frantically, but there was not a single other person in sight. The trees and bushes swayed in the violence of a brewing storm. The wind blew her hair behind her face, exposing her neck. Cold air billowed her shirt. She grabbed her goosebumped arms as the frigid wind rushed across her exposed skin. Thunderstorms had been predicted all week, and it felt like a storm was coming.

The voice croaked at her again. "*How many people struggle to reach their dream of having a family? What about those who have lost children? You're disgusting, wanting to stray from your vows. Break up your family? Vow breaker! Child hater!*"

All she could do was watch the branches of the oak tree in the front yard bow to the storm. The trunk stood still while the branches surrendered to another aspect of nature even more powerful than itself.

Mesmerized by the tree, she whispered to the intensifying wind with tears choking her as they flooded from the deep parts of her soul, "*Help me. Anyone. Please.*" A split-second image from her dream of the women flashed in her mind. She took a deep breath to shake it off, then walked back inside.

The children were just as noisy as the storm as they fought.

"Will, share or else I will take the toys all away until your next birthday. Catrina, can you come help me?"

"Do I have to?" Catrina whined, her eyes still on the tablet.

"Yes, you don't need to watch other kids play with toys for hours. I learned how to do laundry at your age."

The young girl tossed the iPad to the corner of the sofa and shuffled toward her mother. "Yeah, but that's your job."

Alejandra bit her tongue, feeling her anger rise. What kind of role model was she? A shit one. "No, it's all our job. Let's put these dishes away together."

The burst of anger at this exchange wetted her skin with a sheen of sweat. It wasn't just Catrina. Not a day before, Alejandra asked toddler Elodia to help pick up the cookies she had crumbled on the carpet while she laughed with glee. The small child looked up with her chubby angel face and replied, "No. You clean. You vacuum." Elodia giggled, toddling off to play.

Another time, Will sat at the dining table while Alejandra prepared dinner. Matthew lounged on the two-seater sofa in the kitchen checking the sports scores on his phone. "Mama," Will had said, "you know it's like going to a restaurant every day here. We tell you what we want, and you make it for us." The heat from the sizzling fat on the steaks burned her face. The charred rind curled as it blackened and melted to nothing.

She had always hoped Catrina wouldn't grow up resenting her the way she resented her adoptive mother, who had had to give each of them attention as a group and not one by one: Her little army of Christian soldiers saved from their circumstances. The older ones made responsible for the younger ones, with no time for play. Children taking care of children. Despite having many bodies around during her childhood and teen years, the feeling of neglect never left Alejandra.

While Catrina helped her put the dishes away, she looked at their four hands and arms moving in harmony with their nearly identical birthmarks. The image caused a sudden urge within Alejandra to see her birth mother again. It also fed her desire to explore her bloodline, glowing embers that never seemed to die. The winds of age seemed to only stoke the fire.

This made her think of a letter she'd been waiting to open until Matthew would be away, to avoid sharing it with him or hearing his opinion on it. The timing was perfect, and perhaps Catrina would find it interesting. When they finished with the dishwasher, Alejandra caught Catrina before she could escape back to the iPad.

"Hey, you want to see something cool with me?"

Catrina's eyes brightened, and her voice perked up. "What is it?"

Alejandra led her to the entrance of the house. She took out an A4 envelope from DNATree detailing her extended family scattered across Mexico, Portugal, and the United States. This information was available online, but she had requested a proper printout she could keep and hold in her hands or give to her children. To Alejandra, it felt like it could be a treasure map. The small child within her filled with excitement. What secrets did past generations possess?

"After your grandmother Cathy contacted me through a company called DNATree, I wanted to know more about where we came from, and I wanted you to know too. Here, you open it."

Catrina looked puzzled, as if she had expected a lavish gift or a surprise puppy. She still took the envelope and opened it.

"It's a big tree and acorns with names and places. And numbers."

"Yes, isn't it magnificent! All those seeds are connected to us. They are our relatives, their location, and the percentage of

DNA we share with them. There are also spaces here for us to add relatives we know of that are no longer living so we can connect them to us. How cool is it to know this? Would you like to go to Mexico one day? Maybe meet more cousins in Texas?"

Catrina's eyes scanned the paper in mild disappointment. "I guess. If it would make you happy, make you smile."

Alejandra opened her mouth to speak then closed it again. A sadness clouded her previous excitement. "We can talk about it later. Go play, but no more screens."

Alejandra watched Catrina go back to the kitchen. It hurt that her daughter did not want to share this with her. The dull ache throbbed in her chest as she scanned the paper. This would be a project just for her. Maybe in her free time she could piece together her past to distract her from the present. She had to find the motivation first, for anything. What was the point of any of it?

The worst part was that Catrina would only do it if it made her mother happy. Alejandra knew she needed help to stop spreading her heartache and people-pleasing ways. She feared that eventually this dark cloud of depression and habit of constantly subverting herself for others would be passed to her children. Alejandra looked at the blank spaces that were small, shaded boxes where you could add the names and dates of dead relatives. The branches without printed names hung lifelessly in shadow. She wondered what lurked there.

Atzi

Mexico—1522

A tzi sat in her single-room hut in the thick stranglehold of humidity after the rainstorm and thought of death.

Death was the only escape from the curse of being a branded and conquered woman, as Atzi was. She was a thing they used and ridiculed. They called her brown skin *inferior* and *savage*. Yet they lusted after it, and her. Not even the goddesses carved in stone were safe from desecration. The great temple in Tenochtitlán had been recently destroyed to make way for a new god, who offered eternal salvation if only you surrendered every part of yourself.

It occurred to her that generations upon generations would suffer. She thought of their stories. Their voices. Their histories, all up in flames. All of it, unwanted. It was after their defeat at the hands of the conquistadors that the real nightmare had begun for her people, especially for the women and girls who had to submit to these strange men. Atzi knew she carried the seed of the invader inside of her. It made her very soul sick.

Never mind the disease they had also spread, wiping out thousands like an invisible sword sweeping across the land.

As she thought of it, she swayed between vomiting and outbursts of sobs, the seething hate never leaving the front of her skull. Nothing could quell the aches from her captor forcefully taking her sexually whenever the mood struck him. His assaults had landed daily. Soon she began to feel an aversion to the aroma of cooking meat, followed by nausea: the first signs she carried the foreign invader's child.

The man might as well have been a demon. All of them were demons: They had arrived in a horde, in waves of conquest and exploration and destruction, all done in the name of their king and god. Unfortunately, the disease that killed her people had somehow passed over her. By some unforeseen stroke of luck, her firstborn daughter, Yaretzi, remained safe. Yaretzi had fled with Atzi's sister and grandfather as far away as possible, though Atzi wondered if any place could be safe forever from the new world being created by the invaders who had arrived with a cross in one hand and sword in the other. The conquered would be cut down with one or the other if they did not submit.

"Go!" Atzi had told her family. "I will offer myself to one of them to buy you some time. Just flee and hide. What other choice do we have?" They reacted at first with collective shock that soon turned to anguish.

No one could ever stop Atzi from the time she was a child from doing whatever she set her mind to. It had taken the end of their world as they knew it to steal her inner light. Atzi and Yaretzi embraced each other tightly, hoping they would always remember each other even beyond death. Atzi breathed in Yaretzi's unwashed hair, remembering her small infant head cradled in her neck soon after her birth. She whispered to her daughter without looking her in the eye, "Live your life the best you can. Don't forget me. Don't forget your importance."

Her surviving family members all knew the fate that awaited Atzi. Her grandfather could not look at her. His sagging brown eyes betrayed his sense of shame at being beyond the age to fight. They had been abandoned by the gods, who could offer no hope. They had to create their own hope.

With her family gone, this new reality had become too much to take. Atzi decided to take her own life using the small brown seeds of the ololiuqui. In small doses they created visions, but she had heard that if you took enough, death would welcome you home. She could rid herself of the conquistador's seed, but no herb could prevent him from planting another. Death was the only sure escape. Atzi took the ololiuqui seeds into her mouth and swallowed. She lay on her mat waiting to travel to another world. Their bitter taste lingered in the back of her mouth. It seemed fitting for the fate that awaited her and everyone here. A rustling in the corner of the hut disturbed her meditation. Heavy breath that smelled like the head of a newborn filled the room. Was she dead? The seeds couldn't have worked that fast.

A grayish-white figure floated across the dirt floor like smoke rising from burning corpses. It had to be a vision from the seeds. Atzi shook her head and blinked. She was thirsty, so thirsty she could empty a cenote. Perhaps she should have jumped into one instead.

"You have two inside of you. I want them."

Atzi managed to turn her head toward the voice. "What are you? A deathbed vision?"

"I am very real. I want those souls inside of you. Their tender flesh will be delicious. I can smell your malice and pain. I find it pleasing."

Atzi's head lolled. Nausea threatened, but she had to keep the seeds down. Let them work their lethal magic.

"Go away. Let me die in peace. I have endured being ravaged. I have endured seeing my people slaughtered. *Please* . . ."

"I want to make a deal."

Atzi willed herself to look at the smoky figure again. "What?"

"You have another daughter already grown, nearly time for her to bleed. I promise she will be safe and escape all this unspeakable horror of conquest. She will live a long, healthy life, ensuring your bloodline continues."

Atzi raised her chin. A seed of hope, something she'd thought was nearly dead, gave her a spurt of energy as the hallucinogenic plant began to work. "Show me you are real."

The shadow morphed, taking the shape of a human with translucent skin that glowed white like a full moon, or a cluster of stars. Each vertebra was calcified to a sharp, bony barb. The figure blew an iridescent gaseous dust into her face, giving Atzi a vision of her daughter as a grown woman living in a village near a river. Her sister washed clothing in the water next to her. Atzi managed a smile with both joy and despair, knowing she would not see it with her own eyes.

But if this demon could save her child, perhaps it could also take vengeance on her behalf. Her contempt rose like the impending doom of a solar eclipse. It filled the emotional craters created by her assaulter. So many scars at the hands of these invaders claiming what was never theirs to take. Let this creature devour them. "Let us make a deal. When I die, take the souls of these demon seeds that were forced upon me. Kill the man who did this to me . . . He has a leather horsewhip. Let him feel the sting. Make it slow. Extract every tear he took from me. From all of us. Take his family and save my daughter."

The creature let out a wicked cackle. "It will be done . . . for a price. You ask for much. As I have these souls, and yours, I also want your blood and tears to be bound to me. Your seeds forever mine. I will take them now, then you will take yourself to the sacrificial cenote and cast yourself inside. As asked, I will bring catastrophe upon the house of your tormentor. More to fill my belly and time."

Atzi's eyes no longer retained any light. The seeds made her feel dizzy. Saliva involuntarily escaped from the corners of her mouth. She growled while heaving, "Yes, curse their houses. If our children can't be safe, then neither can theirs." With a final scream she pounded on the dirt floor with both fists. Never again would she see her beloved daughter. This thing might not keep its promise. It didn't matter. Atzi had nothing to lose. Women with nothing to lose are dangerous. "I accept."

The form hovered over her with its belly quivering from hunger, ready to consume this energetic meal. It placed its mouth over her left eye and began to inhale with the force of a hurricane wind. Blood and salt jetted into its mouth. Quasar-bright eyes widened as it gorged itself on her pain. Clots floated in midair from Atzi's open mouth until it bit down and swallowed the fetuses whole. It coughed a spray of blood onto her left arm, singeing the skin with a sharp heat. Atzi cried out as she looked at the wound. From her wrist to nearly her elbow, dark-brown spots marked her skin.

A starlit sky of a birthmark. Generations of souls, she imagined. A sky full of lives.

"Rise," it whispered. "Your freedom awaits."

Atzi pulled herself off the floor half alive, the emptiness of her womb bringing a sense of relief. From the small wood chest where she kept her clothing she removed a clean white huipil and matching skirt that fell to midcalf. Fresh clothing before sacrificing herself. She walked sluggishly through the village she would not miss because she no longer recognized her people's lives.

From the edge of the village, she walked another half hour to the closest cenote. Every step forced more tears to stream from her eyes. Snot ran across her lips like rippling saltwater on sand. Vines of blood streaked her legs. As heavy as her legs felt, there was a lightness in every step of kicked-up dirt.

Her daughter would live and be saved from this fate. She smiled as she neared the hole in the ground that led to other worlds, the world of *her* gods. If only she could die in childbirth and be given a warrior's welcome. *Their* beliefs. But what was done was done. Soon, she could be at peace. Just before reaching the cenote, she stopped. Her heart pumped frantically. This was the end. *Courage,* she told herself as she continued to move forward with the image of her daughter in her heart.

Once at the edge of the cenote, she looked down at the crystalline water. There were far worse ways to go: She had seen them with her own eyes after the invaders arrived. Whereas the calm water could be nothing more than a soft blue sheet of fabric if only she embraced it. Atzi's death would be her final act of love for her firstborn daughter. What a gift Yaretzi had been to her life. A gift of the divine.

Atzi lifted her weary arms and looked to the sun to feel it one last time before casting herself into the azure cenote. She was crying right up until the impact of her body against the water took her life. Her last thought before shattering: *Yaretzi, you and your seed must find me again so I may guide you through the terror. I will plead to the gods to give you all my strength and love so you may endure.*

Just as the woman tumbled from the edge of the hole in the ground, the creature pulled at her huipil, ripping off a small square. It placed the rough cotton on what would have been its arm, had it been human, while it watched the woman's body float on the surface of the water before sinking. Now it looked like a shadow of a small swimming fish.

The creature never tired of seeing them perish empty. Since this species had learned language, the creature's bounty had never been more plentiful. The humans' fear made them do anything, believe anything.

The creature fell back into the shade of the forest, satisfied by the knowledge that it would have all it needed to sustain itself and multiply indefinitely. Crying women no one could save or believe, broken to the point where they lacked the ability to save themselves. Their tears beacons in the void between energy fields of the world.

Before the invasion of this land by other humans, the creature had known that something just as malevolent as itself sailed on the horizon. Perched on a jagged rock at the edge of a cliff, the creature had watched the bleeding sunset and inhaled the scent of death carried by the currents from the open waters creeping onto the shores. An omen.

That is how it had found this place: from a prophetic vibration of chaotic bloodshed. This species fed off chaos as much as it did the wails of innocents. The thought of that chaos and bloodshed made it shiver with ecstasy as it waited for violence to scar the land. Violence that would scar the psyche of generation after generation.

The sharp edges of its teeth and claws trembled in impatience for that first meal. Its empty innards churned the vestiges of the flesh of its last meal. Soon it would feel the sharp pain of hunger if it didn't take sustenance.

The creature would move across the planet feasting. Boats moved across the water from all different lands, taking captives. The teeth that lined its bowels would smack together as it digested tears—its favorite delicacy. The creature's senses were hypersensitive to desperation, a perfume excreted by its favorite kind of prey.

But first it had to find the offending man. A promise was a promise. The creature would begin by taking his children under the cover of night.

Sebastien missed Seville. He missed everything about Spain, from the cool air of the mountains to the ringing of cathedral bells in the morning. But this new world would bring more wealth than he could possibly spend in one generation. Sebastien had neither a title nor a large inheritance to speak of. That is why he had set off on this expedition. For more. And more he had. By the grace of his god, his life had been spared from battle and disease. From this conquest, there was wealth to finance his wife's journey from Spain now that this part of the New World was tamed. In quick succession his wife bore him two children of pure Spanish blood, his heirs in wealth and title. His name would go on for a very long time, perhaps even earn him respect in their homeland.

The horses stirred more than usual that night, whining and restless. Their large black eyes roved in all directions as they paced in the stable. Sebastien almost feared they would kick down the walls just to escape. One of the native boys was charged with their care. Tonight, however, he fled as soon as the horses were fed and watered. He left a sloppy mess in his haste. *Lazy and ungrateful*, Sebastien grumbled to himself as he did the last check before bedtime. He waved the torch back and

forth to each corner. Nothing. Horses were such skittish creatures. After they were secure, he stepped into the silent night. It
felt still and eerie, mist covering the village. The humidity here
clung not just to your flesh, but to your bones, so that it was
impossible to feel cool sometimes. It reminded him of the fog
they'd seen as they sailed through open waters, so thick you felt
you were being swallowed whole in the hot breath of Satan himself.

He placed the torch in its holder by the door of the stables,
then extinguished the light. Without further concern he turned
to walk back into his home.

The house felt as still as the village. He removed his boots to
avoid bringing manure into the hacienda. His wife and children
slept soundly. He would go check on them before finding the
native woman he had taken for his own. With an oil lamp in
hand taken from the front of the house, he crept toward the
room where his two children slept. The tiles felt colder beneath
the soles of his feet as he approached their rooms.

The cold quickened his step. Fear licked and blackened his
heart like the flame caught in the glass lamp. He opened the
door.

Both of his children's beds lay empty, the linen tossed to the
side as if they had thrown the light blankets from their bodies in
a hurry.

Perhaps they were in his bed with their mother, he prayed as
he rushed to his room, swinging the door open, not caring if the
sound woke the three. At that moment their cries would have
been a pleasant sound.

But there were no cries, only a sight that made his stomach
seize.

This was terror like he had never known, except for on the
battlefield. His wife lay in her once-white nightgown, which was

now drenched in glistening red. He couldn't distinguish between bed linen, cotton night dress, and flesh. Her organs were twisted inside out, messy as an unmade bed. Her flesh had been hacked as if by a vicious animal or an axe. Blood seeped from her wounds, forming black pools on the floor. But her empty eye sockets were fixed toward the ceiling. He had seen this mask on many other native women, but had never considered that it could reach his home.

It had to be one of them. The natives. They would pay dearly. The entire village would be overturned. No wonder the stable boy was skittish. He had to be in on the murder plot. And the horses? Maybe the murderer had hidden in the stables before his arrival.

Revenge would have to wait. He stepped farther into the room praying to god he would not find his children's bodies beneath the bed. "Isla. Mateo. Come out if you are hiding!"

Before he could take another step, the door slammed behind him.

As he turned around, a slashing pain seared his hand, causing him to drop the lamp, which shattered on the floor. A fetid, hot breath filled his nostrils. Out of instinct he reached for his sword that was not there. The only light came from the moon shining through the single window. He ran into the dim beam, holding his wounded hand.

In his peripheral vision he saw a figure standing outside. It was the indigenous woman. She stood with her clothing and hair dripping with water and a large grin on her lips. Her entire body had the luminosity of the moon. Her eyes met his, reflecting his cruelty back to him. Then she walked away with assured steps. Before he could screw his neck further from the darkness to follow her with his eyes, a shadow emerged from behind the door. In its hand it held his horsewhip.

The creature was a demon so hideous that he crossed himself and began to pray out loud. Its eyes sparkled like the stars during a new moon. The form resembled a human's, yet its flesh hung like a garment over bone. A robe of death.

It raised its hand before slashing the whip across his body. And then blood dripped from its open mouth as it spoke. "Your superstitious belief in one god will not save you. I don't come from the places your small minds conceive of. Your blood and your bloodline are mine."

It whipped him again, this time hitting his face. Sebastien took a step backward, hitting the window. He had nowhere to run. He was cornered. Without taking his eyes off the demon he fumbled with the window latch. The whip cracked, followed by pain across his cheek. The creature watched him with wild eyes, laughing as it moved closer. Slung over both shoulders were the shredded crimson nightclothes of his children. Sebastien screamed in agony. A vision of their sweet faces playing in the garden, then flashes of the indigenous children he saw killed in battle, cut into his memory. It burned as though he were looking directly into the sun.

Sebastien let out another cry so sharp it pierced his own ears. He looked to his left at the torn body of his wife, her dead dark eyes missing.

When he turned back, the creature thrust its claws into his belly. Its saliva-filled mouth was wide open, poised to remove his face. At least he had his faith and god would welcome him with open arms. He hoped.

Sebastien from Seville and his name were gone from history forever.

Alejandra

Three days without Matthew passed following the same routine as when he was there, except there was one less drain on Alejandra's nearly depleted internal battery.

The mornings were the best part of the day. Her children would pile onto the bed, still warm with sleep, and curl into her body like they had on the days they were born. In bed, Elodia sucked on her thumb even though a giant callus had formed at the knuckle. Her little brown eyes, surrounded by silky brown-and-blond-streaked curls, looked up at Alejandra with pure contentment. Her love was given freely. In those moments Elodia asked for nothing and needed nothing because the world was complete in that bed with the love of her mother. Alejandra wished the entire day could feel like that, her internal wick burning bright, emitting only clean smoke.

It was difficult to admit, as she gazed into her baby's eyes, that before Elodia had been born, Alejandra hadn't wanted another child. In the midst of the yearlong wait, with nothing but bloody

panties month after month, Alejandra had come to the conclusion that she didn't want a third child. Three children was Matthew's grand vision for the family, not hers. For her, two children
settled nicely with the future she envisioned of getting back to
work, or at least creating a new avenue in her life.

Then it happened: She'd had an "oh fuck" moment when she
found out she was pregnant. The sickness roiling in her stomach
when she made the discovery had been even more insidious
than the morning sickness she'd had with each child.

But with Matthew gone, she felt newly calm. No fear of his
disapproval, no demands. One morning she brought wrapped
madeleines to her bedroom for the children to eat so she could
get a few extra quiet minutes in bed. The crumb-filled sheets
would matter little; it would be a mess worth cleaning up. In
those moments, as they ate and cuddled her, Alejandra saw the
divinity in their little faces.

But then, the piano ringtone of her alarm alerting them it
was time to start the morning wailed on the bedside table, and
the cycle of pain began again.

"I want to stay home," whined Will as he thrashed his little
arms and legs, inadvertently smacking Elodia across the chest.
Elodia burst into tears followed by high-pitched screeches. Alejandra hated that sound because it mirrored the pain she had
carried from childhood to adulthood. Catrina groaned, "Will
and Elodia ruin *everything*." She shot Alejandra an angry look
before tossing the covers to the side and returning to her room
to get dressed.

Alejandra had to quickly soothe Elodia before beginning the
morning routine for school. Loud shrieks continued to fill the
bedroom as Alejandra cuddled Elodia. Alejandra wished someone were there to wrap their arms around *her* and tell her it
would be all right.

But it made no difference that Matthew wasn't there. In the mornings, unless she explicitly asked for Matthew's help getting the children ready, he remained in bed with his eyes shut even when there was chaos.

"Will, can you please get dressed for me?"

"No!" Will shouted before running to his room. So much for her calm morning.

Alejandra could feel her chest tighten with frustration. Her entire body became a clenched fist desperate to smash through a wall until the knuckles bled. This would be one of those mornings when she would forgo brushing her own teeth or combing her hair to get the children out the door in time.

From there those days would keep spiraling into turmoil—except for the two mornings a week Elodia went to a playgroup. Wednesdays and Fridays would instead be a duel between love and discontentment as she tried to push as much food as possible into the grocery cart followed by trying to shove as much laundry as she could from five people into the washing machine before she had to collect Elodia.

All the while obsessive thoughts of death would scratch at her mind with the ferocity of a rabid animal at her front door. Death was easier than living.

Difficult woman. Sick woman. Dead woman.

Alejandra and the children arrived at school with seven minutes to spare. Alejandra dreaded making small talk with the parents. Even so, she gave everyone a nice smile. Most of the school parents worked full-time and stood around in their nice shoes, chatting about the commute into the city. And then there were the women who didn't work, who had formed their own little clique from the time their children began pre-K together. Alejandra didn't fit in with either group. The parents from both groups returned her warm smile before turning their attention back to their friends.

She stood in the crowd of the school parents as they waited for the children to be led into their classrooms by the teachers' assistants. The adults' conversation bounced off her ears. She picked out something about what they'd done that weekend with their kids. Alejandra could only recount bickering with Matthew, spending too much effort trying to find a middle ground, fighting with Catrina over homework, and listening to Elodia's shrieks for attention.

Alejandra tried to reach deep into her mind to find what she wanted to do besides be a full-time whatever-she-was, a piece of offal called "Mother." She didn't know. A burst of laughter from the parents with big smiles on their faces made her feel even more like a failure. Alejandra only knew she couldn't do the next eighteen years like this, then lie on her deathbed thinking of how she'd spent her short precious time on Earth.

I went to and from school to talk about a new gluten-free brownie recipe. How many hours I clocked on my Peloton to give me this figure I couldn't even enjoy because I chose the wrong partners time and time again, because I gave away my body like cheap Halloween candy. I folded mountains of laundry. I watched my husband achieve his dreams while I sat at home wanting to die, forgetting any dreams of my own.

The waking nightmare began in her kitchen. The sun rose as she stood with a mug of black coffee looking at the scattered toys and fallen pieces of food littering the floor. She hated pressing the kids to tidy up because it would only lead to more fighting and tantrums. She would have to repeat herself ten times, every word more frustrated and angrier than the last. Matthew was away on business, the kids were still asleep, and she took advantage of this moment to do nothing but drink coffee while it was still hot.

The hypnotic pitter-patter of rain falling on the skylight sent her gaze to the large plastic paddling pool that accommodated all three children. It was filling fast with rainwater, and something brown, like fur or feathers, floated on the surface. It was difficult to see with the raindrops slithering down the windows like eels.

Alejandra placed her coffee on the kitchen island and walked closer to the double glass doors. If it was a dead animal, she would have to clean it up before the kids woke up hungry, which could be any minute now.

Then the thing in the pool twitched.

The sudden movement made her jump. She unlocked the door to dash into the rain to have a closer look.

Tangles of greenish-black hair the texture of seaweed splayed and floated at the pool's sides. Beneath the pool toys and rubber balls was an almost indiscernible shape.

But then she saw: It was a body.

It had a pigeon in its mouth. Thick gums gnawed on the chest of the bird, sucking out its insides. It moved its glowing white eyes toward Alejandra. The white in the sockets narrowed to dots in pools of black. "You're next," it whispered from its bloody, entrail-filled mouth. Then the creature jerked upright, spraying a mouthful of blood onto the inner side of her forearm, right over her birthmark.

Alejandra screamed against the rain and wind before running back inside the house. Her wet hair and clothes dripped a puddle at her feet. She frantically wiped at her arm with the bottom of her T-shirt and then saw it: There was not a single spot of blood.

This was just like the hallucination in the shower and the shadow in the bathroom. It all came back to her. An internal warning radiated from the pit of her stomach: Something was terribly wrong. She turned her head in slow motion toward the pool, wondering if her pain had finally manifested before her eyes.

She jumped when she heard Elodia cry "Mama" from her crib upstairs. Alejandra looked toward the stairs to the second floor, not knowing what to do. Go to her crying child or face the thing in the pool that couldn't be real? The *feeling* again. Same as the shower. It was real. Her mind chattered on, *Don't be dumb* over the warning she could only sense. Her body trembled from the cold and fear. She turned toward the pool again. The rain pounded harder against the skylight. Or was it her heartbeat? Maybe that creature was here to drag her to hell for being such a shitty mother.

Will stood in the kitchen doorway in his Thomas the Tank Engine pajamas. "Mommy, can't you hear Elodia? She needs you, and Catrina took the iPad from your room like you told her not to."

What she had just seen in the pool made her shrink to the size of a child, and she remembered being a child. She saw again the basement in the house she had lived in as a teen. It was the only place she could have her own bedroom at thirteen instead of sharing with the younger children. But it had never felt like *home.* The room was belowground, and it had narrow rectangular windows, through which she could see just the surrounding earth. It had a cramped bathroom with just a toilet, shower stall, and sink. The air locked in the space was claustrophobic and foul. The basement made her feel trapped in a small world she didn't understand or know how to make her own.

But the place she felt most fearful of was the corner bedroom where the younger kids slept in bunk beds. She would only go downstairs to sleep, placing a T-shirt across her eyes to keep from seeing any shadows that might've lingered there. Despite what she felt inside, she decided her adoptive father was right: *You are just miserable. That is who you are. Stop being dumb, Allie.*

At fourteen she had disobeyed the rules of curfew, and her adoptive father had sent her to this basement bedroom early to sleep and take her punishment. A large brown wooden cross he'd made himself had hung above the archway.

A believer in corporal punishment, her father had given her four smacks across the back of her legs with his belt. She'd lain facedown on the bed. The pain of the belt as real as the fear she'd felt with a grown man behind her, hitting her without mercy. How could wrongdoing be corrected by more wrongdoing? How could you learn about love from someone who gave you nothing but pain? These thoughts had hurt more than the belt. She hadn't wanted to look back when he paused between smacks. Hadn't wanted to see what might've been in his eyes. He had never been inappropriate in the slightest, but something in that moment had felt off. It wasn't right. Even if it would've carried consequences for their family, she'd promised to call the police or someone if he tried to carry out a physical punishment again. After he'd left, she'd remained in the same position, trembling from fear. She'd cried into the bed, the sheet absorbing her tears and screams.

A ghost or demon or whatever thing lingered in that basement could have taken her away in that moment and it wouldn't have mattered to her. Death would've been better than that life. You never forgot the first time someone struck you or the first time you saw someone being struck.

Now, standing in that kitchen, she wasn't that child in the basement room anymore. But had her mind been teetering on the edge since then?

"Mom. What's wrong?" Will's voice grounded her by snapping her attention to the present.

"I'm here, honey, everything is okay." She shook off the fear that clung to her like wet clothes because she had to get the children ready for their day. "Come here." Will walked toward her with a sleepy look on his face as he rubbed his eyes. She wrapped her arms around him once he stood in front of her. "Everything is okay. I love you. Let's get ready for school. I'll put something extra in your lunch box. Your choice." He nodded into her neck. Alejandra left the kitchen holding Will's hand without looking back.

After returning from the school run, she packed away the paddling pool and outdoor toys strewn across the backyard. Focusing on the thing in the pool would not make things better.

Alejandra decided help could no longer wait.

When Matthew wasn't berating her for expressing her feelings, he begged her to speak to a professional, but something inside of her didn't believe in his sincerity. It felt fake, like he was so perfect and she this broken thing that needed all the fixing. Part of her believed he only wanted her to get help because he had grown tired of her no longer catering to his needs with a smile on her face.

Something inside did need fixing. Year after year she could feel herself unraveling like the yarn of the Raggedy Ann doll her birth mother had given her at their first meeting.

While Elodia took her afternoon nap, Alejandra settled on

the sofa with the iPad. The list of female therapists went on for pages. Her eyes ached from reading countless bios. She picked up her phone, intending to ask a few acquaintances from school if they could make any recommendations. Then she put the phone down again. The last thing she needed was to be mom-shamed with gossip about her mental struggles. You're supposed to smile through motherhood. She decided to type "Mexican American therapist." It would be helpful if someone knew where she came from and the struggles in her home life.

She found a Melanie Ortiz. According to her bio, Melanie was also a practicing curandera, a spiritual medicine woman.

A curandera.

She couldn't remember the last time she had entered a church. So much time in her childhood had been spent in and out of church, revivals, vacation Bible school, Sunday school, even one summer camp with a lecherous camp leader in his thirties with children of his own. Avoiding him for a week had become a game of Whac-A-Mole. She had always sought out friends and men who were not religious.

But most nights Alejandra found herself praying to no specific god or saint when she closed her eyes in bed. She needed to speak on the things she didn't understand.

Alejandra grabbed her iPad to find out more about Dr. Ortiz. There were countless articles Dr. Ortiz had written advocating for mental health awareness in women of color, generational trauma, and even entrepreneurship. *Generational trauma. Generations of people.* Alejandra glanced at a framed photograph of her children and thought of her DNATree report. She continued to scroll through the abstracts and articles written by Dr. Ortiz.

Dr. Ortiz not only had her own practice but also owned a botanica called Sol filled with products made by women from all over the world. Alejandra's heart fluttered at this thought. There were also videos of Dr. Ortiz speaking. One in particular gave Alejandra chills. Dr. Ortiz walked onstage at a conference for mental health professionals. She wore indigo beaded earrings that fell to her shoulders and brown huarache sandals paired with a simple white blouse and dark jeans. With a hand on either side of the podium, she spoke with a passion derived from a place of churning fire as she talked of using indigenous beliefs combined with modern medicine to create deep healing. Her confidence mesmerized Alejandra. She wanted to find that within herself. This woman who had nothing but fight in her to make both herself and her community better would be the one to guide her. *Guides.*

The women from her dreams flashed in her mind with the brightness of a lightning bolt before her fingers tapped across the iPad to send Dr. Ortiz a message. Alejandra made an appointment online and booked a babysitter for its duration, plus an extra hour after. Her pulse raced as she completed these tasks, perhaps a small sign that she was taking the right steps. She then messaged Matthew, who would be back in a week, about the session. It would show up on their bank account and he would ask.

It beat the idea of going to some hotel bar alone and ordering drink after drink. Although how good would it feel to indulge in such a fantasy, because what else did she have just for herself? She imagined sitting on a barstool. A stranger, or an acquaintance, against her back. His or her breath on her neck. A hand on her hip sliding to her thigh, lifting her skirt up slightly beneath the bar where no one else could see. A forefinger finding its way under the lace garter belt. A voice telling her, *Room 305.*

Alejandra cast the iPad aside.

She continued the fantasy: The bar was now empty, and a

man was in front of her. She could part her legs for his hands to explore as he held her gaze. Their parted lips met. Room 305.

Alejandra allowed her body to sink into the sofa pillows that smelled of chips and cookies. She pulled the blanket off the back of the sofa and onto her body. The only way to break the tension in her body was with pleasure.

Alejandra didn't stop after one orgasm but came again as she physically loved herself with every stroke. Immediately she thought about what she needed to accomplish on that day while the baby slept. The thought dried her sexual desire. She rose from the sofa to wash her hands and change her underwear. Only a few hours until the school run again. Better check the fridge before leaving the house.

The kitchen appeared dark with the gloom of cloud cover outside. The clouds moved, and shafts of light streamed across the floor. The ice maker bashed out ice cubes, and she looked in the direction of the sound. Her eyes caught her reflection in the glass of the oven. Behind her a dark halo of a shadow hovered.

She whipped her head back. Nothing there but the tall liquor cabinet and the light from outside moving in and out of the room.

Just get on with it, Alejandra, she told herself.

Alejandra checked the expiration dates on the food in the refrigerator in preparation for heading to the supermarket and planning the meals for the next few days. But her mind drifted to Matthew. When she searched her thoughts she couldn't remember fantasizing about their life as they aged. The cold air from the fridge hit her face. And she realized she already knew in her broken heart that she wanted Matthew for all the wrong reasons.

The shadow drifted across the reflection in the oven glass as she closed the refrigerator door.

The path leading to the side entrance of the home where Melanie's office was located was lined with pots of herbs, vibrant flower beds, and large lavender bushes humming with fat bees. As Alejandra neared the back, she could see a small greenhouse. The property smelled wonderful, felt peaceful. A small patch of Eden, a large garden full of life stimulating all her senses.

She knocked once on the pale-green door, not knowing what to expect, yet the beauty of the garden had put her at ease. The word "safe" popped into her head. A woman not much older than she opened the door. Her black hair, parted in the center, fell to her shoulders. She wore thick-rimmed red glasses. The word "gratitude" was tattooed on the side of her left ring finger. "Alejandra, welcome." Like the garden, this woman exuded peace and empathy. She could've easily been one of the women in the circle in Alejandra's dreams.

Alejandra followed Dr. Ortiz into a room with a large window overlooking a backyard with a birdbath and bench. Just outside the window was a hummingbird feeder. The natural light brightened a room that was also filled with color. Color in the Georgia O'Keeffe and Diego Rivera prints. Color in the striped rug beneath their feet. Two large certificates from the University of Pennsylvania hung on one of the walls. In the corner stood an altar with personal objects next to a shelf with rows of essential oils. On the end of her desk was a single bonsai tree trimmed to perfection with a yin-and-yang symbol on the black pot. Alejandra sat in a comfortable red armchair in front of Melanie. Melanie gave her an inviting smile. "I read over the profile you filled in. Thank you for all the details. Some people don't bother. Married to Matthew; three children named Catrina, Will, and Elodia—gorgeous names by the way; adopted at birth and raised in what you describe as an Evangelical home.

"So, tell me: What is not in your profile? Why are you here?"

Alejandra didn't know how to articulate that she would rather die than experience another day in her current existence, as herself. Her soul felt so dim, the slightest shift of wind or breath might snuff it out. She was seeing things and didn't know if anyone would believe her. But she had to answer the question. Where to even start?

Alejandra began, "I'm not who I used to be, but I didn't like that version of me much when I think about it because of regret . . . I guess I don't like this version of me either . . . My husband suggested I do this, but I didn't. I don't know.

"Sorry, I'm not making sense. Maybe I should come back when I'm less confused and can . . . I don't want to waste your time."

Tears fell from Alejandra's eyes as she began to rise from her seat. Melanie stood from her seat and grabbed a tissue from her desk and a bunch of herbs and lavender wrapped at their base with twine. She handed both to Alejandra.

"You can leave if you want. But will you first take a deep breath and wipe your eyes? You don't need to make sense. That is part of the process. If everything made sense and was in perfect order, you wouldn't need my help. My question isn't a test. Don't overthink it. What is the first thing that comes to mind?"

Alejandra nodded and brought the fan of herbs and lavender to her nose as she sat back down. It smelled wonderful. She fiddled with the stems before looking around the office. Her eyes drifted to a spiny aloe plant in a pot painted with La Catrina, the skull-faced woman in a wide-brimmed hat.

Melanie noticed her looking in a different direction, slightly distracted. She turned to her left. "Are you looking at my pot with La Catrina? Like the name of your daughter."

Alejandra smiled and nodded. "In high school I spent a lot of time alone in the library. I came across an art history book with her in it. My deep curiosities about the world went against my upbringing, which constantly repeated 'The wage of sin is death.' I took in the information about my ancestry from books, but I didn't allow it to take root. I loved that she was the image of death, that was her essence, yet she didn't try to be anything less. It's like she is saying, 'Look at me! I can dress as fine as I want, but death will never elude me. Might as well live and love.' I guess I believed freedom from fear like that wasn't realistic. When I was thinking of names during my first pregnancy, I remembered a depiction of La Catrina. The name was chosen in that instant. That is why Catrina is named Catrina."

"I like that story."

"What does La Catrina mean to you? I watched your videos and read a few of your articles. Very impressive."

Melanie gave her a warm smile as her body relaxed into her chair. "Our ancestors revered death. One female depiction of death is the goddess Mictecacíhuatl, the lady of death whose visage is flayed. And then she was absorbed in the process of assimilation into the dominant culture like our ancestors were after the invaders arrived. She had to become something perceived as less powerful in order to survive. She became a symbol of death as a decorative image of a skeleton in Mexican art and famously in the artwork during Día de los Muertos. She was drawn this way, smiling in her fancy dress and flamboyant hat, as a sort of middle finger to the oppressive ruling class, because death is an inescapable fate for everyone.

"We as brown women from two different cultures have been

on a similar journey to the goddesses of our ancestors. Don't forget, Alejandra, that you have the power to transform anytime you want. Look how La Catrina laughs, as she is still in existence and revered despite her change. You don't have to be the woman anyone else wants you to be or tells you you should be to make them more comfortable in their own existence. Yes, our ancestral culture has changed, but you can still find power in it."

Melanie's eyes softened. "I am sober. I didn't go to AA or have a morning-to-night drinking habit, but my drinking was once enough to cause me to suppress all the gifts I had been given to help others. I made the choice to stop drinking and be empowered enough to be who I wanted to be without alcohol to lean on. Sometimes in life we have to endure the death of others and the death of parts of ourselves. But it is just transformation. La Catrina reminds us that death is life.

"My child is grown now, but when he was born, my mother lay dying in the same hospital a few floors away. She passed away as I lay resting from the birth. A nurse took my son away when they broke the news to me my mother had died, in the event I reacted violently toward myself or my child. She had been in a coma from encephalitis. We never knew how she contracted it."

"I'm sorry to hear that." Melanie's honesty gave Alejandra the confidence to be candid. Melanie wasn't some stranger sitting across from her and scrutinizing her.

"I want to stop crying. I want this dark cloud that feels like it's preventing me from fully loving my children or myself to go away. I'm hurting. I'm scared."

"What are you afraid of? Is someone harming you or your children?"

Alejandra opened her mouth to speak. Her lips trembled with the words trying to form, yet her mind was scared of what someone else would think. Yes, she was afraid of something, and she was also afraid of judgment from other people.

"The more honest you are, Alejandra, the more I can help you. There is no risk in being truthful with me. I'm here for you."

Alejandra had to start somewhere, and as scared as she was, she wanted to know the truth of what was occurring in her life and inside of her.

"I'm seeing things. I love my children, but I feel my patience and motivation to live fading. I get along with my husband but haven't decided if I'm still in love with him or not. I feel increasingly like our relationship was never what I thought it was. Not really sure the direction my life is going in. I'm a horrible person, I know. I chose these things. And all of this makes me want to die. It hurts so bad I don't know how to make it stop except through death."

"You may have chosen all of it. We want to find out what led you to it. Go on."

Alejandra wasn't sure how to read Melanie. Her face remained calm and attentive. Part of Alejandra expected a scolding any minute. But this moment of being completely honest with another person was like the relief of walking for miles and finally putting down a heavy suitcase.

"What are you seeing? You mentioned in the contact form you have no history of mental illness or taking any medication?"

"I'm seeing a woman, no, women, in my dreams that are so vivid I almost think I am awake. Always crying, but not wailing. Their tears roll down their cheeks silently. They are dressed differently, I guess from different places and times. Sometimes I close my eyes to remember as much detail as possible to understand more. There is another phantomlike figure that hides in steam and shadow that tells me to harm myself, feeds the awful things I think about myself. I'm not sure if it is real or in my mind. I just want to feel free. Free from whatever is haunting me. I've ignored it too long. My children deserve better."

"And you? Don't you deserve better? They are part of you. How can you not think of yourself as you think of them?"

Alejandra could only sit there with her exhaustion hanging on her back. A warm sensation began in the center of her shoulder blades then radiated to the rest of her body, raising the hair on her neck. Those words felt *true*.

"Do the women look like you?"

Alejandra refocused from her body to Melanie. "No. But they are brown women, Mexican, I think. And wet, like they have been in the rain or in the water."

"Water, crying women. Sounds like La Llorona. We are both very aware of her story."

"Yes! In fact, I told my daughter her story not long ago. Didn't want to say anything to seem . . . I don't know . . . like I was manifesting my shit with a tale. I was told she was a woman who drowned her children for the love of a man, and now she wanders the Earth looking to take the children of others. I had a moment in my shower, one of my lowest points, and I could swear the steam looked like a woman in white."

"Do you believe in the supernatural or ghosts?"

Alejandra shook her head and let out a sarcastic chuckle. "The only ghost I was supposed to believe in was the Holy Ghost. It never made an appearance, so no. I don't believe in any of it. I'm fascinated by the concept of another world, energy that doesn't die. I haven't made up my mind if that energy lives in us or we are just maggot food. Sometimes I get the feeling it's all real."

"What makes you think the story of La Llorona isn't true?

Stories always begin somewhere. Even those ideas in the imagination come from somewhere. Tell me more about the things you are seeing."

"The women seem kind. Not threatening. It's like they are waiting to help. I saw the other thing only twice outside of my dreams. The first time I was crying uncontrollably in the shower. Without question I doubted myself, my eyes. Then, it appeared as a creature devouring a bird in my children's pool. I ran inside. Then my children woke up crying and hungry. I saw to them, carried on like usual before going back outside. There was nothing in the pool, and it appeared as if there was nothing there in the first place. But doubting myself is all I do. In everything. But I can't stop thinking about the creature or the way the bird looked half eaten."

"Let me ask you this. Why do you think those images have stuck with you?"

Alejandra leaned back into the chair, inhaling the scent of some oil she couldn't identify. It calmed her like a glass of wine or a joint. She allowed her shoulders to fall in surrender. "I feel like the creature and the dead bird."

Alejandra paused. "You know, it's interesting you mentioned La Llorona. Growing up I loved spooky stories, had an interest in the occult and horror. I wanted to know more about my ancestral beliefs, but my adoptive family were so Christian. Christian to the point I got a minor role in the play *Dracula* in high school as one of Dracula's wives, but had to give it up because it was too demonic. God, I was so angry and hurt. I found something that interested me, but it wasn't in line with the faith I didn't share with my adoptive family.

"Anyway, I chose you because it also mentions on your website you are a curandera. Whatever is happening to me feels beyond what I can see or touch. I'm in a place where I have one foot on the ledge of a cliff and the other dangling in the air. The rest of me is in the middle, trying to balance so I don't fall. I don't know how to get both feet on solid ground."

Melanie nodded. "My duty as a light worker is to help others navigate through their darkest times. Part of that is for them to know I have experienced my own demons. I want to thank you for being so open with me. You can trust me. I get the impression you don't trust many people. I want to go back, away from these visions and feelings. Away from your adoptive family. Tell me about your mother."

"Well, for starters, my mother gave me up, and I never knew my father. It was only a few years ago we met for the first time."

"Let's start there."

The first meeting with her birth mother had flowed with the surreal light-headedness of a daydream. On so many occasions she fantasized about being face-to-face with Cathy from the moment she found out at nine years of age that she was adopted. Her Evangelical parents adopted and fostered children from different backgrounds across Texas. Her adoptive mother, Patricia, liked to joke that their family theme song was "Onward, Christian Soldiers." God's will to save souls in this life and the next.

Alejandra carried questions around with the same weight as the stations of the cross. She wanted to know the details about her birth parents and where they were from. Her adoptive parents didn't like to talk about the past and focused only on where they would be going: "kingdom vision," they called it. Everything you needed to know could be found in one book. Alejandra dismissed every word. One day she would leave and find out the way, the truth, and life on her own. Alejandra broke from her adoptive parents for good when they refused to give her any information about her birth parents on her eighteenth birthday.

Years later, technology created another path for deeper communication and connection. A company called DNATree offered clients family profiles, medical information, and ancestral location history. If anyone else on their database matched your DNA, then a connection would be made. For just over one hundred dollars and a tube full of spit, they would give her detailed information about who she was, down to the building blocks of her existence.

Alejandra had fallen asleep in the afternoon during her second pregnancy while watching old *X-Files* reruns on cable TV. It had been impossible to stay alert after lunch during the first trimester. She heard a large bang in her mind, an explosion of sound like a door swinging open and hitting a wall. It jolted her awake. Startled that someone was trying to break in, she grabbed her phone. Not a sound. She called out for Matthew. No response.

Before she could rise from the sofa, a commercial began to play on the television that caught her attention. Hundreds of birds perched on a tree. The leaves and feathers were so vibrant she couldn't take her eyes off the screen. They sang in unison. DNATree. Without any previous thoughts in her groggy mind, she heard, *Order it*. She immediately bought two kits off the website for her and Matthew to do together.

Two months later, DNATree alerted Alejandra to all her blood relatives, where her DNA originated (Nuevo León and Guadalajara, Mexico), and the breakdown in percentages of her ethnicity. On the website you could view an extended family tree spanning all over the globe, including how close you were based on common DNA.

One alert changed her life: A Cathy Castillo sent her a relative request.

The DNA proved their relationship as mother and daughter, a bond knitted and strung all the way back in time. In her bittersweet darkness of being a new mother again, she hoped that healing this wound would bring some solace or at least a step toward greater healing. Turned out that her birth mother lived in Texas and worked at the Bexar County Hospital as a general practitioner.

Still full of surging hormones, Alejandra cried for days, swinging from elation to overwhelming anxiety. Watching Catrina hold little Will in her arms pushed her to decide to contact Cathy. If Cathy didn't want to be contacted, she never would have sent the request. Alejandra possessed the power to make a dream a reality.

"Don't get too excited and don't expect too much. You can't rely on someone like that. You have your own family now," Matthew warned her. Alejandra had to contain her anger. He knew nothing about this person. She ignored him and followed her heart.

On the day they met at a diner, Alejandra and Cathy could only exchange awkward glances, eyes darting between each other, their coffee, and uneaten muffins.

"You must want to know why."

Alejandra nodded, holding back the tears, wishing Matthew hadn't planted those seeds of doubt. This was why she wanted to meet in public. She thought it would prevent her from breaking down, but it took all her self-control to avoid doing so. "Of course. But I also want to know about my past. My family."

"I was very young, still in high school, when I found out I was expecting you, and I had to make a choice. You or myself. I figured giving you an opportunity with a family who could provide meant I was choosing us both. You could have a good life and I could have a life."

"I understand. I took the morning-after pill more than once in my twenties."

"But I also want you to know, and it is probably little comfort, I never had any other children. I sterilized myself. I realized I would never be ready or want children.

"I'm so happy you contacted me. I would like to get to know the woman you are, know my grandchildren. If that is something you would want. Did your family give you a good life? Choices?"

Alejandra bit her lip and nodded. Depended on what she meant by choices. "There were eight of us, all from different places. I think they looked at us kids like doing God's work. We were homeschooled with a Christian curriculum heavy on the Bible verses and light on the science. I spent most of my time looking after other children, helping in the house. There was no play or being a teen with other teens outside of our house. It changed a bit when a few of us were allowed to go to high school. It was a shock. I had to repeat a grade because the homeschooling credits didn't all count. I left as soon as I could just to get a sense of life without someone's thumb on my head. But I will be honest with you now. There have been so many days and nights when I wondered why I was even born. To what purpose?"

These words had to be said, even if they hurt Cathy. Alejandra needed to say them out loud for herself. All her life she had wanted love from the one who brought her into this world, her own flesh and blood.

She had never understood the people who took her into their home. Her adoptive mother was half Mexican and half white, and her adoptive father was white. Alejandra just passed as their biological child. Both her parents were completely entrenched in their faith and demanded obedience above anything else. Her father especially was firm and strict. Alejandra flinched every time her adoptive father smacked the back of the legs of the little ones when they didn't take to potty training. Matthew never raised a hand to her, but goddamn if sometimes the energy radiating from his words didn't impact her like a punch or a slice of a straight razor.

She changed the subject so as not to diminish this life-altering moment with the lingering pain. "How do you like being a doctor?"

Cathy's face brightened with this question. "I love it. I love it so much I never had any other children, as I said before. Never got around to marrying anyone either. Always seemed to be let down by the ones I did meet anyway. I guess some part of me also felt it would not be fair to you. You would always remain my one. What are you doing now? What do you enjoy?"

Alejandra's cheeks flushed. She felt as hot as the steaming coffee. The fact she felt ashamed made her even angrier. "I'm at home. I stopped working after the third because it made more sense financially."

"Oh. That is very nice. I'm glad you enjoy it. And it sounds like you have been married for some time. Good for you."

Alejandra didn't bother to correct her. Perhaps it was her own insecurity, but she thought she could hear a hint of disappointment. "Thank you for the gifts. The kids will love them."

"You can ask me anything. I want you to feel comfortable talking to me and getting to know me."

Alejandra did want to know something. "Tell me about your mother."

Cathy stiffened. The brightness in her face faded.

"My mother, Frances, left me and your aunts and uncles when we were children. I don't know much about her. We've tried to find information, but nothing. It's like she dropped off the face of the Earth or fell into a dark well. And back then there was no electronic footprint. Disappearing could happen easily. I have two photos if you would like to see them. I have other bits and pieces of information about other relatives. But thank god for technology. DNATree has been thorough connecting millions of people. Millions of souls connected instantly from different parts of the world. I'll email all that I have. I also have a box of very old items. When my grandmother Elodia died . . ."

"Wait, what did you just say?"

"My paternal grandmother Elodia."

Alejandra took a bite of muffin to distract herself from her tears again. She sipped the coffee to wash it down and contain her emotions.

"That's my daughter's name. I wanted something to reflect my heritage. Just did a Google search between running to the toilet to puke or pee. I just . . . I liked the sound of the name as soon as I said it out loud. I'm named Alejandra, but my family insisted on calling me Allie, which I hate. My husband didn't love the name Elodia, but he got to name our son."

Cathy stared at her with a large smile on her face. She brought a single manicured hand to her mouth at this unexpected information. "Wow. Spooky. Elodia had a beautiful fig tree in her backyard that looked like the head of Medusa in the winter. Next to it was a type of storage shed. When she died, I cleared it out and found a treasure trove of handed-down items, relics, you might say. I'd love to share them with you, if you want."

This information and the coincidence were too much for Alejandra to process, so she changed the subject, again.

"So, your mother left you and you left me. A pattern maybe." Alejandra immediately regretted saying this as she noticed the small change in Cathy's eyes.

"Yes. It would seem so. I wish it could have been different for all of us. I'm sorry. Thank you for responding to my request. You didn't have to. I cried for days, then I cried more when you reached out. What did I do to deserve that?"

Alejandra reached over and touched her mother's hand. "This is a start of something we both needed, wanted." Out of curiosity she looked at her mother's inner forearm to see if she had the same pattern of birthmark that looked like splattered oil. Nothing but a single café au lait spot, not much bigger than a freckle. Maybe the mark skipped generations, or she was an aberration.

"And my father?"

"It's going to sound ridiculous, but he was just a high school crush. We bonded over albums in music class. And I liked that he could grow a mustache at his age. During my second trimester of pregnancy, he dropped out of school. Through friends after graduation, I learned he got his GED and joined the army.

"I still have a few of the albums he gave me that you are welcome to have. Every time I moved, I promised to throw them out, yet some part of me could not, no matter how much my brain screamed to do it. So I carried them around in a sealed box. Maybe they were waiting all this time to be handed to you. Anyway, he lost interest. As I found out, he lost interest in women very easily. He was born with a wandering eye. I'm sorry I can't tell you more. He agreed to the adoption, and I have no way to find him now. But back to my mother."

Alejandra could feel the muffin sticking to the roof of her mouth and in the back of her throat. She swallowed hard before taking a sip of her coffee. The caffeine and adrenaline in the moment caused her to sweat. It dawned on her that her life would never be the same after this day. Cathy remained calm. Alejandra thought it was probably because of her profession.

"My family did not have any personal information about her. She kept her life before Texas private. From what I can remember she was a haunted woman who walked around like she didn't know if she belonged in this world or the next. I'd catch her staring at nothing with a look on her face as if she was listening to someone speaking to her. She blew hot and cold. She wanted to love us, but the intimacy of it perhaps was too much for her to handle. And let's be real, she had a lot of children to deal with on her own. My final memory is her standing in the kitchen with a zombie expression. The dark circles and smeared makeup beneath her eyes from crying made her look so frightening. I don't know if it's a false memory; however, as a child I could feel her sorrow.

"Now as a doctor I look back and think she needed real help, but times were so different back then. I'm not justifying her leaving, but it is easier for me to attempt to understand and try to move on with my life. I'm sorry I don't have more. I wanted more when I was younger. Many times the truth in our lives remains veiled until the time is right and the blindfold is taken off for us, or we have no choice but to rip it off kicking and screaming to free ourselves."

Cathy's words resonated with Alejandra.

"I couldn't move on with my life without trying to find out more. It would not have been possible without technology. What made you sign up for DNATree?"

Cathy's eyes began to build tears. "It was my absolute last attempt to find her. But it doesn't matter, because I found something better . . . You. When I found you, it gave me the space to put her to rest instead of keeping her as a ghost in my heart."

Alejandra grabbed Cathy's hand as she cried in front of the entire café.

"Why don't we make this a standing date?"

Cathy nodded. "Once a week is perfect for me."

For three months they met as often as possible, until Matthew received the job offer and they decided to move. "I'm all the family you will ever need, Alejandra. I'm the most important person in your life. Why does it matter if we move? This is what you do when you love someone. I need this, and I need you to realize this."

Before Alejandra left for Philadelphia, she collected the box of records from Cathy and said goodbye to her mother. She cried all the way home. When she walked through the door carrying the box of records, Matthew gave her a confused look. "What's all this? We just got rid of a bunch of stuff before the move."

"It's a box of albums from Cathy. They were given to her by my father."

"Albums? We don't even have a record player. I mean, you can keep them if it's sentimental, but they will just be in a box."

Alejandra didn't respond as he continued to walk up the stairs to his home office. First the pain of leaving Cathy and now an even deeper feeling of loneliness. She sat on the stairs with the box in front of her and looked through its contents. She forgot Matthew and could feel herself smiling. Boston, Kansas, AC/DC, *War of the Worlds*. Stuck between two records was an old sepia-tinged photo. She lifted it out of the box. Two small brown boys stood in front of a shop called Rosas.

She couldn't tell what kind of shop it was because the shutters were down in the windows. Only the intricately painted word *Rosas* was visible. The face of one of the boys looked and felt familiar. Both had little round noses that reminded her of Elodia. She placed the photo across her heart and closed her eyes.

They say that the eyes are the window to the soul, and in that moment perhaps she was trying to peer inside to find the answer as to why the photo gave her such a sense of nostalgia. The boy had to be someone related to her father. That explanation rang true with the facts she knew about her family and the feeling within. It was the fluttering of knowledge that can only come from blood or spirit, from her soul. "When the time is right," she said under her breath. She placed the photo back and closed the top of the box. It would be labeled with her name. When the time was right it would be something for her.

Cathy

San Antonio, Texas—1978

C athy Castillo felt awful in spirit and in body as she sat in front of the toilet with the taste of cheeseburger vomit in her mouth.

So much for free fucking love.

This could mean the end of her dreams and ambition, and for what? It was the time of women's lib, even if the concept was lost on the older folks in her family. Her body was hers to use for her own pleasure just as her mind was hers to dedicate to a field outside of the family home. Times were changing, and it was a wonderful thing.

It still wasn't easy being developed physically at a younger age, which made older men think you were a woman when you were still a teen. That's why she'd liked Rogelio. He was a simple guy, the same age as her, with messy brown hair and sideburns. And he gave her exclusive attention. His gaze felt like sunshine on her skin. The wet kisses they shared in his car the moisture she needed for her guarded heart to grow.

When he'd asked her out in the middle of the hallway as the others slammed their lockers before scrambling after the morning bell, she'd stood looking at him slightly confused. Usually, they sat next to each other in music class, passing notes about modern music: rock, not Chopin. Cathy wore oversize glasses and had the best grades in the class. Everyone knew she would be the one to make something of herself with those brains. *Her discipline is impeccable for someone so young,* as the teachers liked to comment on her report cards.

Whatever happened between her and Rogelio would be a light thing that would go nowhere, since Cathy had big dreams of medical school. Of being a female Mexican American doctor. Women's lib was for her too. She liked Rogelio, but settling down was not in her plans. Love was too much of a gamble, a game with winners and losers. And women were usually on the losing end, from what she had seen. Cathy didn't want to be pushed so far to the edge that she would choose to abandon her family. Just like her own mother had. Cathy would always choose herself first.

Between her father always working and his grandmother Elodia taking care of the younger ones, no one took time just for her. To tell her she was doing a great job, or say she was beautiful. The only identifiable thing about Cathy was that, as her family liked to say, "Cathy is wonderful because I don't have to worry about her. She always does the right thing." Her father liked to announce this in front of the extended family or his golfing friends as a point of pride.

Now she had to face the fact that she was shaking on the bathroom floor because after four months of dating she had made the decision to go all the way with Rogelio. The passion that stirred within her had needed to be released. Cathy knew without a test that she was pregnant. It had happened after an Aerosmith concert four weeks before.

Knowing she finally would experience sex with him had made her entire body electrified with confidence when he approached her after school to arrange their date. "How about I pick you up about nine?"

"That's perfect. I should be done with homework by then. My dad is in Mexico with his friend Clarence. I'll have no problems getting out of the house."

Her dad, David, often drove to Mexico for long weekends to have fun with his friends, and probably to enjoy the company of women, because there had been only one girlfriend after her mother left, and she hadn't lasted long. He filled his time golfing, going to dance halls to listen to Tejano music, and drinking with his male friends. He always brought gifts back from his time across the border. His mother, Elodia, gave him a disgruntled look when he came to claim his children. Time after time she told him to find another wife, but instead he filled his days living like a bachelor, mending his heart with the things that were at arm's reach and didn't tend to leave. He passed away having never married again.

Cathy and Rogelio's previous dates had all been simple: walking along the river walk, hanging in Guadalupe Park, sitting on a picnic table with beers. The concert would be something special. Her very first big rock concert, not just a Tejano band at a party or downtown on the River Walk. There would always be a romanticism in the mariachi music and classic corridos, but times were changing. The vibe was long hair, sideburns, tight jeans, and music old folks hated.

Music and marijuana smoke filled her head. They intoxicated her senses as the guitar and drumbeat vibrated through her body. She felt free. Free of her siblings and the pressure to be good. Be better. This was just for her. After the concert they went back to his house, where his parents didn't mind him bringing girls home. Everyone was asleep anyway. Cathy was ready to experience sex for the first time. "Dream On" played as soft as his touch to take her away. She allowed herself to let go.

"Cathy, you don't look great. You all right?"

The dizzy spells alerted her to accept the inevitable, but she didn't want to say it out loud to anyone yet. "Yeah, I think it's just stress. Tests, my brothers and sisters. But I need to be sure."

She knew she should have never slipped off her panties, lost in a fantasy, without contraception. After losing her virginity, she walked through the door to her dark house, replaying how tenderly he had kissed her. The memory of what appeared to be love made her entire being float and flutter, like a flock of beautiful birds taking flight at once. The second thought made her dash to the bathroom to urinate then shower to try to wash out whatever was left of his semen inside. She tried to calm her panic. *It was just one time. He said he tried to pull out. Just once. There can't be much inside.* She wanted to cry with the hot water burning her skin. Then a knock from her grandmother on the door. "It's late and you are going to wake up the house. Why are you showering so late?"

Cathy opened the door to her grandmother's disapproving face. She wanted an answer from Cathy. "My hair smelled like cigarette smoke. You know I don't like that." Elodia looked like she didn't buy the story but knew there was nothing she could say or do. Whatever was done was done.

Cathy lay in bed, unable to sleep, feeling angry at herself. The one time she needed her smarts they failed her. The fleeting excitement did not measure up to the possible consequences. Far from it. She loved her siblings, but she could not imagine herself spending her youth taking care of children, then spending her adulthood taking care of children, not without first giving her dreams a good go. Something unknown told her to not let go of that ambition. *Fight, girl!* The impossible could happen. *If your skirt is tripping you up, put on trousers.*

She didn't have a clue where the money for higher education would come from, but a little vision buried in her chest assured her it would arrive at just the right time. She cried to herself, holding on to a dream as tattered as a security blanket given to a child at birth. *It's you and me, La Virgen, from now on. We are the only ones in this world who believe I can do it.*

Four weeks later Cathy took the bus to her cousin Sylvia's house. Sylvia was twenty-eight, working at Sears because she could sell white goods better than any of the men with her long hair and even longer legs. The women admired her grace as she talked about juggling a baby and working while the men stood there on the borderline of falling in love. Cathy couldn't stop looking at Sylvia's son, Daniel, as he played with his toys then clawed at his mother's legs as she tried to talk. Cathy didn't want that, not now. Sylvia was the only one who would understand her predicament and not judge. Things had worked out with Daniel's father, who was in his thirties, but Cathy couldn't take that chance with Rogelio.

"Can you please pretend you are my mother and make the appointment?"

Her cousin Sylvia reluctantly picked up the phone. "All right, but only if you let me drive you. You are too young for any of this."

Three days later Cathy sat next to Sylvia listening to REO

Speedwagon. The music reminded her of Rogelio and his prized rock album collection he kept in plastic beer crates. He recently gave her a stack of records. Her favorite was Jeff Wayne's version of *The War of the Worlds*. They would smoke a joint while listening and staring at the gory depiction of an alien invasion on the album cover. Rogelio was not the academic type. He was the fun one, the cute jokester with bags of charisma. A good flirt. It's why she felt attracted to him: He was someone different from her.

She shook off the fond memory as the motion of the car made her want to vomit. She wondered if she'd forever fucked up her life. Her imaginary castles she'd built in her bright future for herself couldn't be battered to the ground and set alight like this. She didn't remember her own mother, the cruel bitch named Frances who had abandoned her and her three siblings.

Cathy wanted more, despite being Mexican American, which meant all the odds were not in her favor. She would still try. There was only one way. She would give this child up. Abortion would not be an easy option because of her age and the cost. And she didn't want to have the abortion conversation with anyone in her family, because it was not an acceptable option for a Catholic. Getting one illegally was too risky.

And keeping it was out of the question. She'd heard from her older siblings and from her aunt on her father's side how her own mother had struggled with children. Her mental health broke down after each one until eventually the seismic movement of it all drove her who knows where. When they moved to Texas, she seemed happy draped on her new husband's arm, but as time went on, she became increasingly distant. The offers of help and to be more involved in the family were not taken up. When Cathy pressed for more information, none of her father's

family had much to say. "Your mother was extremely private, quiet. A mouse."

No, a baby was not in Cathy's future. She would still have to break the news to her father and his family, who helped raise her and her siblings. They would try to convince her to keep the baby, but she would be eighteen by the time it arrived. She could do whatever she wanted. And what she wanted was to be free. Her older sister, Grace, had decided to keep her baby, and that was her choice. It wouldn't be Cathy's.

She didn't judge Grace. Cathy just wanted to find her own way. She walked into the doctor's appointment alone hoping for a miracle. The wait for the pregnancy test was the longest wait of her life. That moment spanned longer than her wait for her mother to return and filled her with an anxiety unlike any other test she had taken. There was no way to prepare for a test you didn't want to be positive.

The doctor and nurse both gave her a look of disappointed disgust when she asked about adoption options.

"What do you mean you don't want your baby?"

"I can't do this right now. I'll carry it, but after that please find a good home for it. I'm too young. I can't handle this. I have things I want to do."

The nurse gave her a small smile. "You should have thought about that before."

Fire and anger rose from Cathy's breastbone. If she could have flung the embers toward the nurse's face she would have. A cannon's boom of determination burst in her mind.

"It was a mistake. One time."

"Well, young lady, that is all it takes. That is why the good Lord says to wait until marriage. Nothing good comes out of premarital sex. Your mother should have told you that."

The nurse could not have known how that last sentence crushed her in an instant. Cathy would not cry for her. She placed her hand over her belly. In her mind she spoke to the baby. *You will be my only one always and forever. Leaving you won't be for nothing. I promise. One day we will find each other again when you need me most.*

The doctor maintained a neutral expression. "I have a pamphlet here on how to take care of yourself and what to look out for. You're lucky your father can pay for your healthcare with his military service. One more year and you wouldn't be covered."

Cathy nodded while trying to avoid the eyes of the nurse, who had more to say but knew she couldn't tell Cathy her real thoughts. Cathy hated the sound of crying children. No wails. Ever. Just the silence of her thoughts in a library. Now she had to do the most difficult part: tell her father, David. She had to tell him in one swift cut.

Her father sat in front of the local news, just like he did every evening, a can of Budweiser sweating in his hand. His brown leather recliner his throne, with his slippered feet elevated. He usually fell asleep in this spot, preferring it to his bed.

"Dad."

He looked toward her, slightly startled from dozing off. "What is it, mija?"

"I'm pregnant."

David's face fell. Cathy could see his disappointment. He took a long gulp of his beer and remained silent. Actually, it wasn't disappointment. It was guilt. His shoulders sagged without a spark of anger. He'd never spoken to Grace, Steven, Cathy, or Dolores about love, sex, or their changing bodies. He'd left it to the women of the family. Cathy didn't blame him. She knew he was doing his best as a single father at a time when mothers and fathers had their own domains.

Cathy didn't hesitate to speak fast before he assumed anything. Everyone knew she always made the right choices with a level head. He could rely on her to be independent. "I'm sorry. Don't worry about me. I don't want to keep it. I had Sylvia take me to the doctor, and I've already asked about the adoption process. You don't have to do anything."

He continued to look at her in silence before turning his attention back to the TV. He took a long gulp of his beer. "You will be eighteen soon. It is your choice. I wouldn't want you to raise a child on your own. It's not easy. Sometimes there was a reason I worked a lot. But we all reach an age when we have to make those hard choices."

Cathy turned to walk away, not sure what to expect over the next eight months except knowing she had to make it in this life. She didn't expect anything from her father despite wanting an outpouring of love, someone besides herself to say it would be all right. What she yearned for was to hear that the hardship and pain she would endure would be worth it in the end.

"Cathy."

She turned to Father in expectation, wanting to fall into his arms and cry.

"I love you. You will be fine."

She smiled, nodded, and returned to her room to study. Her lips quivered as tears waterfalled down her face once she shut the door. One door closing by her own hand to hopefully open more. Cathy had read about autopsies. If an autopsy could be performed while a person was still alive it must've felt like this. She could feel the bone saw cracking her sternum and bone dust covering her eyes.

Experiencing the discomfort in the doctor's office sharpened her sense of self and what she wanted to do in life. She would give up this child and become a doctor and work in the Bexar County Hospital to help women like her, whatever the cost or sacrifice. Her father's words stung, but that paled in comparison to the pain he must have felt being abandoned with a house full of children by the woman he loved.

What did her father think about when he lay in bed alone? Or in the recliner that could only fit one? Was that why there was always beer in the fridge and large garbage cans at the side of the house for their cans and bottles, which they took to the recycling center for pocket money? The stench strong and acrid when they were ready to be emptied.

If she was going to be the best damn doctor and go the distance, she would face worse smells and sights. She would eventually face death as a doctor. It would have to be something she couldn't fear but had the resolve to fight. Wasn't that what most of modern medicine was? Holding back death for just a little longer? Life was meant to be lived so death could be a little easier when it came for you. Her path was clear. It would be the only road she would travel.

When Cathy couldn't sleep from anxiety over school or the noises of the house with her brother and sisters, she would stare at the dark crack in her closet. She imagined her heart was like that closet, a small space with just enough room for herself.

A week passed between the time she found out about her pregnancy and her telling Rogelio the news. During that time, she didn't respond the same way to his notes, instead staying cold, eyes on the teacher or head down taking notes. As soon as the bell rang, she sprinted out the door, leaving no time for him to stop her. She knew she had made the right decision when she confronted Rogelio in the school parking lot at lunchtime. It was obvious he was high, his eyes glassy and bloodshot. Music played from the open windows of the car he leaned against. She got there just before his group of friends arrived.

"So now you want to talk?" He tried to look cool and aloof smoking a cigarette.

She took a deep breath to keep her heart hardened as she looked into his brown eyes. "I'm pregnant. I'm not going to keep it, and you can't stop me."

His face tensed as he stood alert. "You sure?"

This statement snatched any softness arising from her emotions. "You know I'm sure. The only chance I have ever taken in my life was with you."

"I guess you don't think I'm worth it."

"No. Look at you. Look at me. We are too young, and I don't want to be our parents. We should be breaking the cycles. Look at what all the white people are doing now. I want to be doing what they are doing."

"Whatever. It was fun," he sneered. His eyes mocked her.

"Wait. Do you want all your albums back?"

He walked around to the driver's side and got into his car. "Nope. Keep them. A souvenir." Within a minute he screeched away, leaving only the scent of burned rubber in the air and dirt in her eyes.

Rogelio soon moved on to another girl. Cathy saw him with his arm slung around her shoulders as they walked the halls together. She had nicely styled hair. Thick black eyeliner. Tight shirts and jeans to show her beautiful figure. He just walked past Cathy without a glance as if he didn't recognize her.

And Cathy soon didn't recognize her own body. No one at

the school had a growing belly like hers. Big brains and an even bigger, ever-expanding belly topped with sagging breasts. *He'd come back if you had the baby.* This voice spoke to her when she tried to get a full night's rest during the school week. She already couldn't find a comfortable position, had to pee every five minutes. Afternoon lessons were the most difficult time of the day to stay awake. Her own voice would shout back as she reminded herself how they parted ways when she told him of the pregnancy. *For how long would he stay? How elastic is any love? Even the love inside the cord between mother and child is not enough. Look at me. No one stays. Maybe physically, but minds and hearts change with time. If your heart isn't there, why stay? Why be a fraud?*

Nine months of feeling ashamed. Nine months of questions from friends, family, and teachers. Everyone had a different opinion. It all sounded like a concert of torment. One day she felt her confidence soar as she submitted applications for scholarships while she investigated schools. She worked with a warrior's grit looking for the money to study. *Think about the future,* her own voice would whisper. The following day another voice sneered in her ear, *You have no future. A girl like you is nothing. Why give away the only thing to give your life meaning and worth? Make everyone happy but yourself. Do what is acceptable and right.*

Cathy wanted all the voices to just stop. She wanted to get through this pregnancy in a vacuum or on a distant moon orbiting Pluto. Nothingness.

The time arrived for her to give birth.

Cathy couldn't wait to have her body back. It wasn't the shape that concerned her as much as the control. The weight of carrying another being was too much for her few years of life. She possessed only an inkling of who she was. How could she possibly guide or financially support another?

This thought got her through the pushes and screams. She stared at the wall with feet high in stirrups, imagining an invisible foe. The bright light overhead mixed with sweat and pain. Nothing mattered but delivering this baby who already had a home. A new, healthy baby going to a Christian family. From what she knew, they claimed they were people devoted to doing God's work. They seemed like decent folk with a perfect résumé for parents. With the final push she screamed, *"No!"*

Then came the screams of the child. The doctor inspected the child before moving to hand the baby to her. She shook her head before flopping back into the bed. "Take Alejandra to her new mother. I have nothing to give."

Without a word the baby was rushed off. Cathy felt numb. She closed her eyes as the nurses cleaned her body, attended to the wounded parts that Cathy wanted no knowledge of. Did they also have stitches for the heart? For her memories?

There was no price on what she had just done. She promised herself to live the best life she possibly could. She would dedicate her life to making it all worth it.

Time passed. She did not know how long. She could feel herself being wheeled through the hospital. Two curtains on either side of her. The sound of women cooing. Infants crying. Cathy placed the pillow over her head. She did not want to hear or see any of it. She just wanted to be released so she could start her life again. So she could be in this hospital, but on the other side of the curtain.

The one making decisions. The one in control.

Between sobs into the mattress, she remembered her own mother walking out the door.

She punched the mattress before willing herself out of bed. She didn't care if something tore. The pain in her body didn't matter. She looked down to see her gown soaked with unused breast milk. She could smell it. Every step hurt as much as every breath without her child. Step by step she made it to the door of the maternity recovery ward.

"Nurse. I need a nurse."

A woman rushed toward her. "Are you all right?"

"I need something strong. I need to sleep."

"I can only give you something for the pain."

Cathy hung her head and squeezed her eyes. She looked up again and grabbed the nurse's hand. "I am in pain. More pain than you can imagine. *Please*. Just once. Just tonight."

The nurse looked at her wet gown, then back at her face. She scanned the hallway before nodding. "Wait here. Just this once. I . . . know you don't have a baby with you. I understand."

"Thank you." Cathy wanted to kiss this stranger. Instead, she leaned against the entrance with tears streaming down her face as she watched her walk away. The nurse returned a few minutes later with two pills and a small paper cup of water. "Go straight to bed. Close your eyes."

Cathy knocked backed the pills and water, then handed the cup to the nurse, whose soft eyes were filled with compassion. Cathy's desire to comfort people roared inside like a torch being lit in a cave. The thought occurred to her that succeeding in medicine would allow her to be a fire so others could warm their hands.

Cathy shuffled back to her bed ready to fall into a deep sleep. The pills worked fast and her head went fuzzy. The scent of a hundred new babies filled her nostrils.

When she closed her eyes, she could feel herself being pulled beneath a cenote. The cold water surrounded her. She opened her eyes to see a gossamer yellow opening in the shape of an egg. Blue tendrils of a deeper shade of indigo shadow floated from the sides. An invisible force lifted her suspended body until she rose again to the bright light of the sun. She floated on the surface, basking in an incandescence that could only be described as the essence of peace with no mental static. Her spirit would wait in that silence.

Something bumped into her arm. She couldn't move her head to see what it was, but sensed it was not a threat. It felt reassuring, familiar. Warmth encased her entire body, and she fell asleep.

The following morning, she woke to a baby crying, but it did not bother her. She thought of the tests she had to finish. A simple beige breakfast of oatmeal and toast waited on a tray next to her. She grabbed the toast then hopped off the bed pain-free. Her bag waited on the floor with a change of clothes. Not wanting to waste more time crying, she dressed to leave the hospital.

A bonfire burned in her heart as she walked out the door without telling anyone. No one noticed her, either. Why would they?

But one day they would.

The creature stirred in frustration. It didn't want to lose another seed in this particular bloodline. The pain of the first victim possessed deep trauma inflicted by the war that raged around her and left a searing imprint on her soul. Her wound remained open energetically and flowed with the swiftness of a treacherous river into the next in her line. Unhealed pain and rage growing riper generation after generation. Not every soul experienced pain in the same way or released it. This bloodline held on tight to their

heartbreak, which made them irresistible and valuable. One meal from them could satiate it longer than a victim with less subconscious rage and sorrow. The more hopeless the soul, the better the feed. Their inner light flaked away with the softness of slow-cooked meat.

This one called Cathy had an ancestor who gave her a sliver of her light. That love was a seed deep inside of her that gave her the strength to attempt to do the right thing for her future. The bond between them was strong despite Cathy's mother, Frances, being long dead.

The creature stirred in the closet with one eye on the sleeping girl. It ripped holes into her clothing. To the human eye, they would be nothing more than the work of moths. This one had so much anger and fire. The woman-girl called Cathy tossed and turned for months with her big belly.

Sometimes tears would streak from the corners of her eyes when she dreamed of her mother, a foggy apparition of a memory. This dream was a ghost of love that haunted her when the world went silent without the noise of being busy. When people left without saying goodbye or giving a reason, it always created a phantom cut. On the occasions when Cathy cried in a deep sleep, the creature would open the closet door, silently float across the broken tiled floor, and catch her tears on its tongue. The creature loved the taste of her suffering and the way her pain made it shiver. The tears also told it she would not keep her baby no matter what it did, that much was certain. But that baby would one day bleed, and the creature would make sure she did slowly, in constant agony.

Alejandra

Since beginning therapy, Alejandra felt slightly relieved, as if being exorcised day by day over the three weeks. Therapy was an hour just for her to work on the emotions and memories that haunted her, including the uncertainty of the future.

She walked through the door and sat down ready to do the hard work.

"How are you today?" said Melanie.

"I've been thinking a lot about what I am worth. I have a lot of things. I want a purpose beyond being a glorified housekeeper. It seems like my existence is one big thankless job. I want something to call my own that I worked for and earned."

"Have you spoken to Matthew about this?"

"A little. He says his money is my money and my job is in the home. That it is a job to be proud of. And for some it is. But I don't feel fulfilled. That makes me feel even more ungrateful and shitty. And resentful of him because he responds with 'This is what we agreed when we had children.' Like I can't change my mind, or even feel like I can."

"That's a heavy load to carry. Let's work on this."

Alejandra inhaled deeply before exhaling. She loved the scent of the incense and oil filling the room. An herbal barrida used to cleanse her was fanned out on the table between them, giving the room a woody smell.

"Close your eyes. Palms up."

Alejandra did as she was instructed.

"I want you to imagine a tight ball of yarn in your hand. This ball is made up of the strings of events from your ancestral history. But not just anything. The pain, the hurt, envy, anger, jealousy, unrealized potential. All the things that keep you locked inside."

Alejandra's palm felt heavy. A ball of thick yarn sat in her left hand. The tough fibers scratched her skin. She wanted to let it go but could not. The fibers clung to the lines of her palm, stuck in the grooves of hair follicles.

"Now, with your free hand, take one piece of the yarn. Snap it off with all the power inside of you. Focus your intent. Place the strip on your lap."

Alejandra pinched the yarn. It took all the strength she had to pull it off. It didn't want to budge. Then she remembered the time she'd had to pull out the smallest of splinters in Catrina's hand after a fall. The little girl had not been able to stop screaming in pain. Alejandra couldn't panic. She had to be the one in control to relieve her baby from pain. It was Alejandra's turn to free herself from her pain.

"Now I want you to blow up a balloon. The largest breath you can take. As if you know you are about to be dunked under water. Inside your breath is everything you need to release. All your pain, hurt, anger, self-hate, jealousy, and envy. Blow it into this balloon."

Alejandra filled her lungs until it hurt. There had already been heaviness in the right side of her chest, just off center. She blew out all this breath. Imagining all the fights with her parents. The tears of loneliness in the past and the present. The rift with Matthew. The lack of love she had for herself. It left her and went into a white balloon.

"Now I want you to place the balloon next to the string. Let them find each other. Coil around each other."

Alejandra saw in her mind the string moving like an eel. Sharp teeth biting at the air until they found the spot where Alejandra had pinched the balloon closed. The string attached, forming a tight knot.

"Now let it go. Let that balloon fly high into the sky and burst far away from you. You don't need it. You don't want it. It is gone. Forgive yourself for holding on to it. Say goodbye."

Alejandra pushed the balloon above her head and let it go. She watched it soar to the clouds until she could no longer see it.

"Open your eyes, Alejandra. And see."

Free as a fucking bird was all she could think to say to herself. She thought of her insatiable desire for sex with strangers. But it wasn't sex she wanted. It was love. She didn't need multiple partners. But she didn't want stale sex with Matthew, either.

She wanted to eat and take like that monster in the paddling pool with the bird in its mouth.

This truth caused Alejandra's entire body to tremble. Her body a balloon deflating from stale, toxic air.

"How do you feel?"

"Exhausted. Free."

"You have to do the hard work. Love is not hard work, but

repairing the damage is hard. Opening yourself to being loved and giving love is only difficult when there are objects attached."

"Like a balloon or string?"

"Exactly. Avoiding the truth is just as difficult, because you will always find yourself facing off with it until you decide to acknowledge it."

Melanie waited a beat before asking another question.

"Can you describe to me how deeply connected you feel to Matthew? What values do you share?"

Alejandra could only stare at Melanie, slightly bewildered by a question she had never asked about anyone, including herself. "What do you mean by deeply connected?" Alejandra didn't have the language to describe what it could mean to be truly connected to another, because physical closeness was all she could give. It seemed to be the only thing people wanted from her. Be pretty. Be quiet.

When Matthew and Alejandra spoke on any subject, he had the tendency to talk in circles with him in the center. She had long given up trying to be heard. Every time she felt shut down, another stitch pinched her lips, leaving her feeling like a shrunken head. She could feel herself shriveling year after year. When they got together, he had liked having the attractive dark woman on his arm who was just interesting enough at parties but not loud enough to be the star of the show or have too many accomplishments to brag about.

Melanie pressed Alejandra to dig deeper. "What binds your souls?"

Alejandra couldn't help but laugh at this; chuckling was easier than breaking down. The last time she'd taken stock of her life with Matthew she had fallen to the floor of the shower under how devalued she felt in the world. She had nothing of her own.

Children were never going to give her a real sense of ownership or belonging. She looked at her sparkling two-carat diamond ring in its simple platinum setting. "We have nothing in common. Except he likes good food and I happen to be a good cook. He likes pretty women, and I am decent-looking, or was. When he first saw our children, the first thing he said was, 'They are so beautiful. I was afraid they wouldn't be.' He didn't want someone with ambition. I didn't have much when we met. He fucking told me that exact thing over dinner and I ignored it." She could still hear him speaking in that moment, leaning toward her over takeout sushi in his apartment.

"I'm still single because I don't date women on the same career level as me." He'd said this with a charming laugh as he poured her another glass of champagne.

"The sparkle of his green eyes made me forget he said it. Then we went to his living room to choose a film. As I browsed the DVDs on a shelf, he wrapped his arms around me. I wanted to watch a movie until he moved his hands all over my body. Before I knew it, he led me by the hand to his bedroom. I didn't really want to go, but I didn't know how to say no. I went along with it."

Alejandra let out a scream as she threw her head between her legs, grabbing her temples with two hands. "I hate myself so much. The signs were all there. What have I done to myself? My life! I keep stuffing it with stuff I never wanted. Stuff that will never love me back."

Melanie rose from her chair and kneeled in front of Alejandra.

"That is why you sit in that chair, to focus on your foundation first. Your children were meant to come into this world. You have choices. You are not stranded. You can still experience a deep connection with someone. Connect with yourself first. You have yourself to love. You have love with your children. Your hands are not empty. Pockets can be filled later."

Alejandra lifted her head. "Thank you. I feel so alone. Three kids and I couldn't feel lonelier."

"Heal yourself so they won't know that feeling, even if your family changes."

Alejandra looked at the floor with her cheeks feeling bruised with unearthed shame rising to the top of her flesh.

"What is crossing your mind?"

"I gave him my power because I felt he, or at least his wallet, was a better keeper of it. He commanded that when we first met. It was intoxicating to be taken care of in the material sense."

"Tell me about that."

Alejandra and Matthew

It was their first Christmas together and not long after their first date. Strings of lights lined the streets, and glowing shapes of angels and silver bells illuminated shop windows. "Where are we going?" she asked in the taxi before dinner at a swanky bistro that had just opened in Alamo Heights.

"It's a surprise. I wanted to give you a gift, but not just any gift." Alejandra loved the sound of that. He made the plan for dinner and now this. He planned everything, and she felt his genuine interest in making her happy.

The ride was one long kiss and hand-holding until the taxi stopped in front of Saks Fifth Avenue. "Follow me." She followed him into the department store and allowed him to lead the way until they stood in front of Gucci. Spotlights brightened all the beautiful items on pedestals and behind glass.

"The shoes are over there. Let's buy you a pair, something elegant. It's Christmas!"

She didn't take another step. In that moment she felt almost undeserving of the entire date. She didn't know how she contributed to the relationship, because she couldn't do the same for him. "This is too much."

"No, it's not. You'll look amazing in most of these, and I want you to look and feel good. You said you liked shoes and wished you could afford to shop more. This is an easy thing for me to do."

The light in his eyes made her feel like no one else existed in that store or as if he was her first and only lover. She would find a way to pay him back or at least earn his generosity.

First, to be lavished compliment after compliment on her looks all night, and now an expensive gift. Alejandra felt *special*.

He walked next to her with his hand on the small of her back as she browsed. The amount of choice made her feel overwhelmed. She would reach out a hand to grab one then withdraw it. What would he think of her flipping it over to check the price? The thought of what he would think of her if she chose either the most expensive or the cheapest item mortified her. It felt like a test.

He picked up a blue patent leather sandal with a three-inch heel. "These are great. What do you think?"

Alejandra didn't know what to think or where to look first. They would do. "I love them. Navy goes with everything."

He smiled in the suit he had worn to work that day, which was nice enough for dinner. "I'll grab the saleswoman to see if they have your size. I love that you can wear heels and not be taller than me. What is your size?"

"I'm a size five."

Alejandra sat down and waited to see if the shoes would fit. She smoothed out her little black dress that showed her shape. Not too much cleavage or leg because she knew he would be dressed in his work suit. They had to match, be a pair. It was important to him. The saleswoman returned with the box. "Great choice, they go with everything."

Matthew gave her a wide grin. She slipped off her Steve Madden black heels that were sexy enough. The Gucci sandals were gorgeous and fit perfectly. She adjusted the strap and stood before taking a few steps. Her legs wobbled a bit with such a thin heel. These would be strictly for going out and not power walking. She glanced at Matthew and the saleswoman, who were both nodding with smiles. He looked almost proud of her. Even if she didn't like them, she would find it hard to say no and appear ungrateful or difficult to please.

"Perfect. Thank you."

At dinner that night he flipped through the hefty catalogue of wine brought by the sommelier. "I love wine. As long as you do the cooking, I can provide the perfect wine." He looked up momentarily to flash her a smile before returning to study the list. When the sommelier returned, he made a show of discussing the tasting notes and regions of three. Were those good years?

Alejandra enjoyed wine, not to the extent he did, but she could learn. And going to nice restaurants was something they both enjoyed. Up to that point all his suggestions had been perfect. This was what she imagined being cared for meant. Being with someone sophisticated and accomplished made her feel that others might view her the same way.

Three children later she found herself floundering in a dream within someone else's dream instead of chasing her own destiny, seduced into silence with expensive wine and shoes. He took her on vacations to places seen in glossy magazines, but never locations he had previously visited and didn't enjoy.

When she mentioned she always wanted to visit Ireland, he'd casually shrugged. "I didn't really like it."

"But I want to go."

Instead of leaving it at that, he had to dig in his point. "It isn't enough for me to tell you it isn't great? I mean, don't you trust me?"

And so they went in circles over every decision. Goddamn if these carousel conversations didn't leave her stomach churning year after year.

Their relationship was fool's gold. Matthew was happy, though: He could depend on having his needs taken care of as he traveled for work and changed jobs twice.

Sometimes she thought of her lover in college, Denise, the Italian girl with green eyes and soft lips. The friendship and occasional hookups ended on a dance floor on the eve of Y2K, Alejandra high as kite dancing to terrible electronic music and Denise watching in disgust because Alejandra was too fucked up and hung up on some guy. They had both always moved between lovers, but this time Denise had had enough. She wanted a proper relationship, but Alejandra wasn't ready. Alejandra still fantasized about their sex.

When Alejandra thought of Denise, she wondered why she hadn't explored that part of her more—taken it more seriously. She liked both men and women but would never say it out loud because things were different in those days. Everything is different when you come from a Bible-thumping home telling you hell is filled with people with "unnatural" desires. How do you express a desire you have no language for?

After graduating from college and working a few years, Alejandra found herself alone, not knowing what she wanted, until she met Matthew. He was stable and checked off all the requirements for lasting love, the ones we are told matter. He was good-looking, educated, confident, had a well-paying job, wanted a long-term relationship. Everyone must grow up sometime.

But the compatibility test she took on the dating site to find her love match never covered the gray area called the future. Computers don't have a crystal ball button to tell you how life will feel and look ten or fifteen years later, when the storms roll in and the power lines of love get knocked down. You might as well jump into a cenote. Is that why they call getting married "taking the plunge"? No book, no advice, nothing can prepare you for the details of parenthood or marriage.

There is also nothing to prepare you for when the cords of marriage begin to unravel. When you know in your bones it is truly over and you leave before it becomes the end of you.

It had never been a marriage of equals. Madly in what she thought was love, fucking all the time, devolved to madly shouting at each other with tongues as sharp as knives, always unsheathed to make a cut.

When she gave birth to their first child, Catrina, Matthew lovingly looked into Alejandra's eyes after bringing her the first sushi she would have in nine months.

"You know you don't have to go back to work if you don't want to. My money is your money. You don't have to worry about work or anything. All you have to do is enjoy our family. I can take care of us." And for a time that was enough. Five years later Will arrived. Alejandra couldn't imagine Catrina not having a sibling. It was a natural progression.

"One more baby. Don't you miss how cute they were?" Matthew had his arm across her belly as they lay in bed. Her mind raced with the repercussions of how her day-to-day would change with three children. His life would change very little except for the weekends.

"I'm not sure. It's a lot."

He sat up slightly. "But you said you wanted a big family. You like kids. Our life is amazing."

His words felt like a burden. What could she say to that? She didn't want a wedge between them. This marriage had to work. She could say no if she had a good reason, like a job. It didn't dawn on her to say no because it wasn't what her soul wanted. "If it happens then it happens."

As she sat in the doctor's office during her final trimester with Elodia, she garnered the courage to speak up. "When you perform the C-section can you please tie my tubes?"

The doctor stopped writing in her chart and looked up. "Of course. Based on your age and the fact this is your third, it's no problem. I will make a note of it now. It will take all of five minutes after the birth." She went back to writing on the chart. Alejandra felt air withheld too long exiting her body. The only thing left was the knowing this was not how love with your partner should feel.

Now there would be no accidents and no other options. There would be no more children to bind them together. After the birth of Elodia, she hated how her husband still cooed at small babies, like she was denying him his right to as many children as he wanted. When she was pregnant, she told him she would have a tubal ligation after giving birth. He remained expressionless before responding. "It's your body. If that is what you want. I just hope you don't regret it later." Alejandra had left the room before he could say anything else.

As resentment in their relationship began to build, she hoped he would meet someone else and do the leaving. How easy to watch him pack his bags and walk out the door without a tear shed. If he wanted a fourth child so damn bad, it could be with someone else. Thoughts of leaving him began while she was pregnant with their third child. But that would devastate her children. More consideration had to be done. If a break were to happen, it would have to be clean. She didn't have a dime to her name or credit history to speak of. All the power that matters in the world was not within her immediate reach. She gave it away so easily.

But if there was a way, she would take it.

The creature hovered in the darkest corner of the cabin bed in the bedroom of the little boy. So close. His mother was already so broken. Lost and alone. A stranded jellyfish drying out in the sun, shrinking and quivering as it nears the end.

The mother's name was Alejandra. The creature had been tormenting this woman for years, toying with her, watching her cry, eat herself emotionally alive. The creature extended a bony finger and tapped the hanging planets attached to the ceiling of the canopy over the boy's bed. The plastic glow-in-the-dark orbs knocked against one another violently, Jupiter cracking in the process. The creature thought again of how little this species knew of anything. Their brains locked with no key, save a few who could truly tap into the cosmic flow.

The creature had once thought it was perishing. It had come from another realm that had been extinguished when universes collided. In the process, the creature's realm had been torn asunder.

During the explosion, particles of the creature's consciousness floated in different directions in the dark. Echoes from different frequencies in the many universes of our multiverse let it know some part of the creature was still sentient. Energy within the multiverse is never truly destroyed, only absorbed. The creature's kind relied on absorption, perfected the process for its own survival and life cycle.

The creature floated in despair until a new sensation from an unidentified being piqued its interest, desire. Hunger became the gravity bringing its form together again. Pain. Anguish. Torment. Floating to find this ephemeral substance the creature craved, it found itself in a new place, less violent than other planets. It wandered in curiosity toward an unknown vibration, gaining speed in a tight ball of electricity. Sparks crackled and jumped as it approached to touch this new source of energy.

The need to consume grew stronger. Without a clear direction it found itself hovering above a woman in a cave next to a dying fire. The shadows from the orange flame created ghastly shapes across the cave walls, shaped like bellowing spirits. The creature scanned the weakening thoughts of the woman and learned that this species had no language, only actions and emotions. Their life span was relatively short and existence vulnerable, like these two. Easy to destroy with soft minds and bodies.

A mother about to fall into darkness in the battle of childbirth lay there alone leaking blood between her legs as an unknown substance wafted from her pores. To the creature it looked like snow rising toward the sky, tiny crystals reflecting light. The creature unfurled itself into a humanish form to sniff the length of her body. The ether had to be the female's bond with the already expired young in her arms, yet still attached to her body through a long cord.

The creature slinked closer to her flushed face. Her body burned with a fever caused by a microscopic indigenous entity that had no power to harm the creature. Oily hair plastered against her bare skin sodden with sweat. A salty liquid fell from the corners of her eyes. The demon stuck out a glowing, tentacle-like tongue to absorb this fluid. A single drop satiated something inside of it. The energetic current within its core flared. It wanted more.

And not she nor anything in this strange realm could stop the creature. It focused all its will to extract more tears until she cried her last one. She had no control of the disease inside her body. No control over the nature of the young world she was born into. No control but to surrender to the circumstances. To death. And to the will of another with the power to make her succumb to what it wanted.

Seeing the power of death over humans excited the creature. It made it feel alive. The creature would never be torn apart like it had been before. The dying fire blazed, with flames licking the low ceiling as it reacted to the creature's energy. The skin beneath the fading woman's eyes sagged to her cheekbones after it took its first taste from her. The flesh giving way as her body and spirit were too weak to fight back. And she was trying. What a spectacle to see her try. It began to take more of her through her eyes. Spheres of liquid floated between them like a frozen asteroid belt. She mustered just enough strength to pull away for a moment with the last of the fight she had inside. Her energy wanting one last experience during this plane of existence. She jerked her face away violently. The human's final breath and act was a kiss upon the head of her young. Her lips lingered as long as they could until her head fell limply to the side.

Gone at last, *it growled to itself. The scent of blood continued to create a frenzy within the creature's consciousness. With the flint knife next to the woman, it sliced the tangled cord of flesh free from the dead human. Dark red liquid oozed onto the ground. Before the contents of the cord could be emptied, it latched on to the torn end. The creature's entire form vibrated wildly as the emptiness inside of it became less painful. Sharp barbs shot out from its mouth and sucked harder on the blood-rich tube until only an empty husk remained.*

The cord. The bond was where the power lay and how they made more of them. So much emotion. A connection it never knew. The creature broke the pieces of flint knife into smaller shards and placed them on what would have been its hands had it been human. With great care it wrapped the cord around its waist in the same fashion the woman had wrapped a strip of animal skin around her waist. Then the creature took the child from her rigid grip to devour later.

Since that first encounter, it slowly evolved at the same rate as the species it fed upon. It mimicked and mocked them, watched the patterns they created within themselves and with one another. And patterns are everywhere. In the unseen universe, the natural world, with creatures great and small.

The creature listened in the dark corners of rooms, hearing the secret desires they whispered when they thought no one could hear. In the shadows it moved swiftly to pounce upon opportunities to consume the humans' pain. The creature slowly gained the ability to interact with the species. To speak their many languages, make deals they couldn't comprehend, because this species believed the creature didn't truly have the power of the stars. If it couldn't be seen, it didn't exist. The humans liked things simple, quick.

The games the creature played with the humans kept it amused and satiated, so it kept its promises. However, the hunt required energy and time. Instead of roving through shadow, it set its intention on single bloodlines, or families. Generational curses provided a steady source of energy to devour, not without torment first to inflict more energetic pain on its victim.

For Alejandra's bloodline, the older girl, named Catrina, carried the curse, the little boy it frightened for fun, and the toddler and mother it would devour down to the marrow. And then it would start all over again.

Alejandra left her eighth session feeling light despite delving into her relationship with Matthew, the father of her children and the person she had spent the last decade with. He was gone again for another night. A hazy autumn light and breeze filled the air. It caught the scent of the growing herbs. The yellow leaves in the trees applauded themselves in the wind for no reason except for being what they were, part of this universe and world. She wondered why people didn't do this more for themselves. Alejandra would do more of it even if she was the only one who noticed. Changing her family situation crossed her mind. Being two households instead of one. Until now she hadn't had the courage.

You are doing a good thing, Alejandra, she told herself as she walked to her car. Twice-a-week sessions were grueling but it was worth it.

Light began to creep back into her heart more than when she was younger. Little torches ignited, warming her from the inside. She didn't resist whatever was happening to her. There were fewer instances inside where she wanted to scream and harm herself because she felt so out of control with a situation involving her children. Her patience felt restored, even if slowly. Her sleep was dreamless and there were no longer any visions. The less she worried about what Matthew thought or how he would react, the more she gained confidence.

The calm ended with a phone call from Catrina's school. "Is everything all right with Catrina?"

"Yes, she is fine, but one of her teachers is concerned. Do you mind coming in?"

Alejandra wasted no time rushing to the school. Her heart pounded with fury as she drove, like a metal drum solo at the end of a gig.

She entered the principal's office feeling clammy all over

from sweating during her drive. The sun shone directly in front of her, radiating its heat.

"Please sit down."

Alejandra became aware that her hair was scraped back in a haphazard ponytail. She feared they could smell her sweat, see the dark bags beneath her eyes. Without hearing a word of their judgment, she judged herself as she imagined the horrible criticism they could be thinking.

She lowered herself slowly onto the chair with their gaze following her. As soon as the cushion touched her thighs, she braced herself for a tongue lashing.

The teacher, Ms. Lane, spoke first. "Is everything all right at home?"

Alejandra wanted to scream *NO,* but to an outsider they were the ideal family. "There is nothing going on that would cause Catrina distress."

"Catrina is a good student. No problems, but lately I see her staring out the window. It is as if she is transfixed by something. When I confront her, she is nasty and snaps at me. Not like her at all. Her entire demeanor changes . . . her face."

"Is that all?"

"She says a woman in white wants to be let in. If she isn't, it will eat her alive. When I pressed her after class, she said the woman stands outside the window at the end of the playground and eats birds."

Alejandra exhaled, feeling like shit. She had tried to bond with Catrina by telling her a story and caused a mess. She hadn't mentioned any of this at home. But how did Catrina know about the bird?

This had to be more than a coincidence or bad parenting. Fresh panic caused her neck and cheeks to feel hot. She felt as though she were back in the car, but driving straight into the sun on the top of a meteor. The sense of losing control caused her to tap one foot on the floor. But Alejandra had to remain calm. She breathed in deeply through her nose and out again to the count of ten in her head. Her emotions were not some fixed projectile hurtling through space. She could handle this even if it took the last of her energy.

"I'm sorry. Catrina wanted a story, a spooky one from my ancestry. I told her about La Llorona."

The white principal and teacher stared at her without expression.

"It's a story about a woman in white. But I never said she eats children or birds."

"I understand. Children have active imaginations. That's why those kinds of stories are not appropriate."

Without censoring her thoughts Alejandra spoke and freed the caged, foaming-at-the mouth frustration she felt inside. "Have you watched an old Disney film recently? Heard of the Brothers Grimm?" A voice popped into her head. She imagined it could have come from one of the women in her dreams. *Pick your battles. They cannot help with the opponent you face.* Alejandra let this one go. "It won't happen again."

Alejandra walked out wanting to vomit, her energy completely depleted. She had to believe that what her daughter was experiencing was real. When Alejandra was younger, she had desperately wanted someone to believe her sadness was more than a mood. Her mind was sometimes jumbled with the tangles of wet hair. She wondered if Catrina possessed the same sadness, and if it could be treated to give her back her spark. Catrina was perfect just as she was, however Alejandra wanted her to know that confusing dark conversations in the mind did not determine who she was. Perhaps Catrina should see a therapist too.

Alejandra shuffled to her car in a daze. She sat in the driver's seat and placed her forehead against the steering wheel. In the pit of her jugular notch she could feel a bubble of energy rising. With the same mechanical motion that got her into her car, her lips opened. She screamed until the pain shot out of her throat. The sound was the frustration of not understanding what life was telling her. Suddenly a dark cloud was covering the headway she thought she had been making. She cried out in pain from the bottom of her abdomen: *I need help! I am so fucking alone!*

Why had she ever thought having children would fill the bottomless void where her soul should be? She then looked to the passenger's seat, wishing there was someone she could call, curl up to. Matthew would just blame her. Make her feel worse. Maybe she was better without him. Not only did she not trust herself in that moment, but she didn't even have a partner whom she could lean on. The idea of wanting to die entered her mind again.

This will pass. Just breathe. You are getting the help you need. Just live for another minute, then it will be evening. Then it's a new day, Alejandra said to herself. Sometimes in bed or when she was alone, she would clasp her hands together, imagining that someone was holding her hand. She would run her thumb against one of her index fingers to soothe herself. At the very least she had herself.

Be your own company, baby girl. She did the breathwork that Melanie had taught her to calm down enough to wipe her eyes with her sleeves. At bedtime Alejandra would have to talk to Catrina about what was happening at school, then contact Melanie about therapists for children.

Catrina lay beneath her comforter with dark circles under her eyes. Alejandra sat next to her on the bed. Will and baby Elodia had already been sound asleep for half an hour. She thanked the heavens for having children who slept. All her friends complained that their kids refused to sleep or spent most nights in their bed. Alejandra had smiled and said, "It's all down to a firm routine from birth."

Alejandra disliked sleeping next to her children. First, when they were infants, there was the anxiety that she would inadvertently smother one of them, so she feared falling asleep with them in her arms. Then as they got bigger they also got more active, and their little legs would kick her spine, or she'd catch a fist in the neck that would make her recoil. She already struggled to sleep. Their presence made it worse. Unless it was an emergency where they needed that comfort, she never let them stay the night.

On the rare times she allowed them to sleep next to her, she knew she was choosing not to sleep herself to make sure they were all right by checking their breathing or temperature. Now that they were bigger, they could pile in the bed when she was awake, and she would sit next to them before bed.

Alejandra found herself needing increasing amounts of physical space to herself after the birth of each child. There was always a child pulling on her or jumping around nearby. Year after year of having one kid or another climbing all over her demanding something added to her exhaustion.

Alejandra kissed Catrina on the forehead. "Last time I told you a story. Now I want you to tell me a story."

"Me?"

"Yes. Maybe one that's a little frightening? I want to hear about the little girl who daydreams in school. Tell me about all the fantastic things she thinks of when she should be listening to the teacher."

Catrina frowned. "They aren't fantastic. No unicorns. The

little girl sees a ghost. Maybe a witch. It says the little girl is horrible. That her mother doesn't love her . . .". Tears began to well in her eyes.

"Honey, all mothers love their children. But love isn't one-size-fits-all."

Catrina jerked up in bed. "It says you don't love me, and you want to hurt me, break my neck because I'm a worthless baby bird."

Alejandra's instinct was to jump up and wring the life out of the monster who would tell her child this, but she had to remain grounded for her daughter. "You are not a worthless bird! You are a strong little girl with the heart of a dragon, or better yet a jaguar. Do you understand me? I love you. It was a daydream of the worst kind. I love you more than anything in this world."

"When is Dad coming home?"

"I don't know. It's only us. That is enough. We are jaguars or dragons, and we are fine on our own. And when you are older, you will be a big jaguar."

Catrina's hazel eyes darkened before she lowered them. A single tear rolled down her cheek, and then she squeezed both her eyes and her mouth shut. Alejandra wanted to do the same: She had once been that small girl crying in bed because of the scary thoughts howling in her mind. She had also been the small girl trying to contain the sound of her sobs. Catrina's little face was far too innocent to have that kind of torment etched in her eyes. The pain had scratched the light out of them. And Catrina shouldn't feel that she should be silent about her worries. Alejandra's anger at the monster became a soft white down to wrap her baby girl's heart in. She wanted to always be the one to provide soft feathers for when Catrina fell. But she also wanted to be the one to show her how to get back to her feet again.

"You can cry as much and as loud as you need to on my shoulder, okay? Whatever it is, I want you to get it out. But know there is no need to worry, because I have you always and forever. I understand how you feel. I love you."

Catrina threw her arms around Alejandra's neck. She unlocked her lips to let out a deep breath and tearful whimpers. "Thank you, Mom. I love you."

Alejandra held her daughter tight. She felt as if a funnel of warmth opened from the crown of her head to the pit of her belly. The longer she held her daughter, the wider the funnel. It spun slowly at first until the funnel dissipated within her body like the white smoke of a candle being absorbed into the air. She accepted the love from her daughter and gave it back. As she stood up to leave, the closet door caught her eye. Catrina had placed an ivory-colored IKEA chair in front of it. *Good girl,* she thought. *Don't let that thing in to begin with. Let it know it doesn't have a home here.* She closed the bedroom door, determined to fight for her daughter.

Alejandra couldn't sleep after the school meeting and her conversation with Catrina. She knew she had to tell Melanie about it, but that old sense of doubt, of not wanting to be a burden, snuck into her thoughts. What would she say to not sound stupid? She knew intellectually that Melanie would not think that; however, Alejandra could not fully embrace that notion. The old wounds were still not completely cleaned out and sewn shut.

She wanted a small dash of rum with three ice cubes to sip in front of the TV. Despite the hardships of the day, Alejandra now felt better equipped being on her own. She had to get used to organizing her emotions and thoughts in peace. *Any crisis or chaos will pass. The anxiety will ease. They are your children, and they just want your love. You deserve their love. Just be open to it.*

You don't have to impress them. You don't have to impress other parents. You are enough.

As she watched a show on TV about hot vampires half her age, her body felt rigid. Part of her wanted to masturbate and think of a beautiful woman kissing her or a younger man with no limits on his stamina thrusting hard inside of her. She could work out all her vitriol with the movement of her hips and then end her day with an explosive orgasm so strong she could fall asleep with a smile on her face. But she couldn't get the hurt far enough out of her mind to do that. It still hurt so much that she couldn't turn to Matthew for tenderness in her confusion.

Alejandra drifted off at some point during the program. She found the woman in white waiting for her in the darkness of her sleep. Alejandra looked to the horizon, where calm ocean waters met a billowing clouded sky. The clouds expanded with gray air, becoming a fog, rolling in from deeper, volatile waters. Through the cotton sky, a silhouette emerged. A woman in a dress moved closer. The same dress, just like in the shower.

Though her garment appeared white, the closer the woman approached, the clearer it became that the dress, and the creature, were created from different textures of flesh and fabric. From what Alejandra could see, the creature was constructed of loose threads of old lace and dried strips of human and fish skin blanched from radiation. The face was wet and soggy like the skin of an albino toad. The eyes flared white-hot with the cosmic radiation of destruction.

Alejandra could only watch the woman increase in speed as she neared her with an open mouth of box-cutter-sharp studs for teeth. They seemed to pulsate from her reddened gums. "Sick woman. Difficult woman. Dead woman," it croaked.

Before it could attack her, Alejandra awoke terrified. She looked around the room. Even though Matthew's presence could be oppressive, she still wanted someone next to her. Soon the nightmares and pain in her heart would be gone. She would talk to Melanie about it at their next session. *You're not a fool for speaking up. It's folly to think you are ever alone in struggle,* she told herself.

She got up from the sofa at three A.M. and went to bed. However, she just lay there staring at the ceiling, wide awake. Every hour on the hour she looked at her phone until it was nearly seven A.M. and the children would begin to wake up. It was going to be a long day from not sleeping. Alejandra waited until the clock struck eight to contact Melanie for advice on the dreams. She sent her a text hoping she had time.

> Hi. I know this is last minute. Do you have any time for me to drop by for a chat? I don't need a full session, but I could use some advice. Thank you. Alejandra

Melanie messaged back straightaway.

> Absolutely. Drop by after your school run.

Melanie answered the door with a warm smile and guided Alejandra inside.

"Everything all right? You mentioned needing advice but nothing else."

"I've been up since three A.M. My dreams are vivid and frightening. Like I mentioned before. What can I do to sleep or understand what they could mean? They seem more like visions than dreams. What should I do?"

"Based on what I know, I want you to consider building a

small altar in your home. Connect with the women, the benevolent forces in your dreams, as part of you connecting with yourself. Acknowledge your needs. They might give you some insight either through intuition or dreams. The worst feeling is one of desolation, but you are not alone. Read about our history as brown women. And continue to share yourself with your children."

"What do you mean by altar? I have briefly read about them before but mostly related to Día de los Muertos."

"It can be whatever you need any day of the year to create a better connection with yourself and those who have passed. Or it can be a place to celebrate those who are living. Include items of personal significance or things that bring you joy. Fresh flowers are a wonderful way to bring even more life and fragrance to the experience when you pass by it or sit and meditate or pray. The point is, it's up to you. I'll write this down in a little list along with some traditional flowers."

The concept of an altar as a form of connection resonated with Alejandra. She knew Melanie was right. Alejandra lacked the motivation to keep in touch with her friends because it took effort—effort she didn't have. Liking her friends' posts on Facebook and Instagram was easier than communicating or admitting the troubles in her mind. By her age you were supposed to have your shit together, be ready for life, or at least be at peace with the decisions you have made. None of that applied to Alejandra, so she stayed at arm's length from others. She needed to surround herself again with family and friends. People who believed in her. "I want to build an altar in my home. It could be good for the children too. Can I ask you something? If it isn't appropriate you don't have to answer."

"Absolutely."

"You're a therapist, a doctor no less, and a curandera? How

does that work? Where does the supernatural and spirit live in a world of science?"

Melanie chuckled and sipped her coffee on her counter. "I believe in two worlds. This one and everything else we don't see including the multiple universes and galaxies above our heads. I don't really know what form the other side takes, but I *feel* it. Always have. I've come to learn that thoughts often get in the way of intuition. You have to turn the dialogue down and listen to the music of your soul. It's different for everyone. No one can tell you what that sounds like. But our thoughts can be influenced. I'm not sure if you noticed from my home, but as a curandera my specialty is in plants and herbal medicine. However, I still prescribe medication when needed. My mother was also a curandera, a midwife. Our gifts have been passed down generations too. Curandismo began as healthcare. Our ancestors were deprived of so many things by the colonizers. We had to do for ourselves. Our men were not even allowed to ride horses yet were forced to care for them. The women were forced to be their lovers."

"I hope my children aren't anything like me."

"Don't say that. Your resilience is something to be proud of."

Alejandra didn't like compliments of any kind. She automatically assumed that everyone felt sorry for her, that they just wanted to be kind to the kid who didn't belong, to the brown girl who had nothing going for her. "Do you think it will be back?"

Melanie's lightness turned serious. "Yes. I think it's going nowhere. It will only grow bolder as you grow stronger, as it feels you slipping away. Which is why it's important you fight for yourself and your children. I want you to come with me."

Melanie guided Alejandra to a small closet in the office. She opened the door. Inside were shelves lined with oils, crucifixes, candles, dried herbs and flowers, crystals, cards with images of saints and prayers in Spanish and English, figurines of Christ, La Virgen, and another with the words *Santa Muerte* on the red robe. "I want you to choose something. Don't second-guess. And you don't need a reason why. That is how intuition works. Take whatever you are guided to first.

"Now, I know you aren't religious, but I want it to be something you hold in your hand, and whatever faith and love you have inside of you I want you to share it with this. Put it by your bed or the altar. Share it with your children. Let it be a source of hope and protection when you need it. You are more powerful than you know. These are just man-made objects until you set the intention behind them."

Alejandra gazed at all the items. She didn't know what to choose. In the back of the row of crystals, she saw a large piece of obsidian that stood upright. The bottom was rough; it looked like it had been hacked away from a larger piece. But the top was a smooth point. It appeared sharpened. She reached out and took it. This piece had weight to it. "I want this one. It looks like the head of a spear. Thank you."

"My pleasure. Now take care. Believe!"

The altar must be built as she had rebuilt herself. Instead of lying down to rest, she drove to the supermarket to buy the flowers on Melanie's list and more of her favorite cookies with dark chocolate on one side.

In Texas it was easy to find candles with saints, La Virgen, and Jesus on them in all the supermarkets and gas stations. But the Main Line in Philadelphia was an entirely different place.

She would have to order La Virgen online. When she arrived home, there was enough time before the afternoon school run to start the altar on the credenza next to the family photos. If Matthew didn't like the altar, then he didn't like it. She didn't care what he thought. This was for her benefit and didn't harm him in any way. She placed the photos Cathy had sent her next to photos of her children, as well as the fresh flowers she'd taken from an expensive bouquet: roses, baby's breath, and gerbera daisies. Marigolds, an important element in Día de los Muertos and in her culture, were not typically sold in the supermarkets. Perhaps they should take a trip to the garden shop with the children so they could plant them in the backyard over the weekend. Catrina might enjoy that.

Alejandra stepped back from her altar. She smiled and looked forward to giving her children hugs at the school gate and seeing Elodia's face light up when she opened her arms to her when she picked her up from her playgroup, feeling her baby's heartbeat in her chest.

She paused at the key jiggling in the lock of the front door. Matthew walked through, and his gaze immediately fixed on the altar. "What is all of this? Do we need more decorative stuff out? It doesn't really match the rest of the house."

She had forgotten he was coming home today. "It makes me feel good to do this and more connected to my roots. It's also part of my journey with therapy."

"That is what we are paying for? You still seem miserable."

The elation she'd felt deflated at his words and the cross look on his face. He focused on the chaos and not the transformation. Her need to grow and heal was lost on him. She would not back down or apologize.

"Why don't you help me? Be part of this?"

"Because I'm tired. I've been working. I have back-to-back calls after a long flight. Please keep the kids under control after you pick them up."

Alejandra stood there alone as he walked up the stairs to his home office, thinking of all the times she wanted to flee, flee even if it meant death. She wanted to open the door and run. But in reality, she didn't want to run from her children.

What she was running from was something bigger, more sinister. A chill ran the length of her spine as a draft could be felt creeping through the mail slot in the front door. She looked to the altar and said a silent prayer.

I want to be a healed woman. A strong woman for whatever comes next.

As she drove through a residential area with the radio off, she passed a home with a yard sale. With the speed limit so slow, her eye caught an old, clunky record player on a table. She quickly glanced in her rearview mirror to see if anyone was behind before putting on her blinker and pulling over.

A white woman who looked to be a similar age to her sat behind the table scrolling through her phone. She wore no makeup and her hair was pulled back. The pink sweatshirt and patterned leggings clashed. As Alejandra approached, she could see dark circles beneath her eyes. Her skin was dry. She looked up and gave Alejandra a quick smile before lowering her sad eyes back to her phone. This woman had probably been up late and awoken early to put this sale together. Alejandra stared at the record player with a fluorescent yellow sticky note labeled $30.

When Cathy had given her the pile of her father's records, she'd brought up the idea of a record player to Matthew. He'd scoffed, "Why? What's the point? We have the Amazon stream-ing service. Everything is on there. That's why we pay for it. Plus, that new speaker I bought cost nearly a grand."

Alejandra wanted to play her records, the music of her par-ents. She didn't care about his fancy stereo system.

"Hello, does this still work?"

The woman put her phone down, looking somewhat aston-ished. "It does. I checked it after taking it from the attic."

Alejandra gave her a friendly smile. Thirty dollars wasn't much money. She had enough in her wallet after she'd acciden-tally punched the wrong AutoCash button on the ATM.

"You having a big clear-out?"

The woman cocked her head and raised her eyebrows, scan-ning the table of random items. "You could say that. Need to downsize. Sometimes you have to know when to let go and what to let go of."

The longer Alejandra observed her, the more she saw sadness in the woman's eyes. There was an urgency to move forward that could be from a job loss or divorce. She was happy to buy this today, for both of their sakes. "I'll take it."

The woman's face lit up. "Sorry I don't have any records for you to look through. He bought it with the promise of listening to records with me but never did. Don't ever think you can change people. Take them as they come or don't take them at all."

Alejandra took the cash from her bag and handed it to the woman, hoping it would brighten the rest of her day the way spotting this record player had done for hers, maybe or maybe not by chance. Melanie believed in serendipity. Alejandra was beginning to believe in it too. Melanie also told Alejandra to not second-guess herself when it came to gut instinct, and Alejan-dra wanted this item. She knew exactly what would make her happy the following day. Her children were going to love this find; she smiled imagining Catrina and Elodia dancing together. Will would pull silly faces for sure.

She placed the record player in the trunk to prevent it from getting bashed around.

"Hey, wait!"

Alejandra looked toward the voice. The woman from the yard sale was running out of her house with a blue square in her hand. "I forgot I had this album. It's what I used to check to see if that machine still worked."

Alejandra loved the image on the cover of a large Eye of Horus. The album was simply called *Eye in the Sky.* "I'm sorry but I don't have any more cash."

"Take it. It was a gift I bought for someone. They didn't really care for it or use the record player with me. If you can use it . . ."

"Thank you. It will be the first one I listen to."

When the album passed to Alejandra's hand, she sensed a need for release in the woman. This was her letting go. Her heart had already begun to heal by passing this on. It had been on her mind for some time. She had to muster the courage to take the first leap of faith.

"Take care and good luck letting go of all the things you no longer need or are taking up too much space. You are going to be fine."

The woman smiled and nodded. Her eyes appeared glassy from tears held back to form a shield. "Thank you."

Alejandra placed the album on top of the record player before moving to the driver's seat. As she glanced in the mirror to pull away, she noticed herself still smiling as she thought about her children. *Thank you,* she whispered to the atmosphere before pulling away to pick them up.

The next day she had to watch a few YouTube videos to figure out how to connect the speakers from Matthew's hi-fi unit to the record player. Usually, he did all that stuff. Now she would do it before he had a chance to scold her for spending money on something so ridiculous. It wasn't about the money; it was about the fact that he had no say in what she spent money on. He wanted final approval on everything. He could never appreciate things she did for her own joy.

Alejandra jumped up and down in excitement when the record player worked. The Alan Parsons Project would be first. *Eye in the Sky* played. She moved to the beat while listening to the lyrics. A surge of energy coursed through her body. The urge to *move* overwhelmed her senses. The yard sale popped into her head followed by the words *let go*.

She looked around the living room. What to let go of and what to keep? To let go also meant to release. She needed a release from whatever was taking hold of her heart and soul. The woman at the yard sale allowed herself to relinquish the things and the sentiment behind those items that were dear to her. There was pain in her eyes, Alejandra could see it. Someone didn't want to experience music with her. The woman went through with her yard sale anyway. And when you were released or let go, freedom could welcome you at the other side. But Alejandra didn't know where to start with more than forty years of emotional clutter to go through. When the song ended, she put it on again to sing out loud. *Let go, Alejandra,* she said to herself. With her mind empty she naturally began to walk upstairs to the bedrooms. Three of the bedrooms were on the second floor; Catrina's room was on the third. It didn't feel like walking, more like floating. How fucking great to be led by what was inside of her.

She started in the master bedroom, going from closet to dresser, dumping out everything. The pattern on the bedspread caught her eye because it was white with plain blocks of muted colors, not something vibrant like she would have wanted. It was one Matthew chose, and she agreed because he would never go for the brightly colored floral one. An epiphany bloomed in her mind. She had no set values because until now she had placed no value on herself. How did she define what was valuable? She would turn this six-bedroom house upside down to find it, clear it out until all that remained were the things of value, even if it was only herself and the children. Value. *How valuable is your soul, Alejandra? Let go.*

Old makeup she hated to throw away was the first to go. A dried red lipstick called Red Corvette made her think of her friend Caroline, who always wore a black choker. Caroline taught her how to apply lip liner in the school bathroom. Black mixed with red. She brought her tweezers to school and helped Alejandra pluck her eyebrows for the first time. The only time Caroline came over for dinner, her adoptive mother, Patricia, was as nice as ever. The perfect mom with a big smile telling her she was always welcome. After Caroline left, she turned from the door, her face as hard as a gargoyle's. "That girl looks like trouble. I forbid you from hanging out with her. That makeup with hair so short she could be mistaken for a boy? Dressing in all black? No daughter of mine. Do you hear me? No wonder you wanted to be in that play about Dracula. Not at all acceptable."

Alejandra didn't have to hoard old bacteria-filled makeup. She was a grown woman free to wear any shade of lipstick she wanted without anyone's approval, including Matthew's. With that task complete, she moved on to clothes and shoes she hadn't touched because she'd bought them at Matthew's suggestion. When they first met, he suggested that she buy nicer sneakers and gave her a list of a few brands. So she did, but they were hardly worn, as she favored flat high-top Nikes. It was almost embarrassing for them to walk out the door dressed alike in the same brands and style. Her petite frame looked best in form-fitting dresses just above the knee or shorter, but he questioned why that was her style, showing her curves all the time. She would keep the low-cut tops and the dresses she did like to accentuate the curves of her body. He could wear polo shirts and the brand of jeans he liked. She wanted to throw on what felt right on that day or look wildly sexy without him feeling insecure.

He liked the idea of them dressing for each other because, "You should always try to please the other person in the relationship. That is what a relationship is. I would never wear something you hated." The anger balled in her throat, bringing down the good mood the music and cleaning out the house had created. *I'm done worrying about you,* she thought before taking a deep breath to exhale her negative emotions toward him.

As she moved from room to room, singing and clearing, she realized how barren the house was of her own taste or style. Nothing reflected *her*. None of the art belonged to her.

When they had moved in together in a new apartment, he'd already had framed photography and modern art prints. Some she found interesting and others she didn't find aesthetically pleasing at all. Over the years as she explored more of her roots sporadically online or in bookstores, she discovered more about Mexican artists and history. She wanted those prints and brightly painted skulls. Vibrant colors or photography of the ocean, her favorite place. Melanie's home made her feel welcome.

The new home she had moved into felt devoid of her personality, who she really was inside. But this was *her* personal pattern, always so eager to please the person she was with to be accepted, loved. To blend in seamlessly without a fuss.

No more. She would allow everything she was rediscovering inside to be reflected in the outer world. On Elodia's bed were all the stuffed bears Matthew had bought Alejandra during the course of their relationship. She would enter his apartment to see a bottle of wine and a stuffed bear next to it holding some sort of heart or other item with a cutesy message. "I have a little present for you. Cute, huh?"

She would hold the stuffed animal close. "Adorable. Thank you." She couldn't scare him away by being ungrateful or telling him she didn't like soft toys. They would just sit in a pile in her apartment. This was Matthew's life; she was just a thing inside of it. It wasn't his fault; she had allowed it to happen that way. She gave him that power with a bow wrapped around it. She was getting rid of the clutter, the unnecessary things that could not love her back.

She placed the Hervé Léger dress she had worn for her wedding reception in a bag to take to a consignment shop along with the matching gold heels. All the cards over the years from Valentine's Day and her birthday she placed in another bag for recycling. The box to go to charity was filled with the belts and matching shoes she'd bought because he suggested they would look good on her. Her jewelry box was filled with little things she bought on their vacations as a reminder. Most of it she'd never worn. Those would go. And all the stuffed animals he'd given to her as gifts were already in a bag that would be donated as well. It would be an important lesson for her children to learn too, considering they had so much stuff.

She overturned four drawers onto the bed to sort through the clothing she no longer wanted, especially the items Matthew had gifted her that were not her taste.

The loneliness in that moment made her feel like she stood at the bottom of a mine shaft looking up to the sky, asking a solitary figure at the top for help, only to be ignored.

She flipped through a pile of cards she kept in a small box in her closet. One was the first birthday card she had received from Cathy; it had a kitten wearing a birthday hat. Alejandra could understand the decision her birth mother had made, remembering what her own life had been like as a teenager. And it wasn't just Cathy. Cathy's mother had opened the door and fled. All the women in her family seemed to run, but here she was chained in place.

Inside the birthday card were photos Cathy had included. One was of a man and woman, glamorous in their stylish clothing from the 1950s. They appeared to be the perfect Chicano couple from that time, with a glint of lust in their eyes. It was one of the only photos Cathy had of her mother, Frances. Cathy had told Alejandra that she had no desire to ever hear from her mother. She had stopped seeking answers that no longer mattered. Alejandra still wondered what the full story could be. Her heart filled with compassion for Cathy, thinking of the pain she'd endured, followed by gratitude that at least she and Alejandra had the opportunity to make amends. It was not too late for Alejandra to change the course of their family tree.

Frances had vanished with the same mystery as La Llorona herself. Was Frances just as unhappy as her? What if Frances wasn't living her life in bliss somewhere?

Alejandra had an hour before the school run. She continued to clear out the house item by item, allowing her mind to drift back in time.

Frances

Texas—1961

Frances cried as she held her fourth child in her arms. Her breasts still ached from undrained milk. They were refusing to relinquish their liquid and might as well have been rocks. Again.

The last thing she wanted was the baby's mouth on her, taking from her like the other children. It would drain her until nothing was left, then she would place the baby's mouth to the other breast, wait a few hours until the feeding had to be done again. This painful ritual was needed to nourish her flesh and blood—the child Frances was still struggling to gather the energy to love. Unconditional love needs space to reside. Frances scarcely had enough love for herself.

Everything hurt. Frances's heart stabbed with searing pain, as did the tear between her legs. This baby had split her in two: Her perineum had needed stitches. *Wretched woman. Difficult woman. Dead woman,* a voice whispered in her ear. Frances looked around the hospital room. A breeze from the open window blew the white curtain toward her. Watching the fabric float evoked a fear she had never experienced in her life. The shadow and the fabric had seemed to take on demonic shapes as the sun set. Frances blinked away her tears, then turned back to her child.

She didn't know who the father was. But her husband had to believe the baby was his. Her lover, Kevin, was long gone, and her husband, David, had come back from his trip with the air force to Korea exactly around the time this baby would have been conceived. All he'd wanted was sex upon his return, even though she suspected there was no way he would have remained faithful during his time away.

When he was overseas it had dawned on her that she wanted a respite from everyone taking. The house and her head were filled with unrelenting noise: chatter, arguments, shrieks, clattering cutlery, breaking glass, toys thrown across the room. Not to mention the laundry and mounting diapers in the garbage. Runny noses to wipe.

But she couldn't be sure who had fathered her child, since she was having sex with two different men at the same time, and time had lost any meaning because this life held nothing that gave her lasting joy. Many things were slipping away from her these days.

It was probably only a matter of time before David decided to leave her. She had gone into labor three weeks painfully early, because of the shock of seeing, with her own eyes, the new woman David had taken as a lover. It was by chance she went to the military base to get her hair done because her usual hairdresser was on vacation. Frances didn't want to wait two weeks feeling out of control in her heavy body. She wanted to sit back and feel someone massaging her scalp and bringing her a coffee as she sat and did nothing. The hairdresser spun her in the chair to face the window. Across the street there was no mistaking David's tall frame. His hands were around the small waist of the woman. It was in the shape of a woman who had never carried children. And the expression on her face appeared as if she didn't have a worry in the world.

She was what Frances knew she was not. David was looking at this woman with light brown hair and who was at least five years younger the same way he had once looked at her. Frances could feel the heat of the coffee rising from the pit of her stomach to her cheeks. The men she had taken as lovers while David was away had only been for the sex, a quick jump-start of attraction. And she pursued other people when she discovered he was doing it first. If he could have an escape, then why couldn't she?

But seeing them together caused her entire body to tremble. She never held hands with her lovers. The affairs had to remain superficial. No, what David had with this woman was something else, she knew it was. Frances couldn't sit there any longer. She stood from the chair and placed the coffee on the hairdresser's cart, then ripped off the gown. "I'm sorry, I don't feel well."

The hairdresser looked at her belly, then back at her face. "Are you all right?"

Frances didn't bother to respond and walked out. She could still see David and this woman strolling with their bodies touching until they stopped in front of a dress shop. The woman pointed to the window, then they disappeared inside. It was too much. Without a second thought Frances began to run to her car. The cement hit the soles of her feet hard through thin white slip-on shoes. When she approached the car, she stopped to catch her breath. Her pelvis and cervix contracted. She breathed through it, thinking it was only a Braxton-Hicks contraction, not the real thing. *He would never leave you. Not with all these kids. Get on with it.* She got into the driver's seat of her car and refused to cry.

At eight P.M. that night her water broke.

Now she lay in a hospital bed not wanting to live. She didn't want her children anymore. Something inside of her niggled. The only solace she had before this baby were the handsome men she brought to her bed while her husband was away with the military or someone else. The men had always brought treats and fruit for her children to keep them occupied for a few hours. Behind closed doors she cried in pain and in pleasure until it was time for her husband to come home. The electricity of something new, like a dress or pair of shoes. But instead, this lightning storm came from flesh.

Since marriage, Frances had felt trapped: She had no education, and she and David had just enough money to cover the bills. David's pay had been adequate when it was just the two of them after she had lost her job. But his paycheck covered less with every extra child. Every mouth deducted another number from their bank balance. And seeing him buying gifts for another woman flared her rage. She doubted the money he placed in their shared account was all of it. This was too much too soon.

Their marriage hadn't always been a game of toxic tic-tac-toe.

Just as in a romantic movie, she'd first seen David at a dance hall with his friends, looking like a brown movie star in his air force uniform, tall and dark. His thick black hair had matched his mustache. The women around him were giving him an eyeful of what they had to offer, with their tight skirts and low-cut blouses. When their eyes met, she knew she wanted a man like that to take care of her, but also to look good next to her. Frances was eighteen and didn't want to be one of those girls who couldn't snag a decent husband. At the same time, the main criteria on her list for a man were "hot and fun."

All it took was one rum and Coke with David for her to fall in love with him. Together they drove around in his baby-blue Buick with the windows open and the California wind in their hair. After their dates, they would return to his one-bedroom apartment for hours of sex, during which he'd focus all his attention and love on her. Those dark eyes, hypnotic in their intensity, made her forget that other men existed. He taught her that life was as sweet as the ocean breeze while watching a sunset next to someone you love. And David made a decent living with the air force, excelling in all he did despite fighting the response to the color of his skin. Laughter came easy over diner food—they always ate out because Frances hated cooking. He'd promised her a comfortable life, and for a year it was, until the military stationed him in Texas and they had to leave California.

"It will be fine. You'll make new friends. All my family is there, and they can help with our children when we have them. My career needs this. This is my chance to fly! How many Mexican Americans get this opportunity?"

Without any hesitation she agreed, because what did she have to lose? What else did she have going for her? She had no idea what in life she wanted to do. And she didn't want to become a stereotypical domestic worker, work in a field, or cook. Maybe she was meant to just have a few kids and settle down to be a homemaker, a military wife. There were so few ways to get ahead for Mexican Americans, and the GI Bill meant the military was one of them. Frances preferred to stay out of politics. Maybe Texas would be different. Her mother had passed away from a stroke while working at a vineyard in Sonoma, and she never spoke to her father. She had no real strings to keep her attached to California. And so they packed up David's Buick with their belongings and drove off into the sunrise for a new start in Texas.

Every day rolled into another with consecutive pregnancies and caring for small children. The military base community consisted mostly of white folks keeping to themselves. Although military life could be a transient experience, everyone else seemed to know one another already. No one wanted to embrace the brown mother, with all these kids in tow and with another on the way. She felt the stares when she walked the aisles of the base supermarket, with one child crying with a runny nose while the other jumped in the aisles, dangerously close to knocking over a glass jar of something. The noise had no end. Her struggle to shop in the store felt like a garrote made from pantyhose. That was when she decided to shop off base, to avoid the eyes and whispers. And the voice in her head repeating, *You are the worst mother. Look at them. Look at you.*

When they went to visit David's family, she felt like an outsider because she didn't like to cook or be in the kitchen gossiping. That was how his two sisters and aunts spent their time. Besides, Texas was hot enough, even without the steam from a boiling pot or the heat from an oven. Frances longed for the days when she and David could decide last-minute what to eat or to pack a picnic for the beach. Here in Texas, David's aunts and cousins gave her recipes they knew by heart, but that Frances had no desire to memorize.

She didn't know where in this new world of marriage she belonged. But it had been a new place to run to at eighteen. And then she had her first baby at nineteen, followed by the others quickly.

When at twenty-one years old the second child had come screaming out of her body, Frances cried day and night, unable to shake the feeling that something bad would happen to her children. The anxiety flooded her mind and body as quickly as the milk in her breasts. When it was just one, you could devote all your energy and time. After the third was when she first found out that David had been unfaithful, because when he asked her to clean out his duffel, she found he'd forgotten to remove the condoms from a small inner pocket. She wasn't enough for him; the life they'd created together was not enough for him. The rejection was a combat boot to the belly that kicked out any self-esteem she had left.

But Frances couldn't leave him. Instead, she just sat on the floor sobbing with the condoms in her hand, her sorrow turning to rage. How dare he leave her alone all the time, expecting her to be his little wife? If she couldn't leave, then she would get even. She wiped her face and placed the condoms in her apron pocket to keep for herself.

Frances wanted to feel wanted too. She made the decision to take a break, a short escape from her life for just one moment in time. The widowed aging neighbor Carla was available to babysit.

Two days later, Frances put on her best dress that cinched in her waist—or at least the loose skin that resembled a deflated balloon after her pregnancies. To brighten her tired face, she chose red lipstick and earrings. And she wore the little pearls her husband had given her when they first met. It had been a long time since he bought her a gift. The pearls would look beautiful next to her glossy dark-brown hair, freshly curled. Her reflection in the mirror reminded her she was still a woman.

She headed to the Redwood Inn, a historic hotel with a bar made of dark wood and draped in heavy fabrics, with plush chairs you sank into and found impossible to leave. It smelled of cigarette smoke, whiskey, and cologne. At one time she'd loved the scent of David's cologne on her skin and clothing after he left for work. The scent would linger until he returned, and then they'd spend the evening together talking over beers.

Now his cologne could no longer be detected over the sour scent of baby spit-up that was always dribbling off the burp cloth onto her clothing, and her hair smelled of cooking oil. When it was hot, and it was always excruciatingly hot in Texas during the summer, the constant layer of sweat made her feel like a wet dishrag.

But that night, she walked into the bar alone without a worry to weigh her down. The soft murmur of adult conversation surrounded her.

"What can I get you?" the bartender said. She loved that sound: *What can I do for you? How can I help you? What do you need?*

Her mind went blank. There was a list of things she needed and wanted but had had to put last to take care of her family. "Rum and Coke."

The Black bartender gave her a smile before turning to make her drink. In silence, she exhaled a thousand breaths and countless sobs. When the drink arrived, it had a single maraschino cherry in it. Something sweet just for her. The first sip went to her head, and the taste eased her tension.

This was exactly what she needed. Halfway through the drink, as she flipped through the *Vogue* magazine she'd packed in her handbag, she felt eyes on her. A white man at the end of the bar gave her a smile when she glanced at him. She quickly looked back down. Her face felt flushed. When was the last time a man looked at her like that? Her husband still wanted sex from her but only with the lights off. His playfulness had ceased long ago. She missed it, but at the same time she hated the idea of kissing him for a prolonged time. She wanted to spit out his tongue when he tried to slip it into her mouth. An unwanted invader. The mustache she once adored feeling on her neck now prickled against her.

She continued to sip on her rum and Coke until a body stood next to her. "You waiting for someone?" She looked up to see the man from the end of the bar: He was good-looking, clean-shaven, and smelled of expensive aftershave.

"Get another one for the lady," he told the bartender.

Then he turned to her. "If you aren't waiting for someone, you must work here? In an unofficial capacity?" His smile was greasy, the handsomeness ugly after saying this.

"Can't a woman sit and have a quiet drink alone?" She fiddled with the straw in her glass so that she could flash her wedding band.

"So you aren't offering anything?"

She clenched her jaw. "No."

He huffed and drummed his fingers while looking at her up and down. "Cancel that drink, bartender." The stranger left the bar, leaving a meager tip.

The bartender handed her another rum and Coke anyway. "Don't even let that bother you. I got it worse before from the patrons here."

She drank the remnants in her glass before starting the second one. "I came here to have a break from my children for a minute."

The bartender chuckled. "Yeah, I have two myself. I know the feeling."

She looked at him, peering beyond his uniform and the formality with which he served drinks. He was a kind and handsome man. And it felt nice to hear that someone understood her even in the slightest way.

He gave her a smile. "Enjoy the drink."

Frances was nearly finished with the second rum and Coke. She and Paul the bartender had been in conversation for what seemed like hours, talking about Little Richard and Etta James. His stories about the hotel patrons made her laugh out loud. She felt that old sparkle inside, now that there was nothing to interrupt her joy. As she sucked on the rum-soaked cherry, she noticed him watching her lips. He had been nothing but a gentleman, but an unmistakable yearning bloomed inside of her. For what, she did not know: only that she had an appetite.

Paul was the one.

"When do you finish your shift?" she asked.

He looked at his watch. "In about half an hour."

Paul's body and companionship gave her the momentary release she needed. She passionately kissed him like she'd been longing to kiss a man. She felt the eagerness of that first time of touching someone new, someone forbidden. The windows were open and the curtains fluttered, allowing in slivers of light that shivered across their bodies. And his mouth also shivered across her neck and his hands on her thighs. It was the kind of sex she needed.

Paul was gorgeous and gentle, and because of that she was able to let herself go and fuck her pain away even in this spare hotel room that wasn't used because of water damage. The room was hot too, un-air-conditioned and smelling of cigarette ash and cleaning supplies. Still, when it ended, she was sad for it to be over, and she kissed him gently before saying goodbye.

Frances returned to a quiet house with no dishes or cooking because the sitter had done that while there. Her body was alight with a calm she hadn't enjoyed in a very long time. As she lay in bed, her false sense of serenity ended, and the deepest shame burned between her breasts and spread like fire between her legs. What was she looking for? The emptiness was even deeper than her shame. It was a shaft full of toxic air in which no canary could survive.

Then she heard a croaking giggle from the corner of the room. It couldn't be one of the children. She had checked on them before getting into bed. They would have made a commotion as they came into her room.

Maybe it was a demon ready to take her to hell. She believed she deserved it. Her life meant nothing. As long as the demon didn't touch a hair on any of her children's heads, she would let it take her. Frances lay on her back, watching the ceiling fan turn in circles. The fan was a closed circuit of movement. It couldn't stop on its own. Eventually she fell asleep and forgot her pain again.

In the boredom of the next day, her thoughts drifted back to sex and its adrenaline rush. As much as she enjoyed Paul, she didn't want to make any specific someone a habit. An affair couldn't be that bad as long as it wasn't love, she told herself. After all, at the end of the day David always came home to her, even if their eyes never met.

And so Frances found what she needed to cope, in sexual encounters with men she would see a couple of times before ending the affairs without any remorse. The ritual of preparation gave her the rush of excitement and expectation. And then there was the pleasure she would feel with no other sounds but their wet skin slapping and their moans of gratification.

This continued for years until darkness began to creep in again inside of her. The emptiness was there again, crying to be fed something, anything. To be pacified from people and things outside of herself.

Meanwhile, David worked hard; he had to, being brown and proud. He'd even received recognition in the form of pins on his uniform. Part of her was happy for him, but another part resented his accomplishment. The only thing she was told to be proud of were her four healthy babies.

The first hallucination happened at the supermarket.

As she passed by the meat counter, the young man slicing deli meat gave her a smile and a wink. How good it felt to be noticed, to be wanted for something more besides prepping meals, changing bed linens, and starching her husband's uniforms. Though she never missed an opportunity to fix her hair, slather on bright lipstick, and put on a low-cut dress, David never took her dancing anymore. So the supermarket was her only outing.

The butcher wanted her to approach the counter, she could tell. She looked down at the gold band on her finger. Such a funny little trinket. She wondered who the first people to be married were and how such an unnatural thing became commonplace. *Wretched woman,* she could hear. Her first instinct was to look around, but no one was there. Then it dawned on her that it could be the voice of her shame for the affairs. Frances shook her head of black hair. It was half pinned up, half loose. The butcher was serving another customer but managed to flash her a smile and an alluring glance at the same time. His arms flexed as he pushed the meat back and forth on the deli meat slicer. He knew all about tempo. She would wait until the customer was served before heading over. To appear busy, she reached for a tin of soup.

Just as she had the can in her grasp, a brown, decaying hand grabbed her wrist and flipped it over. The index finger was capped with a long, jagged green nail shaped like an arrowhead. It punctured her flesh slowly. It sounded like the ticking of a clock. Every tick raised the temperature of the room. A countdown to an unknown terror.

Sweat trickled between her breasts. She tried to pull back, but the thing's grip was greater than she could wrestle away from. Her strength amounted to nothing compared to the thing's. Without warning it ripped into her flesh, leaving a deep horizontal gash. Blood gushed from the wound and pooled on the floor. *Die,* a voice hissed from the dark gaps of the shelves.

Behind the rows of cans, two white glowing orbs appeared. And from the darkness of the shelf, a flurry of blood spewed out and landed on the birthmark on her left forearm before the unseen assailant released her.

Frances screamed with what little breath remained in her as she stumbled back. She nearly hit the opposite row of shelves and dropped her basket onto the floor. The loud crash caused patrons to stare in her direction. Easy jazz played from speakers above their heads. Without looking at the butcher she ran out of the shop to her car.

The cool air hit her face as she flew through the doors. It felt refreshing, freeing. As she reached for her keys in her bag, she noticed her wrist was fine, with no visible blood, just her birthmark with its brown spots in different shades and in the shape of what could be a galaxy. Her heart still pounded from running. Without any control she leaned against the car, breaking into sobs. Something had to give.

This life of hopping from bed to bed no longer had any meaning. She didn't want to return home to the noise, the washing, the obligations. It must be stress, she told herself, all this pressure building inside of her when she wasn't in a stranger's bed or driving away from her home—both the only things that gave her relief.

And then there was that dark shaft of shame. It was obvious that fucking around would never be enough to calm her cry for help, would never be a rope to lift her out of that dark shaft. Frances remembered the look on her mother's face as she lay in her casket. She had a slight smile across her grooved lips. She wore a mask of peace. Would her own death be the only answer? She wiped her tears with her hands as if trying to take away the traces of these thoughts. There were more tangible matters at hand, like the fact that the refrigerator would still be empty if she didn't go to another supermarket.

The next two weeks passed in sameness until the few strands of sanity she had left untied themselves, leaving her feeling loose. After the incident at the supermarket she ended it with all her lovers. She had no energy or desire left. Numb. She could no longer sleep because the relentless spinning of the ceiling fan kept her awake. The sound of the air circulating through the room whispered, *You're a rancid piece of meat not worthy of your children or life. Give in to the darkness.* The voice from the supermarket had returned.

One evening, after being awake since three A.M., she shuffled into the kitchen, trying to leave behind the little voices. It would be dinnertime soon. She prayed that the desire to grab a knife and end her own life—or her children's lives—would not come to her again. But did she even have the strength to lift the steel knife? It felt like her thoughts of suicide controlled her like a puppet. Only vestiges were left of her resolve; it had been so hard the last time to fight back. To fight *herself*.

As she chopped garlic, she could barely control herself. She gripped the knife so hard that her fingers tingled before going white. Her young daughter, Cathy, pulled on the hem of her dress, wanting to eat. Cathy's pleading drowned out her willpower; she couldn't keep her eyes open for another second. Frances could feel her heart quicken with her breathing. It would be so easy to lift the knife over her head, and then . . .

She tossed the knife into the sink and then backed away, disgusted at herself. Horrified at what she had become.

"Mama. I'm hungry. What's wrong?"

She looked into the child's beautiful eyes. They were the same shape as her own. Cathy's little hand still tugged at her. The love in Cathy's eyes was a knife itself slicing into Frances. Frances didn't believe she deserved such love, even though she wanted it more than anything. She didn't know where to begin to allow herself to fully embrace unconditional love. If only she could give all of them all the love in the heavens. But she was too wretched for that. They deserved better.

"If you go play with your brothers and sisters, I promise to give you an extra candy."

"Like your friends? Those boys you let in the house when Daddy isn't here?"

Frances wanted to drag herself to hell and throw herself into the lake of fire for the sins she thought she had kept hidden. The voice was right all along when it said she was not worthy of the light because her darkness was a stain on everyone around her. She reached into the jar next to the sink and gave Cathy two cookies. "Take these instead, but promise to never say or think about that. Do you understand?"

The little girl nodded before running off straightaway. Frances remained where she stood, trying to calm her breathing.

Her trembling hands gripped her apron. She lifted the fabric to her mouth, balling it tight before screaming in frustration. She screamed until the sound and her tears could be absorbed. Why couldn't she be as good of a mother as her mother was? What the hell had happened?

After the children were fast asleep, she called David's sister Theresa to come stay with the children the following day, something she rarely did. Frances lay in bed all night thinking of a plan. The brown swirling wood made her think of river water. Fast, treacherous water. She would take a bus to the border. Walk however long it would take to throw herself into the Rio Grande. Just another body no one would bother to find out about because she would have no identification on her. It would end. All of it.

The curse of her existence and the curse of her ability to tolerate life. Just like the story of La Llorona. One of the most reviled women in folklore. Frances wondered what tale she would tell if she could speak. Unlike La Llorona, she didn't want to harm her children, just herself. Her death would save them.

Frances didn't bother to say goodbye or write a note. What would that do? No matter how she played it out in her mind, what she was about to do was unforgivable. What other choice did she have? She made her choice long ago.

She walked out the door as the children gathered around Theresa, who brought fast food burgers in paper bags with her, distracting the kids. Only little Cathy looked directly at her with inquisitive eyes. Frances could swear the girl knew. Or the girl would know sooner or later what her mother had been through. A cry choked Frances into silence. All the more reason to leave.

No one bothered her at the station or on the bus. She drifted in and out of sleep with her head against the glass. The quiet lulled her into a false sense of relief. Maybe she could just get off the bus somewhere and start a new life. Still feeling groggy, she opened her eyes to look out the window. A shifting shadow made her jump. She rubbed her eyes and looked toward the seats across from her. They were empty. Slowly she looked toward the window again. Her hands gripped the edge of the seat.

A ghoulish dead thing in a white mantilla peered back at her until seconds later she saw her own face again as light rain slid down the glass. Thunder cracked outside.

No, she couldn't ever lead a normal life. This thing would hound her. The only way out would be for the dark water to take her to where she belonged. Hell. The place created for people like her. People beyond redemption.

Frances stood at the bank of the river. She buried a picture of her children and her identification in a hole nearby. She kissed her hand before touching the earth. The lining in her stomach ached with biting acid. Her final meal had been half a bottle of cheap rum she'd bought at the bus station. The burn of the liquor kept her company and soothed her fears. She stopped walking when she stumbled across a small clearing.

It was a desolate spot near fast-running water. The ripples of large brown hands motioned for her to jump in. Maybe that was the rum playing tricks with her blurry eyes. Tears ran as quickly down her face as the river currents. Fast-moving dirty water. Childish chatter gone. Arguing and negotiating with David and children gone.

You deserve a better mother anyway, she said to herself. *He will meet someone else better suited to the life he wants to live. I'm no good at it. You deserve better and I deserve nothing. Look at how I behaved. All my mistakes.*

"Do it," a voice whispered.

It sounded like the voice in the bedroom from those previous nights. She turned to her left.

A figure resembling a woman stood next to her. It was the apparition from the window on the bus. Its flesh hung like a dress on the bony frame. The skin was nibbled and pockmarked like lace. Small, delicate bones and fish skin stitched together to create a veil hung from the scalp dotted with sparse wet strands of hair. A dress created from a patchwork of flesh and fabric clung to its bones. The voice had an insidious countenance to match its words.

La Llorona, Frances whispered.

She thought of the doctor's face when she came in after her last pregnancy, the disdain in his eyes and raised eyebrows. "You people like your babies."

The shame in that moment. So much shame in this life. It was second nature. Was her nature one of shame? Her very existence stitched with shame, like the dress of this creature was stitched with flesh? What choice did she have? David felt no reason to use any kind of birth control. "We are Catholic. We are married!"

It occurred to Frances that perhaps everyone wore another set of clothing beneath their human skin, stitched together with all the things they hated about themselves and tried to hide. How does one shed such a thing? But she didn't consider herself smart at all. What nonsense was this.

Now it would end.

"You will never be safe until you let the water take you under the water, Frances. Don't you feel better after you have cried?"

Frances closed her eyes and thought of her children, of all the men she'd bedded to make the hurt and rage go away. Orgasms didn't last long and neither did love. The last image in her mind was of her daughter Cathy. She spoke out loud to nothing and everything that surrounded her. *If there is a god, let Cathy have a good life. A life of her own. The strength I didn't have. Ancestors, give all the women after me any power they need. It is all I ask.*

She stepped into the current, not knowing how to swim.

The creature stood by the riverbank and watched the woman float away without a fight, her mouth swallowing fate without question. When the body got caught in debris farther downstream, it would float to her corpse and rip out her guts. Devour each organ one by one, then let the body go.

Days would pass before they found her. In the empty spot where she previously stood were her shoes. The woman removed them before jumping into the lethal water. The creature had no feet to speak of, yet it formed them out of will and placed the shoes on its new feet. Now that this one was gone, it would flee to another until the dead woman's daughters were ripe for ripping apart. So many souls. So much despair to relish. It admired its own gaining power over this species.

I am a god, *it thought.* A god. I can rule their destinies, thoughts, and actions.

And they are powerless to stop me.

Alejandra and Melanie

A little voice came from the entrance of the TV room.

"Mommy, I don't want to sleep here. I don't want to see the bright eyes again."

Still in a daze from her dream, she sat upright and opened her arms to Will, beckoning him to come closer for a hug. She needed an embrace. *It was just a dream, Alejandra,* she told herself.

"It's okay, baby. It's just your glow-in-the dark planets hanging above your bed."

Will's face looked angelic in his *Star Wars* pajamas. His thick brown hair was combed to the side, his big brown eyes looking up to her with genuine fear. She didn't want him to feel afraid in his own room or of the dark. Not like she had all her life. And for no good reason. This was also very unusual behavior for him. He typically fell asleep within minutes unless he was suffering from illness. She was grateful that her children were all good sleepers. "I'll go up with you and make sure everything is safe."

She shut off the TV and turned off the lamp next to her. Will nodded and trailed behind Alejandra back to his bedroom. The room appeared just as she left it when she'd tucked him into bed. "I'll tell you what, I will shut off the lights to show you there is nothing to worry about."

Alejandra touched his face, then walked to the door to switch off the light. "Here goes."

She reached for the switch, then paused. The feeling from the kitchen when she saw the creature in the pool crept over her again. It was the same sensation, of her guts being pulled from her belly button, and it froze her. *It was only a dream!*

She shook off her residual fear. It was all in her head. A coincidence that the fear felt the same.

But then the room went dark.

Alejandra couldn't stop herself from screaming out loud. The lights Will had seen weren't his plastic glow-in-the-dark planets hanging from the wooden slats of his cabin bed. Above his bed hovered two eyes glowing white-hot. She could also just see pustules that resembled nipples infected from untreated mastitis oozing pus. No real teeth but little razorlike nubs on gums that ground against each other. Its skin glistened wet. Alejandra's shaking hand fumbled for the light switch to flood the room with light.

"Did you see it, Mommy? See, I wasn't being a naughty boy."

The sound of his voice hit her like a bat swinging at her heart. It couldn't be real, none of it. She was having a breakdown. But he saw the creature too? And then there was Catrina. This wasn't a shared vision or hallucination.

The creature was real, and it meant to harm them. Alejandra would do anything to protect her children.

"You can sleep with me tonight. Go on into my bed." She wanted to remain calm to prevent him from becoming more frightened or having nightmares, even though her heart pounded in her chest. Sleeping with her would reassure him he was safe. As much as Alejandra did not like children in her bed during the night, she couldn't risk anything happening to him. He sprinted to her room with his feet hitting the floor like the pounding of little drums. Alejandra prayed Elodia wouldn't wake up.

Alejandra remembered the obsidian. She rushed to her room and grabbed it off her bedside table. She held it tightly between both hands and closed her eyes, imagining the women from her dreams laying their hands upon it. *Wherever you are, I need your help. Protect this home and protect my children. Guide me. Please. I have faith I can get through this. I want to live.*

She kissed the obsidian and placed it in the center of Will's room and walked out backward.

She needed now to keep her calm to figure out what to do next. She couldn't leave the house. Where would she go and for how long? How would she explain a hotel bill to Matthew? The upheaval to the house from her clear out already left him irritated with her. She hoped the power of her faith would be enough until she could find real answers. An exhausted and panicked parent was an impatient parent. Will would have ample space in the bed to spread out with Matthew gone. She shut the light off again and waited for the eyes to stare back at her, or for a creature to lunge at her throat. She took a deep breath and imagined her circle of women. Her finger clipped the switch. Nothing there. She looked around for any sign, shut the door, and went to her room to settle Will in her bed. When she reached the threshold, he was already in Matthew's spot with his eyes closed. She would call Melanie first thing in the morning. What was happening?

Alejandra shut her eyes. *I can do this. I can deal with this.*

Alejandra tried to go through the morning without looking at the clock while she waited for it to be a decent hour to call Melanie. She didn't want to disturb her before breakfast again.

God, she is going to think I'm a needy, hysterical woman. That instinct to worry what people thought and the need to please, be pleasant all the time for everyone's sake at her expense, made her feel irritated with herself. Melanie was trying to rid her of that. In fact, she told her to always be in touch if anything out of the ordinary happened.

But ingrained habits were hard to break. Alejandra would try even if it meant breaking everything she'd learned from birth so she might rebuild. When the clock hit eight A.M. she gave Melanie a call. Alejandra turned her back to the children and stepped away to prevent them from hearing her. After two rings Melanie answered. "Melanie, it's getting worse and it's now affecting my children. Will and I saw the creature in his room. This isn't a dream or vision while awake. For now I have placed the obsidian inside and locked the door. Nothing else has happened. *Please.* I need to see you."

"It's okay. How about I come over? Would that be all right?"

Alejandra could feel herself calming down, her thoughts easing off the accelerator. Her mind had been racing in uncontrollable circles toward the darkest conclusions, until now.

"Yes, how soon can you come?"

"Did what you both see make any move toward you? Did it try to physically harm you?"

"No. Nothing physical, but it was incredibly frightening."

"I can head over tomorrow morning. After the children are in school I think is best. If you see it again, call me as soon as possible. Keep your faith and keep the room locked. Whatever was in there has to get the message you won't be pushed around."

"Thank you. See you tomorrow." Alejandra ended the call

with the determination to get through the day in peace. And through the night.

Catrina stared at her as she ate her breakfast, as if she knew something was not right but did not want to speak about it. Alejandra put the phone away as she crossed back into the kitchen and kissed Catrina on the crown of her head. "I love you. You make my day."

Catrina smiled. "I love you too."

That night, Alejandra allowed Will to sleep in her room again to avoid his room altogether. After the morning school run, Alejandra bought a packet of the nice cookies and fresh coffee. She also put soda and sparkling water in the fridge in case Melanie didn't drink coffee or tea. Before Will and Catrina had gone to bed the night before, she'd made them tidy the toys they'd strewn over the house in an effort to create more boundaries and structure. Melanie helped her feel that doing this would be to her benefit and was healthy. Any tantrums would result in their favorite books and toys being put away for a week. And no dessert the next day. The house looked decent for once. Alejandra waited for the doorbell to ring by pacing the house, looking for things that seemed out of place or smudged by little hands. The business of preparing for company made her forget her fear.

Melanie arrived with a warm smile. Alejandra wanted to throw her arms around her. Seeing her was such a relief: someone to tell Alejandra she was not beyond hope. "Thank you for coming over. This is the second time I have seen that thing in real life. Catrina has mentioned it at school. Now Will?"

"We will talk about Catrina later. Show me the first place you saw it." Alejandra led Melanie to the kitchen and out the unlocked door to the backyard. A breeze caught their hair. Melanie closed her eyes then breathed in and out. She opened her eyes to look at Alejandra.

"What does this place feel like for you? It's a beautiful home, yet beneath there is a heaviness. A dense energy. It is as you have described it to me. I feel it all around."

Alejandra placed her hand to her mouth. "That is exactly right. I know I've told you this before. When my husband is here it feels like a trap, or like I can't do anything right. I feel anxious. When he's gone it's like a haunted house. Every sound and bump like something or someone lurks in the dark. I miss him, the security of him being in the house at least. And he is also an extra set of hands with the children. Catrina adores him much more than she does me. I'm just the awful warden always nagging and unhappy. I feel overwhelmed. It has subsided since we started our sessions, though. I don't know what I'm doing wrong."

"When you think on these things, where in your body do you feel it most?"

Alejandra bristled at the breeze without a sweater on. "Do you mind if we go inside?" Melanie nodded with a look of concern on her face. Once inside, Alejandra looked around the kitchen, trying to take in what Melanie had just said, but she couldn't focus, didn't want to focus. "Can I get you anything? A hot drink or cold drink? Snack? I can make you breakfast if you haven't eaten."

Melanie took Alejandra's hand into her own. "This is not for me. I am here for you. Your well-being. Stop. Close your eyes. Where do you feel all of this manifesting?"

Alejandra's stomach dropped. She began to sob. Her sorrow emptying with the force of a heavy period draining from her body. Melanie wrapped her arms around Alejandra. "You can cry. You don't have to feel ashamed of how you are feeling or who you are."

Alejandra wiped her eyes with her sweatshirt sleeve. "Sorry.

All that emotion is always there. Sometimes I can't prevent it from just exploding out. I imagine my eyeballs hold their shape from my tears. I feel it everywhere, my body always tense. I am ready to let it all go once and for all. It has been a slow process since we began, but I sense this has come to mean life or death. For me, my children."

"You are a brave woman from a long line of other brave women. We all are. Why don't you show me where you saw this thing that frightened you and your son so much?"

Alejandra nodded and led Melanie to the second floor where Will's room was. She opened the door that they'd kept closed since the incident. "Here is where I saw it. I think my son saw the exact same thing, except he only mentioned seeing eyes. And right before this I had a dream of La Llorona. I wanted it to all be a coincidence."

Melanie scanned the room before her gaze caught something on the bed. She walked closer to look at the top of the cabin bed. There she saw some dark-green, almost black smudge marks, which she sniffed.

"Alejandra, where did you say you saw the creature?"

"Right where you are standing."

"Did you see this?" Melanie stepped aside and pointed to the smudge marks.

Alejandra looked closer. Her fear replacing tears. "No way my son could climb up there without falling off. Melanie, what could this be? It isn't crayon or marker. None of my children would have a toilet accident and wipe it there of all places."

"Many coincidences are not coincidences at all." Melanie reached inside her bag, taking out a tissue. She wiped the mark away, then carefully folded the tissue, placing it in the pocket of her bag. "Whatever it is, I don't sense it here anymore. If the manifestation still lingered in this room, I would gravitate toward it. It's a shame my mother is no longer with us. She helped so many children. Had a real way with them and could probably talk to your son more. But I will sweep this room with an herb barrida I brought with me. I have Florida water, too."

Melanie took from her bag a small glass bottle filled with a pale green liquid. She handed another bottle to Alejandra. "You can dab a little Florida water on yourself or use it when you clean. There are many uses when it comes to clearing energy or in specific rituals, but for today we are using it to purify the room. Think of it as a different type of holy water."

She walked around the room while spritzing the air. Alejandra breathed in the scent deeply. The cologne had a unique citrus smell, with many layers: orange, cinnamon, sage, and lavender.

"And now we will use the barrida of herbs from my garden. We have mugwort, lavender, bay leaf, and rosemary. This is a way to sweep the room and the bed to cleanse the area of unwanted lingering energy. It also aids in protection."

Melanie reached into her bag and pulled out two bundles of fresh herbs tied at the bottom with red string. She handed one to Alejandra. The scent of rosemary and bay hit Alejandra's nose first. The room now had the freshness of a garden.

Melanie swept the bed with her barrida as if she were painting it. She turned to Alejandra. "I want you to do the closet." Alejandra nodded, feeling a sense of strength and control.

Both women touched every place where a malicious force would try to hide.

"I think that should do it. You keep the Florida water and barrida. Shall we sit down and discuss this more?"

A barrida of confidence swept across Alejandra's heart. "Yes. I'm ready to do what it takes."

Alejandra made them each a cup of coffee with a plate of cookies, the ones she liked but didn't usually eat because every calorie counted. Recently she had stopped punishing herself with those thoughts and ate what she wanted. She ate the damn cookie if that was what she wanted.

"Did you feel or sense anything here? I'm not that sick, at least not as sick as I thought."

"You do need help to heal your mind and heart. Work through the trauma of your past to help you cope with your present. At first, I thought this was susto, fright. A common ailment brought to us curanderas. But I think it's deeper than that.

"But give me some time to find an answer. Let me think about this and get what I found on the bed to my friend at the university. Why don't you come and see me in three days?"

"I will. Thank you for taking the time to come here."

Melanie rose from her seat. "I must go now, but don't lose heart. I'll see you soon and I will try to find out what that was on the bed. You are doing great, Alejandra. Believe in yourself. Don't doubt your voice. It's there for a reason. If you need me, please get in touch. I'm taking this seriously."

Three days later, Alejandra sat in the comfortable chair opposite Melanie. "Any information on what you found on the bed?"

A look of frustration crossed Melanie's face as she shook her head. This was unusual, because she always had a solid awareness and calm. She looked unsettled. "Unfortunately, not yet. I gave it to a friend who is a biology professor at Penn to analyze its compounds. Believe me, I am just as curious as you. In all my time I have never experienced anything like this. My mother possessed a wealth of knowledge, but never mentioned encountering curses in this form." Melanie paused and glanced out the window in her office.

"I want to bring up an idea. Now perhaps hear me out. What if the story of La Llorona is true? What if *she* is the entity you've been seeing? La Llorona has not survived this long by simply going away. Her story has been passed down from generation to generation and remains frightening. No one can say for certain how her tale originated. Her story doesn't have an end, and we need to find out why. The crying, the dreams, the white dress. The only thing I can think of is some energy source has taken the story as a guise. Wearing it to mask its true intention."

Alejandra didn't know how to respond at first. The idea of a ghost story, a very old story, being true tested what she was raised to believe as an Evangelical Christian, even if she was not practicing. But that type of Christianity had never appealed to her or felt like the right fit for her soul.

"Wow. I know an entity is attacking me. And say you are right and it is La Llorona, why me?"

Melanie answered, "From everything you have told me about your past, your family, your nightmares, and your recurring dreams, perhaps you are dealing with a generational curse that runs through the mother. The women in your family, the ones you know of, seem to be haunted by a force or forces beyond their control."

"A generational curse?" Alejandra asked. The phrase made her think of DNATree and her previous conversations with her birth mother, Cathy, who abandoned her, and the photo of her grandmother Frances, who abandoned Cathy.

"Can you see the patterns of behavior that recur, consciously or subconsciously, from generation to generation of women? As individuals we reflect familiar patterns in our own lives and those we've learned from our parents and environments. But this is a little different. I bet if we could speak to the women who are not alive, they might have more knowledge about this. Perhaps that is why they are in your dreams. They are not here in the flesh, but they want to show you that you are not alone.

"The creature you saw is no vision or hallucination. I believe your generational trauma is manifesting as a creature, and all those women in your dreams probably experienced its torment. And the only way to break a curse like this is by going back to the places where the patterns began and confronting the trauma. Your individual trauma and the generational trauma. The trauma is the culprit, not just La Llorona, or the creature wearing her guise."

Alejandra nodded. It was a lot to process, but it was the kind of work she was willing to put her soul on the line for. "Can it harm me or the kids? I mean physically?"

Melanie pursed her lips and shook her head. "I can only *guess,* but my instinct says it wants you to hurt yourself or them first. Then it attacks physically. Like weak prey in nature are targeted first by the predator. That is why it is important for you to stay strong no matter where you are."

Hearing this made sense on the one hand but was overwhelming on the other. She thought of curses as hexes made by someone else and placed on another, not something you could invite into your life without knowing it. Or passing them on. Catrina's and Will's experiences with La Llorona could only be explained this way. This was a part of her past that had to stop with her. She would be the one to confront this.

But then a wave of exhaustion from all the information made her feel light-headed. Every session left her feeling like she'd been in a fatal car accident. But this was not a usual session. Her brain worked fast and hard to expand and accept that this thing with La Llorona could be both external and internal. What a mind fuck.

"How can I stop La Llorona?"

"That is what we must find out. I will help you."

"I'm ready. I'm listening more to myself. Letting myself be led by my inner voice. It feels great, but fragile. Old thoughts are hard to prevent from creeping in when I feel a setback has occurred or I feel overwhelmed."

"That is okay, Alejandra. You are human. Why don't we get started? Ready?"

Alejandra nodded with La Llorona still on her mind. She was ready to begin the next phase of her life full of deep understanding, even if it meant having to touch the nightmare.

"I want to start with you closing your eyes and taking a deep breath. We need to rid you of whatever we didn't catch in those balloons, whatever that fright has brought back. Tap each knee with your hands. I want you to take a deep breath and say what you want to say today. Say something you have been hiding and want to rid yourself of. Say what you want to burn and let the wind carry away that feeling and thought like ash in the wind. Become a bonfire inside."

Alejandra breathed heavily in and out of her nose. "There are times I would rather die than continue on with motherhood. I would rather be dead than have to carry the weight of it. The fear of it. The fear for their future. The fear I'm not good enough. I would rather be dead than fail them. To deal with their cries. You are supposed to live for your children, but I feel they rob me of my life because I am so consumed by the fear." She continued to breathe heavily in and out of her nose. Tears streaming from the corners of her eyes. In her mind she saw herself lying in the cenote with the other women from her dreams, with Catrina's face looking down on her.

"What makes you think of this?"

Melanie's voice broke her vision. "Catrina. After what happened at school. I'm also afraid of her resenting me for not always having enough time for her because the younger ones need me more. It's like being in the middle of hurricane force winds when they all want me at once. Because she is the oldest, I lean on her to wait, to step aside."

"Keep breathing. I want you to take all that resentment, all your rage, and imagine you have the heat and power of a volcano. Who do you fear? No one. You are ancient and from the Earth. Take the fire and burn that fear. It doesn't exist anymore. You are more than your fear and more than your past. Let's go back to the first night in the hospital alone with your eldest, Catrina. I want you to see everything. Go right back to your first child. Time-travel back to that moment in time. Don't doubt your ability to be there."

Alejandra inhaled a deep breath through her nose. The room smelled of sage and rosemary. Heat gathered in her throat; it felt scratchy.

"I'm alone in my hospital room. We could afford a private room. My baby smells wonderful. I'm so happy she is here and healthy. While I waited for her, I couldn't stop worrying about the cord being caught around her throat. You read about it in all the books. You have no idea if it will happen. What kind of god kills babies with the very thing that is meant to keep them alive? I feel hazy because the drugs from the C-section are so strong. Breastfeeding is difficult. But . . ."

"But what?"

Alejandra's hands began to pat faster.

"Someone is in the room. Even though I am groggy I can sense a presence. Not my husband. He has left to get me food."

"A nurse? Doctor?"

Alejandra grabbed the fabric of her leggings, digging her nails in as she gripped her knees.

"It's a shadow. No, it's lighter now. It's . . . the creature. It's wearing . . . my dress."

"Is it speaking to you?"

"No. It's retreating to the shadows. It's gone. I just think it's the drugs and exhaustion from breastfeeding every few hours."

Alejandra opened her eyes and stared at the floor. "How did I forget that? The fear was so real, my inner voice crying out, but I doubted my instinct."

Fear blanched Melanie's usually vibrant skin. Her mind seemed far away.

"Melanie?"

"Sorry, I am trying to listen for any pieces of information sent to me that might help me understand all these moving pieces."

Alejandra continued, "I think it has been there all along. Watching and waiting for me to have a child. Now it will wait in the shadows for Catrina. Is it possible?"

"You come from a fundamentalist Christian family who shunned anything that did not line up with that belief system, yet evil and demons are thought of as real, as real as the rapture. If those things are real, why nothing else? And on whose authority?"

Alejandra searched her memory of all the births of her children. Searching for the details she'd brushed off. "Not an authority I believe in. I struggle to believe I'm marked by a curse or that La Llorona has been after me. Why?"

Melanie tapped her foot against the wood floor. "I want you

to try to find out as much about your past as possible. Every-thing from your mother and DNATree. I also think it's time you confront La Llorona. On my end I will go over all my notes from our sessions and meditate on it."

Alejandra nearly stood up to leave before stopping herself. "La Llorona? Really? You want me to confront her? What makes you think she will come?"

Melanie glanced around the room. Her arms trembled as if a sudden chill caught her off guard. "I don't think she has left, or whatever entity is taking the form of La Llorona. But we don't have enough information. You are confronting what plagues you. That is what is important. I feel there is something bigger at work here. It remains veiled to me, and I don't do well with those kinds of uncertainties. But don't mind me. How are you getting on with your altar?"

The thought of the altar brought Alejandra great joy and peace. It was something just for her to share with her children, like the record player.

The altar.

After Alejandra rearranged the space on top of the credenza in the entrance of the house, she sat in front of the altar, watch-ing the flame from the seven-day candle, which resembled an amber ghost. Black soot smudged the side of the glass. The lon-ger she stared, the more she saw and the wider her eyes opened. Soon they refused to shut. And as she cried, she could also feel her soul stretch its limbs as if trying to create a better fit inside of her.

Epiphanies and revelations hit her mind with the suddenness of a hailstorm. One in particular burned to the bone. The black soot on the glass made her realize she had been viewing all her relationships with soot-covered eyes. The soot from her adop-tive father, the men she gave her love carelessly to. As the flame grew stronger and the black smoke rose higher, Alejandra's eyes continued to widen.

But her inner flame could not shine through her smudged eyesight. The time had come for her to wipe her eyes clean for good.

Alejandra said a silent prayer for forgiveness if this meant she could no longer stay with Matthew, the father of her children, but possibly not the one for her. It might take time, but her family deserved that grace for her to see this process through.

And she knew now she could live in this world alone.

"The altar has been a beacon for me. I love it. I know it has a purpose. All of it. But I can't make all the connections yet."

Melanie nodded. "Divine timing could be at play. But you need to reach out to it, as I fear it will only grow bolder if it feels you are growing stronger. As soon as I know what the residue is, I will call you. Buy us some time and make a connection with the entity. You are strong enough. Call on the women of your dreams. That is what they are there for. I still call on my mother. In fact, I think I will try to connect with her spirit later today."

Alejandra walked out of the session to a light rain. She looked to the clouds blotting out all the sunlight. She whispered to the sky, "Come to me, La Llorona. Wherever you are I ask you to meet me face-to-face."

A gust of wind blew hard against her body. The force made her move along to her car before it began to pour.

It was almost time to pick up the children from school.

Melanie

When she had a break between clients and the weather was pleasant, Melanie enjoyed sitting in her garden to allow the sun's rays to replenish her spirit.

There she allowed her mind to wander where it wanted. This was where she often heard from her mother and sometimes others she did not know. Not their actual voices, but instead a feeling of comfort and awareness that often handed down sacred knowledge or direction. Many times this intuition had helped her in her own life and with clients. Problems with the mind also needed to be felt and dealt with compassionately.

When she was at graduate school, being the only Mexican American woman in her class, she knew better than to ever speak to anyone in school about this side of her beliefs. Now, at the age of forty-five, with an established practice, she had the freedom to be who she really was. She could use both her gifts of worldly knowledge and her abilities with unseen knowledge to help others.

And she wanted to help Alejandra. Not out of pity but because she had seen her aunt Olgita go through a similar scenario. Olgita did not make it out of her abusive relationship alive, and her boyfriend lived in prison for her murder.

Humans had so many curses to contend with.

Melanie glanced out the window to see if the sun was in the perfect position for her to sit on her bench in the garden next to the birdbath and drink a cup of manzanilla tea. This creature plaguing Alejandra was affecting Melanie in ways that left her with an inner fear that its malevolence could be anywhere.

She rolled her neck from side to side to loosen the muscles, then stopped when her head hit her chest. A sheen of sweat appeared above her lip. The back of her neck felt wet. From her peripheral vision she registered a reflection in the window.

She slowly turned her head to look, even though she knew exactly what it was.

A face sagging from the weight of the water that seemed to be leaking from its scalp stared directly at her with a hatred radiating so intensely that she could feel it in her chest. It had hollow cheeks and the bones of the sternum and clavicle were exposed. The entire form appeared malnourished. Then it disappeared.

A small oil diffuser on a side table turned over and gushed on the surface before dripping onto the floor, creating a circular stain on the carpet.

"Come out. Speak to me. I know you are here. I can feel you."

The room was still. No birds chirped outside her window. A cloud interrupted the sunlight, and the room went dark. Melanie turned back toward the window.

There it was again. The reflection. Its grin full of barbed teeth taunted her. Within a matter of seconds, it transformed from a reflection into solid matter and stood next to her. She could hear and feel its breath on her neck. The hair near her ear rose with static electricity.

Melanie could feel herself trembling. This thing felt so powerful. Its energy pulsated against her body. She continued to fight the urge to run. It brought a bony hand with thick flint shards for nails to the corner of her eye. "You disgusting, blasphemous witch. Stop playing games with what is mine. You can't have her. I own her."

"She is owned by no one but herself. We are given free will. Your power is only in your mind. And I will not stop helping her."

"Then you will have blood on your hands. I will come for you after, when you are at your worst, full of shame and guilt. This is your first warning, witch." One if its hands gripped her upper arm. Melanie tried to move but found herself paralyzed by its grip. It was like an energetic lasso wrapped around her entire body.

It slowly brought its forefinger within her eyesight. Melanie continued to try to free herself. As she struggled, its forefinger pierced the corner of her eye, drilling until it hit bone with its nail. Melanie stood still, saying a silent prayer as she heaved through the extreme pain. She allowed herself to be filled with memories of her loved ones, all she found sacred in life. Moments of unadulterated joy. She remembered her mother showing her how to make a barrida for the first time. The elation when she received the news of being accepted to graduate school. All the letters and messages sent by previous clients who told her of how their lives had changed for the better after seeking help.

"Stop that," it hissed.

The creature snarled before snatching its nail back, ripping the flesh from the corner of her eye to her ear. Melanie screamed out from the sudden pain, lifting her hand to her face.

But the energy in the room cleared. The entity was gone.

She ran to the mirror hanging on the wall to inspect the wound. Nothing. There was nothing to show that the entity had manifested itself except for the overturned oil lamp that continued to drool onto the carpet.

Melanie grabbed a box of tissues from her desk before turning the diffuser upright and trying to absorb the oil. The large circle reminded her of Alejandra's dream. The rings were like the circle of women.

It was at that moment she knew this was indeed an ancient entity stretching back in time. It would take the collective power of all the women in Alejandra's circular bloodline to stop it. She had to make a connection between all of them.

Melanie dabbed the carpet dry, then opened her laptop to make sure her friend was still rushing the analysis of the residue left by the entity. She wanted a little more confirmation before giving Alejandra any unnecessary worry. Alejandra had to continue on her soul journey.

Melanie would reach out to her mother in meditation. Answers did not happen in a linear way. They were more like random words and images popping up in her mind. She would sit outside, barefoot, and try to listen. What she did gather by the way it appeared was that, despite feeding on souls century after century, this thing could never be satiated or nourished. It could not store anything within. So it took until whatever it consumed was no more.

Alejandra

It was another night of Alejandra sleeping alone with Matthew away for work again. Will was in his room. She used the baby monitors when Matthew traveled for work, as a sort of extra protection. The fear of an intruder was always in the back of her mind. Alejandra and Matthew's bedroom was on the second floor with Will and Elodia's rooms. Catrina was on the third floor next to the home office. It scared Alejandra when she heard noises in the dining and living area on the first floor.

Her adoptive father, Jim, had talked about preparedness all the time. *Be prepared for the end times. Be prepared for the devil to tempt you. Don't allow yourself to ever be caught with your guard down.* He kept a large gun in a pocket in the cab of the family truck, wrapped in an old T-shirt. She knew it was there because while she was looking for her book, her hand gripped the hard metal in an unmistakable shape. It made her shudder. Her book, *Midnight's Children* by Salman Rushdie, had been tossed in the open cab, its pages stuck together and wet. Ruined.

She didn't have to ask him about it, because tossing something that was hers with such disregard was all she needed to know.

Alejandra slept with the light on in the hall that connected the two levels of the house and bedrooms. House noises always scared her. She'd been a light sleeper since childhood, when she was always being awakened by one of her siblings crying or getting out of bed; any noise at all would cause her eyes to pop open. She waited there to hear it again and figure out what it was so she might go back to sleep in peace.

But that night, she left her closet door open. She whispered in her drowsy state, *La Llorona, I know you are there. Show yourself. If you want me, I am here. Waiting.* Not a sound. Not even a creak from the closet or a clang of ice falling from the ice maker in the refrigerator. She allowed herself to fall into the exhaustion of the end of the day.

The bang roused her from the drift between dozing and deep sleep. At first, she thought it could be her eldest, Catrina, using the toilet, she too being a light sleeper the older she became. Another bang above her head where the boiler was located, but it didn't sound like the boiler—more like hands and feet pounding inside the walls.

Alejandra glanced at the monitor. No sign of anyone. Panic gripped her. She would never forgive herself for how she felt about her family if something really did happen to any of them. She jumped out of bed, grabbing her phone from the charger.

Adrenaline pumped violently as she expected to confront an intruder. With the hallway light on, she quietly crept up the stairs to the home office and Catrina's room. Her heart hurt as it thumped against her ribs. She could feel her pulse in her neck and temples. She flashed her phone's flashlight to the dark corners of the office and to the closet with the boiler inside. Nothing. Next, she approached Catrina's room. Her hand twisted the doorknob slowly before opening it just a crack. The hall light streaked across her daughter's bed. Her closet was secured with the small chair. Nothing.

A wave of relief. Nothing where the sounds originated. No one could have come down; she would have seen it. She made her way back down the stairs. Her entire body relaxed. Might as well check on the other children. Will lay in his bed, snoring softly with a glowing *Star Wars* Death Star lamp next to his bed.

Now to check on Elodia. She walked toward the crib and watched her daughter sleep peacefully. Her beautiful face at rest with little lips pouting. She loved all of them so very much. Alejandra wondered why she'd waited so long to get help. To begin the process of making changes on her terms.

"Can you smell that?"

Alejandra whipped her head around. Her body quaked before her brain had the chance to question what she saw before her. It was an intruder, but not human.

"Smell the life inside of them. The purity."

Alejandra knew she had to be here in this moment. Not run away. Not wish it away. Face the ugly thing because the confrontation had to happen. She kept her eyes firmly fixed on the creature and then pictured her dream with the women. *Come to me now,* she screamed in her mind. Their arms and chins raised to the heavens simultaneously like soldiers in formation.

In the center of the cenote, a flame similar to her seven-day candle sparked from the bodies of the women floating on the surface. No longer water, the cenote was a pool of oil. Fuel. The fire roared to life before Alejandra spoke.

"You heard my call. You are real. What do you want, La Llorona?"

It looked at her curiously, sniffing the air as if it could detect the scent of smoke from the image in Alejandra's mind. "A soul.

A soul to keep me alive, but not just any soul. I want the souls of children, their innocence. And I want you. All your terror and pain that grows day by day. Every ill word you speak about yourself. All your hate, the despair. I want to devour you as you decay inside."

Something struck Alejandra. It didn't respond to the name or mention children of her own. "Are you La Llorona?"

It gasped with laughter as its eyes rolled to the back of its skull. Loose, putrid flesh jiggled off its bones. Strings of bloody saliva speckled with black dripped from its lips. "No. Silly, human. *You are.*"

Ownership. No choices. No hope. It enraged Alejandra. She would live if only to destroy this thing so it could never harm anyone again. Her resolve to keep her children from experiencing the corrosive anguish strengthened her. Alejandra stepped closer to it, wishing she had a weapon at her disposal. What would it take to end its cycle of destruction? Even a bullet would be useless. "You can't have them. I don't agree with it. I reject it."

"Time is but a cord. Your bloodline is a cord. How can you cut time but through death?"

The creature ran its tongue across flabby, gelatinous lips before gnashing its jaw together to expose a mouth full of barbed teeth. In the gaps, small strings of rotting flesh resembled hungry writhing maggots.

Alejandra reached inside for ancestral fortitude in the face of this nightmarish sight. "I'm telling you now, you can't have us. I am here to tell you no. You have been visiting Catrina. Frightening my son. I will end you."

Its mummified-looking hands curled and flexed in agitation. "Yes, as a punishment for bringing that witch into your life. She has been warned too."

The creature grinned at Alejandra again, causing its flesh to crease like the translucent, paper-thin skin of a featherless newborn bird. Its body swayed side to side and its eyes fixed on Alejandra. Pulses of invisible heat hit the middle of her chest. As she winced it continued to sway and smile a malicious grin.

Alejandra bowed her head and met its gaze. She could feel its energy pressing harder against her chest. Without knowing why, she imagined invisible hands pushing through her rib cage to release whatever this thing was trying to place inside of her. Alejandra's body began to sway. She focused all her will on repelling it and showing it her strength. Her forehead began to throb, specifically a pressure next to her right eyebrow. "You're wrong. I've never felt better. I'm getting help. I do not want to become you. I won't feed you anymore. My ancestors are on my side."

The creature's grin snapped to a tight singularity on its face. Quasar-hot eyes burned brighter as the swaying of its body turned to trembling. "Help? But it won't last. You can't escape me or this curse. No matter where you go or try to hide, I will follow. I will destroy you and them either way. That little pile of rubbish you created with that witch. You think it will help? Tear it down." The wildness of its eyes blazed again with fury as it continued to study Alejandra's face for any crack to allow in fear.

Alejandra knew *it* was the one scared and desperate. "I'll find a way, demon. If you didn't fear me, I don't think you would be here now speaking to me."

The white glow in the eye sockets dimmed slightly. The gums in its mouth gnashed, releasing a black saliva that dribbled down its chin. It rocked side to side again, looking like it wanted to strike. Alejandra could tell it was holding back. But why? Had it experienced defiance like this before?

"You can try. But there is nothing special about you. No way for you to defeat me. I am made of the dust of creation. It never dies. Once you are in the ground that is it. Pathetic. You can't even manage your own life, and you are halfway in the grave."

The heat from the flames in her vision rose from her throat and spread from the crown of her head to her toes. A tornado of molten power spun inside of her. As if invisible hands had pressed into her back, Alejandra lunged with animal ferocity toward the creature. She tried to pull at the patchwork gown of flesh and fabric. Eviscerate it to oblivion. Her hand nearly caught a sash around its waist that looked as if it was made from braided umbilical cords, the ends blackened like the three she'd saved when the remnants fell from her own children's bellies.

She didn't manage to reach the creature before it dashed into her room. Alejandra followed it, flipping on her bedroom light. Nothing but the open closet door that swung to the right. With slow steps, her determination still fresh in her fists, she approached the closet wondering if it waited to attack her from behind the freshly dry-cleaned suits. Her hand trembled at the edge of the clothing before she parted them forcefully.

Nothing. Just fabric. Her sweaters appeared to have been punctured or eaten. Alejandra's heart continued to beat steadily as she looked at the back of the closet.

"Mom?" Alejandra jerked around to see Catrina standing in the doorway in her LOL pajamas. "Is Dad back? Who were you talking to?"

"No one, baby. I'm sorry I woke you up. Just the iPad. I couldn't sleep. Go back to bed, my love."

"All right. But, Mom, can you look at my closet door? It won't close anymore, and my chair is gone. It keeps opening." Catrina walked back up the stairs to her room in a haze of sleep.

Alejandra froze. This mass of evil energy was stalking her

daughter. Her innocent child with so much hope in her heart and a world to conquer. Alejandra wanted to crumple on the floor next to the pile of dirty laundry she had to do the following day. But it wanted her to give up, to feel there was no point to living. She grabbed the obsidian she had previously placed in Will's room from her bedside table and crept upstairs. Catrina was silent and seemed to have dozed off again. Alejandra quietly left the obsidian beneath her bed, then went back to her room.

She would call her birth mother. Maybe Cathy knew something about this curse that she hadn't wanted to share. Alejandra needed to know more. She sent Cathy a text to call her between shifts at the hospital. Then another message to Melanie.

Melanie, La Llorona, or should I say the creature, spoke to me but did not make physical contact. It did tell me running is pointless. I have to find a way to get rid of it. I messaged my mother Cathy. Maybe she can help.

Melanie messaged back immediately.

Continue to light your candles on the altar. As long as it is not physical then try to find out more if it speaks again. I think finding more information from your mother will be helpful. After you speak to her, let me know what she says. We can go from there. Don't be afraid of it. That is what it wants. Maybe it will tell us something we need to know. I'm here if you need me. M

Alejandra lay in bed thinking of the ways to end the impostor La Llorona. But why wait until sunrise? The sunrise could welcome the miracle she needed. Her ancient ancestors believed every day and season was a miracle. She tossed the comforter aside to sit by the altar and ask for guidance, a miracle.

The stairs creaked beneath her feet as they always did. When she reached the bottom, the moonlight streamed through the stained-glass of the door. Instead of broken shards on the floor, the light cast red prisms at her feet. They took the unmistakable shape of human hearts. Alejandra wanted to pick them up and hold them to her chest until they melted into her flesh. Every one a new layer to fortify her own until it no longer beat.

She continued to the altar and lit a white seven-day candle and a stick of copal. The orange flame of the candle flared as the copal emitted its smoke. She kneeled and placed both hands on her thighs with palms upright. She breathed in and out of her nose deeply to fill and empty her lungs completely. The crown of her head began to tingle the longer she did this. The center of her mind cleared to an empty shoebox. She opened her mouth to speak without thinking about what she wanted to say. It didn't matter anyway.

I'm lost. I've been lost for a very long time, but I want to return to myself. I want to be whole. Ancestors, spirit, whatever may be hovering by my side to give me guidance, please send me the miracle of knowledge, strength, and love to rid me of this demon. Show me the way, because I can't see through these eyes. Show me my purpose. I know there has to be a purpose. I can feel it.

She finished speaking but continued to stay in that position inhaling the scent of the copal.

Cathy

Cathy shuffled to the elevator just after midnight, feeling the exhaustion of her shift taking over.

Flu season always meant overtime. It was a good tired, though. The people she helped met her eyes with sincere gratitude. For her patients who could not afford medication, she tried to find a way to get what they needed for free or at a discount. There were times she paid for it out of her own pocket. She didn't mind, because there was very little she spent her money on. All her time was devoted to the hospital. With Alejandra gone, she didn't even have their morning coffee dates. She couldn't stop crying when Alejandra moved away, feeling for the first time the regret that they hadn't been able to stay together from the beginning. But she didn't dwell, because they had each other now. It did worry Cathy, maybe from a mother's intuition, but Alejandra's communication had slowly declined. Her texts and emails became short and no longer felt *open*.

Cathy didn't want to press, didn't feel she had the right. So she waited for Alejandra to reach out to her.

The patients who had no one in their lives tugged on her heart the most. It was the frailty in their waning eyesight, the wisps of thinning hair that could be mistaken for loose spiderwebs, and lips that could only whisper about memories. This was what the end of mortal time looked like.

It made Cathy wonder if her mother was out there somewhere, alone, a ghost of an old woman all alone riding out the river of time. But she chose that when she left them. Cathy tried to spend time with the patients without visitors for a few extra minutes to ask how they were feeling or perhaps allow them to share a memory. Throughout her visit, she would hold their hands, allowing them to feel her presence even if they couldn't see well. Love could be experienced beyond the five senses.

She pressed the button for the elevator, looking forward to going home. A hot shower followed by her bed was all she wanted. The muscles in her neck and the backs of her calves felt tense. Maybe she would take a bath filled with Epsom salts.

When the doors opened, she stepped inside and pressed the ground floor. Her mind wandered as she stood alone, waiting for the elevator to stop. Without paying attention, she walked through the doors when they opened. As they closed behind her, she realized it was the wrong floor. Bright murals of flowers and animals decorated the walls. A tiger with a pin board in its jaws, photos of babies stuck on every free inch of it. How did she end up in the maternity and children's ward?

The elevator had gone up five floors instead of down. No one waited in front of the elevator. "You need a vacation," she said to herself. The thought of visiting Alejandra in her new home to help with her children popped into her mind. Hopefully, her nagging feeling was just her own projection of missing her daughter. Three little ones sounded like a lot of work. More work than she did in a week, because at least she had days off.

A pinch to her heart reminded her of how much she longed to make things right with Alejandra. Being in this ward created an ache within her chest. She turned around to press the elevator button again.

No one sat at the nurses' station. The entire floor was illuminated by only a few lights. Not a sound or single person around. She would have expected to hear at least a few babies crying. Her ache turned to fear.

At the end of the corridor stood a woman in front of the room where the newborns slept. She wore an outdated dress, a style from the 1950s with a sweetheart neck and slightly puffed sleeves. The hem that fell midcalf dripped with water that pooled at her bare feet. It made her think of something her mother would have worn. The woman's features were indiscernible behind matted brown hair full of leaves and twigs. Brown water stained the dress where her hair fell.

Cathy rubbed her tired eyes before looking around again for the nurse. She parted her lips to call out but decided not to cause a disturbance. The elevator remained on the floor above. She turned back to see the stranger now walking toward the baby room.

Shit, she said to herself. Cathy took big strides to reach the end of the hallway, her heart pumping hard. She needed to exercise more at her age. Cathy stopped in front of the glass wall where you can view the newborns. She gasped.

A hideous creature in the guise of a woman in white stood among the babies. And it didn't wear a dress, at least not in the real sense. Its dress was a patchwork of dead flesh and fabric hanging over its exposed bones. Its eyes had a glare of greed while bloody saliva dripped from its mouth. Slimy threads threatened to cover the babies. Footfalls from Cathy's right broke her gaze with the creature. It was a nurse. Cathy didn't care if she appeared foolish. She darted for the nurse. "There is something in here! Please!"

The nurse ran toward her. Cathy ran back to where she had stood. Her mouth dropped. The room was empty.

The nurse stood next to her looking into the room, then back at her. "Doctor?"

"I saw . . . Can you just unlock the door? Please?"

The nurse nodded and did as she instructed. A few babies stirred as they entered. Cathy looked around. Nothing.

"You pull a double today?"

Cathy nodded. "Do I look that bad?"

The nurse smiled. "Probably the same as me." He moved around to inspect the babies, who were fine. Cathy dropped her head, massaging the bridge of her nose. Her eyes caught a single drop of red-and-black slime beneath one of the bassinets. She squatted to have a closer look and used the sleeve of her fleece to wipe up the substance. She rose from the floor.

"You sure you are all right?" He was a good-looking man—though far too young for her—with real concern in his eyes.

"Yeah, thank you. Sorry about the false alarm."

"Not at all. Get some rest tonight."

She followed him back to the nurses' station thinking about what she had just seen. The elevator doors were now wide open.

"Have a great shift," she said to the nurse before pressing the button inside. As she moved toward the ground floor all she could think of was Alejandra and a box she had meant to give her. No more waiting for tomorrow.

Her pocket vibrated as she exited the elevator. It was a text from Alejandra. She needed help.

Cathy's entire body tensed with a surge of energy waking her up. She no longer wanted to sleep or take a bath. She would go home and spend the rest of the night doing everything in her power to get to her daughter as soon as possible. Because of the time of night, she would wait until the morning to call Alejandra. Still, something felt amiss. The sense of unease was exacerbated by the strange occurrence and now Alejandra texting her.

She assumed Alejandra might be trying to sleep. She had no way of knowing how badly her daughter needed her help. Cathy wasted no time booking the earliest flight and arranging emergency leave.

Alejandra and Cathy

Cathy called as Alejandra prepared an easy breakfast for the children: the last of the Cheerios and muesli mixed together, with blueberries to hide the raisins.

"Is everything all right? I saw you texted me in the middle of the night."

Alejandra stopped rushing with the colander as she rinsed the blueberries. Water sprayed everywhere in her usual haste to keep the children quiet and the routine moving swiftly so they could beat the morning traffic.

But today if they were late, then they would be late. She slowed everything down. This was important.

"Cathy, you said you would do anything for me. I need you now as a mother, a grandmother, and maybe a doctor." Alejandra would ask for what she needed without feeling guilty or like a burden. "Do you mind coming for a visit? I want to talk more about our family history. I am going through a tough time right now, and the children should get to know you more."

"Absolutely. In fact, I have already arranged time off. I'm looking for flights right now. It will be nice to get to know Matthew as well." This was a white lie. Cathy had already booked a flight the previous night.

Alejandra paused as she poured milk into three bowls of cereal, ignoring the children's chatter. Matthew. She glanced at the clock. He would be home soon. She had to decide what to tell him. Should she share this nightmare? That is what you do with the one you spend your life with, share. But whenever she tried to share herself, it was met with resistance if he didn't agree. No. She wouldn't share anything with him. Not now, at least. Besides, his rejection meant nothing when she fought for her very soul and the souls of her children. Far too long she had carried every rejection like a badge sewn into her skin. Not anymore.

"Alejandra, is everything all right?"

"Thanks, Cathy. Let me know when you can make the trip. As soon as possible if you can. I'm all right for now."

"Alejandra, now that we have found each other, I would move heaven and earth for you."

Overwhelmed by her emotions, Alejandra squeezed her eyes shut hearing this. It was all she'd ever wanted. Love. The kind that doesn't fail. The ember that starts inside. It does exist.

Keys jiggled at the front door. Elodia squealed as she hopped off her chair to run out of the kitchen. Catrina's eyes went large now that her favorite person in the world had arrived. Matthew had returned.

"I have to go now. Text me when you have details." Alejandra ended the call.

She could hear Matthew dropping his bags in the entrance.

"How is my family!" he shouted, sounding exuberant as he walked into the kitchen.

Catrina and Will jumped off their chairs to hug his legs as he carried Elodia in his arms. She held a new baby doll with a mermaid costume.

"You are just in time to drive them to school."

"I just got home. Still need a shower and food. Besides, I don't want to interfere with your routine. Maybe next week."

Alejandra nodded, internally rolling her eyes. "Cathy is coming to stay."

He stared at her as if she had said she had thrown out one of his expensive bottles of wine.

"You could have asked me first."

"I need this, Matthew. I made the decision." There was no attitude or tone in her voice. She remained neutral.

He raised his eyebrows and looked away, flustered. She wanted to rip into him but not in front of the children. She needed her mother. She needed to put herself first.

At least he would be around to entertain the children so she could take walks with Cathy alone and tell her everything. He was good with them when he wasn't stressed with work, always had time for silly games. Alejandra found games tedious, could never shut out the rattling noise in her head, but Matthew knew how to let work have a corner in his mind and forget it on the weekends or when he took time off. Alejandra didn't have the option of taking time off from family life.

"All right, kids, eat your breakfast, listen to your mom. I'll see you after school."

Alejandra was happy to see him go. She turned back to the kitchen table to start the day with her children.

"Are you ready for a special visitor?"

All three children jumped up and down, unable to contain

their multitude of questions and excitement as they finished their lunch. Special visitors (family and friends) meant gifts, sweets, and later bedtimes. They loved surprises. Alejandra was shocked at how quickly Cathy arranged everything. It felt wonderful. What had been occurring between them since first contact was more than a bandage. Alejandra could describe it as true healing.

She received the text that Cathy was close. Inside she was a small child jumping with excitement, but to her family she was her usual, composed self. The doorbell rang. Elodia with her little legs was the first to dash toward the door, probably with the image of gummy bears on her mind. Alejandra giggled at how adorable she was, her little angel with eyes that were floodlights of joy. She was her beautiful final baby who gave the best hugs.

The children screamed with excitement from the moment the door opened. Cathy smiled with her mouth open and her arms outstretched to receive them. "Look at how big and wonderful you all are."

"Gummy bears!" Elodia squealed. Both Alejandra and Cathy laughed.

"All right. Let me see what I have in here." Elodia and Will ran amok like circus clowns when she unzipped an entire suitcase filled with toys, sweets, and clothes. Even Catrina joined in laughing, though her eyes were a little shy when Cathy glanced in her direction.

"I didn't know what they wanted, so I bought everything."

Will gave her a huge grin. "That was an excellent plan, Grandma." As soon as the words were out of his mouth his eyes darted between Alejandra and Cathy, the smile gone.

"That is true, Will." Alejandra gave him a warm smile. He resumed his eager clawing through the suitcase with Elodia and Catrina.

Alejandra was especially pleased that Catrina seemed happy. When Alejandra would try to get her to talk to Cathy on the phone, the young girl would just shake her head and walk away. A spark of joy tingled inside of Alejandra watching her three children as the moment unfolded with ease. Before she'd taken the time to heal herself, their shrieks of playfulness would grate on her. Now it felt so natural. There was a sense of wholeness.

The happy tears imprisoned behind her pupils wanted to be let out. But Alejandra would not allow herself to cry. She had cried enough alone and with her therapist and she didn't want to have to explain her outburst of emotion. The gratitude in her heart needed time to settle in, to spread itself so it could take deeper root. Despite the threat looming in her home, Alejandra could not remember the last time she felt this happy and at peace. Now she knew: Just because she had surrendered to motherhood didn't mean she could not be something else or ask for what she might need, even if it had to come from her alone.

Matthew walked down the stairs in his robe, appearing slightly grumpy from the commotion. Given the chance, he could sleep until midafternoon. He didn't want to be too bothered on the weekends.

But Alejandra was a morning person. She remembered when they went on their first trip together as a couple. She lay in bed next to him in the dark, wanting desperately to venture out to the pool or explore the resort. They were in Egypt of all places. Halfway around the world. Yet at two P.M. he was still snoring. She didn't want to leave on her own; what kind of good girlfriend does that? After all, they were at the beginning of something. He ticked the boxes. Now Alejandra knew she should have left that bed alone and enjoyed Egypt instead of lying in the dark waiting to impress him.

Waiting for him. But no more.

"It's good to have you. Hope you and Alejandra can get some quality time in."

"So do I. Maybe I can help with the kids so you two can have some time alone."

Before Matthew could say anything, Alejandra spoke up, "How about coffee?"

He raised his eyebrows and pushed past Alejandra for the kitchen. "Well, it's good to be loved so much. Do you mind taking all this mess into the dining room? It's kind of in the way here."

At one time, Alejandra would have lost her patience with the way he communicated with her. But now, after all the excruciating work she'd done with Melanie, she found herself faced with a test. Her body tensed momentarily. Then she switched her focus to her smiling children, because they were a source of joy. Now she could just allow his words to pass her by with the lightness of a falling leaf.

After all, her mother was in her home to spend time with her. She looked at Cathy and gave her a large grin filled with contentment. This moment was infinitely more important than Matthew's hurt feelings or ego.

Immediately after hearing Matthew speak, Catrina stopped smiling and put her toy pony with rainbow hair on the credenza. She looked around at the room before bundling the discarded packaging and taking all the unopened gifts to the dining room. Alejandra made a mental note of this. It was natural to want the approval of their parents, but Alejandra saw the uncertainty in her eyes, the fear as she stood between wanting to continue with what made her happy and her father's words that were not directed to her specifically. When Catrina returned to the room, Alejandra felt compelled to address this head-on.

"Catrina, you can keep playing. This isn't for you to clean up. Have fun."

"But Dad said . . ."

"I know what he said, and it wasn't meant for you. This is the first time your grandmother is here to visit, so we are going to enjoy it. There is plenty of time to clean up. Is any of this hurting anyone?"

Catrina gave her mother an inquisitive look, then glanced at Will and Elodia, who continued to shred paper and play without a care. "Okay."

The light returned to Catrina's eyes when she grabbed the pony again and kneeled down to look through the treasure of gifts.

"You're a good mom, Alejandra."

Words could eviscerate or they could be a miracle. The moment was surreal to Alejandra. Her cup of love and confidence funneled upward instead of down. She looked toward Cathy. "Thank you, Mom."

Cathy and Alejandra spent the day making small talk. The kids interrupted every five minutes with one of their toys in hand and a detailed explanation of it, or to ask Cathy a question about the hospital, which fascinated them. Cathy took it in stride, as did Alejandra. Her connection with Cathy filled her soul.

The day passed quickly into the evening, when Will began to grumble for dinner. They ordered pizza despite Matthew hating Domino's, but it was another treat for the kids.

When the delivery arrived, Matthew stared at the boxes, unimpressed. "What am I supposed to eat? Did you get something for me?"

"The refrigerator is full, Matthew. I just went to the supermarket. I'm sure there is something in there." Matthew gave her another disapproving look before searching the refrigerator with a scowl. Alejandra could feel Cathy's discomfort as she sat with the children, trying not to listen and to maintain her distance. She could see in her peripheral vision Cathy only half focused on watching the children eat.

Matthew continued to move items around loudly to reinforce how annoyed he was. Alejandra could feel her entire body go as cold as the refrigerator. She didn't want to lie next to him tonight or any other nights after that. Alejandra glanced at Cathy, who met her gaze. Her eyes read *I'm sorry,* and she gave Alejandra a small smile of reassurance. But Alejandra was not the only one gone cold. The refrigerator slammed shut loudly, causing the children to look in the direction of Matthew, who was making himself a sandwich.

Alejandra continued to enjoy Cathy's company and watch the children eat with abandon. Pizza sauce and grease smeared across the table and their happy faces. It was enough to make her not feel a speck of guilt over Matthew. The usual fear she possessed when she *knew* he would be displeased with something. Let him sulk. *You are only mother to the children you gave birth to. Let him grow up.*

Matthew had always scowled when she talked too long about her birth mother. "The woman gave you up and now you put her on this pedestal. You're obsessed with this other family. We are your family. *I'm* the one who has always been here for you. What about me?" She couldn't understand how it was a competition. His comments chipped another scale from her eye to truly see him as he was, and not just as the charming bachelor with a good job and nice suits. It was like the crust you wipe away from your eyes when you wake from a deep sleep.

Matthew took his plate, beers in both pockets of his shorts, and an iPad, then retreated upstairs to the bedroom. Cathy helped Alejandra with the bedtime routine, making it feel special. The plan was for Matthew to do it, but Cathy wanted the opportunity to spend time with her grandchildren. Without any fussing all three children went to bed. They were always better behaved with strangers around.

Alejandra went to the bedroom to remove her bra and pull on a hoodie before settling on the sofa with her mother. "I feel a bit left out, Alejandra. Usually when you visit someone it's courtesy to bring the host a gift," Matthew said.

"It's my mother. Did you see how she spoiled the kids? Does it matter? You feel as left out as much as you want to be included."

He snorted at her while watching his game. "Is that something from your therapist? She doesn't seem to be doing a great job with your attitude not improving."

The weight of her diamond ring tugged at her arm. It had to come off. Alejandra left the bedroom without engaging with him further. She had outgrown this carousel ride.

With the house quiet, Cathy followed Alejandra back to the kitchen full of cardboard and all the opened gifts trailed in from the entrance of the house. The scene resembled Christmas morning. Alejandra didn't mind at all. It was a good kind of mess. "Thank you for putting them to bed and doing their bath," Alejandra said.

Then she wrapped her arms around Cathy. The two women held each other for a moment before Alejandra could no longer hold back a lifetime of emotion. Her tears took on a spirit of their own with the power of a flooded river washing everything in its path to places unknown. She held her breath before releasing sobs that caused her body to shiver in her mother's arms with the fright of a newborn baby. In many ways Alejandra felt like a woman being reborn into her own consciousness, now knowing who she really was, the good and the bad. Cathy held Alejandra in a firm embrace to calm her thundering body.

"I'm here now. It's okay. Let it out."

Alejandra gripped Cathy's shirt tighter as she expelled what remained of her heart's desire to be this close to her mother and the sorrow that prevented her from living her life in the light. She didn't have to carry the heavy wish to be with her mother, because it was now a reality.

Alejandra let out one last breath before breaking away from Cathy, who looked deep into her eyes with all her attention. A warm smile spread across Cathy's face as she brushed away the hair from Alejandra's forehead.

"Why don't we share a glass of wine. Alejandra, you have me worried. Tell me what is happening."

Alejandra stepped back and shook her head. She walked to the wine fridge, choosing a red wine from a grape variety she wanted to try but Matthew didn't like. The cork popped from the bottle. She filled two glasses. Before speaking, Alejandra took a deep breath. Then she recounted her story of the last few years with the children and Matthew. The spiral of despair that pushed her to reevaluate her life and seek help. Alejandra left all her heartache on the table like the wrapping paper on the floor.

"Did you see the altar I have been building? My therapist, Melanie, suggested I build it to help rebuild what is broken inside of me and see the bonds I didn't grow up with. Cathy, I need to know everything about where we come from—I'm going through something . . . strange."

Cathy adjusted her body in the seat. The moment felt uncomfortable with the way Alejandra paused before saying the word "strange." It made her think about experiencing the haunting vision in the hospital. She could feel the skin between her eyebrows fold. Her lips pressed tightly together to prevent herself from blurting out her own fear. She had to be there for Alejandra and not show the growing terror that scraped below her navel with tarantula-like legs. She didn't want her fear to wrap them in a web and bleed them of their sanity. This was a time for her to dig back to her days in medical school, when she only dealt with the material world.

"You can tell me anything. And change is not strange. It is empowering. I love the altar. It's beautiful. It's a coincidence because before you texted, I brought more family photos for you. They are a gift for you."

Cathy bent over to her large handbag and took out a lilac-colored box with a purple ribbon wrapped around it. She slid it across the table toward Alejandra.

"Thank you." Alejandra's heart pounded despite already knowing it contained photos. The sense of expectation gathered in her stomach, as if all the answers she would ever need in life were kept inside. She tugged at the purple ribbon and lifted the lid.

Cathy pointed to the top photo. "That one is my favorite."

A man and a woman stood together with double bandoliers across their chests. Each had a worn and weathered intensity to their gaze. People who had been through some shit and didn't take any shit. The woman looked familiar in a way that made Alejandra doubt her ability to think straight again. It had to be a trick of the mind. She had seen that face before. She was one of the women in Alejandra's dreams. Alejandra could see the high cheekbones she shared with Cathy. The strength in her stance gave Alejandra a sense of courage. "Cathy, tell me everything you know about her."

THE HAUNTING OF ALEJANDRA   189

"That is our ancestor Flor, and it turns out she fought next to the great Colonel Amelio Robles Ávila, who was transgender, and fought in the Mexican war for independence. He not only held a high position in the military and received a pension, but he also lived to be ninety-five. From what I have been told, Flor had an altar until the day she passed too. She kept many items and made sure they were preserved to be passed down." Cathy leaned over to reach into her bag again.

"Here is something else. It might be what you need." Cathy placed another box in front of her and lifted the lid.

"I have no idea about some of these items, but I think it's time I passed them on to you. Some are from Flor. There are swatches of fabric, some look bloodstained. Buttons. A rosary. Add them to your altar. I've told you all I know, and these photos and items are all of it."

Alejandra had hoped for more concrete information, stories. She wouldn't give up on destroying the curse even if it took her to the brink of destroying herself. As long as her children remained safe and their future free from the creature.

For now, she would enjoy the rest of the evening with her mother. She thought it wise not to mention just yet that she had seen Flor's face in her dreams. Having a close relationship with Cathy was a dream she didn't want to end. Her insecurity about losing Cathy or driving her away with too much craziness too soon was a real fear. Having her here felt so good. Normal, even if the circumstances were far from normal. They finished the bottle of red wine and ate the slices of pizza the kids had left uneaten. Just before midnight they called it a night. Alejandra took the box of photos with her to bed and placed them on the side table.

Cathy and Alejandra

athy lay awake in the dark. Her iPhone indicated it was four in the morning. A pang of self-hatred pierced her heart when she'd heard the details of Alejandra's pain growing throughout the years of her marriage and after every child. How could she ever forgive herself? In between these thoughts and as she wondered if she should ask Alejandra if she had seen anything unusual, eighteen-month-old Elodia stirred in the room next to hers. Since she was awake, Cathy would let Alejandra and Matthew sleep and see to Elodia herself, something she had never had to do in her life. Cathy wanted to help her daughter, who was not well. She hoped in some small way that she could help to make up for lost time.

Trying to not make a sound, she opened the door to Elodia's room. The light coming from the hallway night-light streaked across the floor. Cathy had to catch her breath. She squeezed her eyes as if the atmosphere were a fog of pepper spray. In front of the crib, in the illumination of the video baby monitor and hall light, crouched the creature from the hospital.

Its skin hung from its form like a raggedy dress on a clothesline. Wheezy rasps escaped from its open mouth, blowing onto Elodia's forehead. Clawlike, bony hands gripped the top railing of the crib. Cathy ran her hands down her eyes and cheeks as if this might take the image away. The horrid creature remained, glaring in hunger at the child. This was not a coincidence or a vivid dream. The creature reared its head toward her. The light of some distant dead star radiated from the eye sockets. Black-and-pink gums with tiny sharp nubs for teeth sawed back and forth in expectation of its next meal. It let out a breath. "You thought you could escape me."

It lifted a single finger and slowly slipped it between the slats of the crib. Acting on instinct, Cathy dove toward the creature. She fell face-first into the carpet, scraping her chin and biting her tongue when it jumped in an instant. Cathy rolled onto her back when baby Elodia stirred from the commotion. The creature jumped onto Cathy's belly. "Cathy, you belong to me. Your entire family. You never wanted them anyway. Give them up again and give up on yourself. You're worthless."

Cathy recognized the voice from the hospital when Alejandra was born. It was the same one she'd heard right before she signed the papers releasing parental rights to her baby. That voice had whispered to her all the times she had any doubts. *Just give up.* But Cathy hadn't given up when she barely had enough to eat in college, when there seemed to be no way to pay for medical school, when she prayed in the dark for miracles to occur so she could pursue her dreams. She had never given up looking for Alejandra, never stopped believing they would one day have a relationship.

Cathy raised a hand and grabbed the creature by the throat. "Not if we kill you first!" It hissed, blinding her with the brightness in its eyes before biting the soft skin between her thumb and forefinger. Cathy cried out at the shock of pain. Elodia kicked her legs up before bursting into screams. Cathy looked toward the crib, then back to the creature. It was gone, as if it had never been there. Alejandra stood in the doorway with the full light of the hallway streaming into the room. Her eyes were wild as her chest heaved with deep breaths.

"Cathy! You saw it. I know you did!"

Cathy paused with her eyes remaining on the carpet. She focused on the small woven fibers as she tried to regain her awareness of the moment. The sounds of Alejandra's voice and of Elodia crying saturated the strings of her heart with fear. She would sacrifice herself to God or creature to keep them safe.

Alejandra kneeled next to her to help her up from the floor. With shaky arms and legs, she took Alejandra's hand, ignoring her throbbing palm. Cathy reached into the crib to pick up crying Elodia. The time had arrived for her to be honest about her experience with the creature. Elodia's head nuzzled into her neck as she rocked her granddaughter. She turned to Alejandra.

"This wasn't the first time. You have seen it too? I wanted to say something, but how do you talk about the horrors of the mind? The fear?"

Alejandra nodded. "Sometimes you need to know you are not alone in the scariest of experiences, especially the ones that push you to the brink of your understanding of everything." Cathy placed an arm around Alejandra. A swell of emotion passed through Cathy's entire body. She knew Alejandra felt it too, because her hands gripped her tighter. The souls of three generations ignited in that moment. "I'm so glad we found each other," Alejandra whispered before giving Elodia a light kiss on the back of her head. The sleepy child already had her thumb in her mouth with her eyes slowly closing again. Alejandra pulled away from her mother and placed Elodia back into her crib.

"Alejandra, does Matthew know?"

"Matthew is sound asleep as we speak. No, I haven't told him any of it. He barely understands me, let alone understands the supernatural. You know he despises Texas and Mexican food? He loves me in his own way, but that is just it. His way."

"I can't sleep now. Tea?"

Cathy nodded. "Yes, I should clean my hand as well."

Alejandra made them both manzanilla tea to drink in the kitchen. Neither wanted to go back to bed or ignore what had just occurred. Cathy's hands trembled, and her tongue ached. She inspected the small puncture wounds.

"I don't know the how or why, but I swear that thing is real. Look what it did to my hand. This was no shared delusion. It physically attacked me. This is not scientifically possible. Everything I have been taught . . ."

"It is real. It is as real as the hurt inside of me every time I looked at my children. The first time was when we first moved in here and I had a breakdown in my shower. Then I saw it floating in the children's pool. It showed itself to the children. It has just been escalating. This is the first time it has made any physical contact. But I think now that it has, it may not hold back from doing it again. My therapist, Melanie, is also a curandera. In our last session she said I should make contact. Well, it found me first. It told me that one of our ancestors promised our bloodline to it. We need to find more about our family. We need to find a way to destroy it, break this cycle of curses."

Cathy tried to take a sip of the tea but winced from the pain of her bit tongue.

"I had a very strange experience at the hospital one night.

Actually, the night you messaged me to come here. I dismissed it, but now I know it had meaning. It was real. I want to talk to your therapist. We need to do something about it."

Matthew had already left for his hour-long commute to work when Cathy and Alejandra sat at the breakfast table with the children spilling milk from their bowls of cereal and bickering with one another. Will looked innocently at Cathy.

"Grandma. Are you okay?"

"Of course, darling. Why do you ask?"

"The eyes in my room said you were next. It won't be just your tongue bleeding. What happened?"

Alejandra and Cathy glanced at each other, trying to withhold their fear in order not to panic the children. Cathy reached out and stroked Will's cheek. "Nothing, darling. I took a big gulp of tea last night before it cooled off."

Will frowned. "Let me kiss it better, Grandma." He rose from his seat and lightly pecked Cathy's cheek. She took Will into her arms and squeezed tightly. "I am lucky to have you as my grandson. I feel better already."

Alejandra silently texted Melanie that she needed to see her as soon as possible. She let Melanie know that Cathy would be joining them. La Llorona was back and had made its intentions clear. Melanie texted back immediately. She encouraged them both to come after they took the children to school and to leave Elodia with the babysitter.

Melanie opened the door wide with fear and urgency in her eyes. She looked to the sky and around the two women as if she expected to see someone or something appear from thin air. "Come in quickly. We have much to discuss and, Alejandra, this is off the clock. What is happening to you is a threat to others. It has to be stopped."

Alejandra knew something was frightening her to disturb her usual calm demeanor. Alejandra and Cathy walked past Melanie, who made the sign of the cross on her body. "Tell me everything. Don't leave any details out. Please sit down."

Cathy spoke: "Let me go first. Back to the hospital room after Alejandra's birth. The time had come for me to sign the papers giving up my parental rights. I named her Alejandra because I wanted her to have something from me. She had to know I loved her enough to give her a name. I told them that was my only term. Of course, they didn't like it, but she was a healthy newborn.

"I told myself this decision would be best for both of us. Then there was another voice. One not my own. I had second, third, and fourth thoughts with the small glimpse of her face so beautiful and perfect. Little white dots on her nose smelling like what being in the presence of God would smell like. Then I thought of the life we would live. I felt like I had two voices in my ear: one telling me how awful I was and wretched, saying I should keep you. See what happens. But I couldn't do that. My personality has never been one of recklessness. Every step in my life was carefully planned. But caring for another human being before I knew how to care for myself seemed insurmountable and unfair to her. Last night the voice was back. It had a face and bit me. But there is more, and Alejandra, please don't be mad at me, I didn't want to alarm you over something I didn't believe.

Right before I arranged to visit, I had a vision of a woman in white at the hospital. It was late and I was tired. Now I know it had to be this thing."

Alejandra said, "It was at the hospital as well when I had Catrina. I haven't said anything to anyone, but I think I found a way to stop it or destroy it. I'm not certain. I think I'm required to take a leap of faith."

Melanie chimed in, "I think this proves beyond any doubt we are dealing with a generational curse. One that is ancient and invested in your souls."

Alejandra needed a glass of water. The words about to be spoken took every drop of moisture just so they could be uttered.

"I need to die. At least it needs to think it will get what it wants without a fight. I must try to take my own life."

Both Melanie's and Cathy's faces turned to shock.

"You want to give it what it wants? We don't know how dangerous it is if you are in a weakened state. We know very little about it despite how far you have come on your personal journey."

"Don't you see, Melanie? That is why the women have been in my dreams. They will guide me. They will give me the power I need when I need it. It is a leap of faith in myself."

Melanie looked to the photo of her mother on the wall with searching eyes as she struggled to make sense of the plan and what her intuition might say.

Cathy placed her hand on Alejandra's arm, giving it a light squeeze. "You want to attempt to commit suicide to trick a spirit?"

"Cathy, yes. I am sure it will work."

Cathy began to pace the room and shake her head. "No, no. No."

Alejandra approached Cathy to look her in the eyes and took both of her hands into her own.

"This is the only way, and only I can do this."

Cathy broke down in sobs. Melanie wrapped one arm around her shoulder with tears in her own eyes. "Say what you need to say to your daughter, Cathy."

"I never thought the day would come I would hold my only child in my arms again. My entire life has been spent giving hope to others, then in the most miraculous way you entered my life and gave me hope. My work has been a skin graft that could never substitute for you. I can't go back to living with a broken heart while telling myself everything is okay. Let it take me. Let me die knowing I did my best and got to know you. I can't let you do this, especially with your beautiful children at home, my grandchildren. I love you too much to let you go now or ever. This fight is also my fight."

Alejandra could feel her body begin to shake as she heard her mother's words; they reverberated to the heart of her atoms, re-arranging everything that made her who she thought she was and what she was capable of in this life. "Mother, that is why I am doing this, for them. And believe me when I say I won't fail. For the first time in my life, I believe in myself, my power."

Melanie nodded. "It makes spiritual sense. We are always guided by the past in one way or another. There are connections between everything and everyone."

Alejandra wiped her eyes. "Just hear me out. That photo you sent me, the one with our ancestor who fought in Mexico's war for independence. She found a way."

Cathy regained her composure. "What? Flor?"

"Yes, Flor. I have seen her before in my dreams, among the crowd of women. Before I woke up to you in Elodia's room I saw her again, alone. But I didn't know her name until you showed me the photo with the name. She was standing in a graveyard filled with fog so thick the outlines of the gravestones were almost hidden. We stood in the rain, our clothing soaked through. She wore a black dress that covered her from the neck to her ankles. The bodice of lace flowers matched the pattern at the hem and cuffs. There was a silk sash around her waist. I believed her to be in mourning. She was beautiful, with brown skin and high cheekbones. Her sloping nose similar to yours. I tried to speak to her, but the storm was too loud for my words to be heard. She walked toward me and whispered, '*Don't fight it. Our fate is death as is everything in the natural world. Even the great creations in the heavens die. She will come to you as you near the end, and that is when you will find her most weak. But do not be afraid because you are not alone.*'

"Before I could speak, she turned and walked into the fog. A loud crack of thunder woke me up. The urge to go to Elodia's room was incredibly strong. Then I saw you there."

Melanie stared at the carpet where the large oil stain discolored the vibrant red. "It was here. In this room with me. It knocked over a bottle of oil. I'm convinced it will do everything in its power to destroy the women in your family. But that is not all. Just this morning I received the report on the residue on your son's bed. The soil, dust, and traces of flint are old. There wasn't enough to do carbon dating, but my friend suggested that would be the only way to get a true date. There were also traces of a species of algae only found in Mexico. This creature pretending to be La Llorona has been around far longer than anyone has ever realized. If we can safely stop it, we have to try. I believe it to be immortal as long as it remains fed."

Flor

Mexico—1900–1919

Dorotea pulled the braided sash so tightly around Flor's waist it took her breath away for a moment. Instinctively, she winced and let out a whimper. The sensation matched the pain in her chest.

She wondered how easy the dress would be to take off that night when she was expected to share a bed with a man for the first time in her life. The thought was exciting, but it also filled her with dread. She found her soon-to-be husband, Francisco, as interesting as cross stitch. He had no real passion beyond building wealth for his family name and building a family of his own to prove his success. That was one reason why her father, Alvaro, approved of him. Flor was not expected to participate in the family business, only to be the support at home for his endeavors. And they had nothing in common except for their parents' ambition. The marriage had been arranged by their grandparents through a matchmaker she'd never met and who hadn't asked what she wanted in a life partner. But also, at nineteen, Flor didn't know what she wanted in a life partner. How could she, when she had experienced so little of life? Dorotea gave her a hard glance in the mirror when she finished creating from the sash a large bow that hung at the small of Flor's back. Usually her mother's rose perfume was pleasant; however, today it stung her nose.

"He is a nice man, Flor. Give it time. Our combined land will bless generations upon generations in our family. Why would you not want to help achieve that goal, give it to your children?"

"You mean sons?"

Dorotea didn't respond to this remark. She took a step back. "There. You are ready to be a wife."

"And then what? To provide a son?"

Her mother did not look her in the eyes. She stared at her own reflection, smoothing her hair into place and adjusting her pearl choker with a small ruby in the center. Flor's gaze fixed on the birthmark on her mother's forearm that looked like a patch of sprinkled brown sugar. It was nearly identical to hers. "Try to be happy. That is my best advice. And when you have your dark days, do what you have to do to get by." Dorotea placed one hand on Flor's shoulder before walking out the door.

Flor sat on the bed not caring if the bow came undone or the fabric wrinkled beneath her weight. This was meant to be a time to celebrate, yet she felt as if she should be in mourning, wearing black. Part of her own will had to die to accommodate a stranger. The thought angered her. She cried until a knock on the door alerted her that it was time to begin the rest of her life.

Sixteen months later, Flor gave birth to her first child, Rafael. Two years after Rafael she welcomed a daughter she named Regina. Dorotea was too "ill" in bed to attend either birth. Flor secretly ached as she cradled Regina. The pain of abandonment during this special and traumatic time had left a scar on Flor's heart. She couldn't help but wonder what she had done to deserve such coldness from her own mother.

Her entire body had throbbed as it pushed a new light into the world. She guided this baby into the world through her physical tunnel, and she wished she had her mother to guide her through the emotional tunnel of childbirth. So many souls had died in this battle between worlds, and it hurt to fight it alone. Flor rubbed her nose across Regina's scalp and thanked God they made it through safely. She also prayed her mother would someday find peace from her bedridden spells of dark moods. No one in the immediate or extended family dared speak about it.

Since she could remember, her mother had often retreated to her bedroom with spells of being unwell. Before Dorotea's children arrived, she and her husband had built a decent business in fabric and leather with the little land they owned. Family members and friends would recall how Dorotea was once the life of the party. Everyone wanted to be her friend. Flor found it hard to believe it: Her mother seemed to view the world through a veil of sadness. Seeing her mother's anxiety kept her fighting as hard as she could so that she would not be like her. Flor's firstborn was a son, which made everyone happy, had them telling Flor how amazing she was. The boy would be groomed in the business from day one. But Flor would groom her daughter in secret to be the woman she didn't have the opportunity to be, with constant encouragement to have the same confidence as her brother, even if someone had an opinion about it.

The most valuable gift her mother gave her on her wedding day was the advice to make the best of her arranged marriage.

After both children were born, the sex petered off. Flor's body felt on fire when she bathed, wanting the scalding touch of a man; however, her husband was not that man. Francisco was only three years older than she was, yet he shuffled around the house like a man twice his age, with a grumpy demeanor no matter what the weather or even if he received positive news regarding the business. Silver linings did not exist to him. He despised anything out of the ordinary or routine. He didn't try to reach out to her for comfort either. They lived in harmonious silent discord on different frequencies. He wasn't cruel or abusive. They were just not attracted to each other, the relationship wholly transactional. Flor made the decision to redirect her fire to learning. When her husband was away, she spent the time studying on her own without his watchful eye. She sat in his office and read all there was to know about the business. His papers on politics, history, and money were there for her to absorb in the quiet moments in the day.

When her children were on the cusp of adulthood, the winds of change blew hard, with the death of her husband from a fall from a new horse he had purchased and the arrival of war that had been a long time coming. Their livelihood was on the line. Her cousin Tomás stood to lose everything he'd worked diligently for all his life as the middle and lower classes were squeezed under Díaz. He was young enough to take up arms in the Mexican Revolution. Without anyone to stop her, she made the decision to join the fight, to become a soldadera and go with her cousin Tomás.

Regina stood at their kitchen table in defiance. "Let me go with you to war. I've seen the soldaderas. If people think I'm old enough to marry and have a baby, then I am old enough to fight for a stable future. With Father gone, I know you feel this fight is important to our business, our future."

Flor loved her daughter's spirit. This was exactly why she had to stay safe, so one day she could have a good life, perhaps make choices for herself.

"You must stay here and take care of your grandparents for the time being. I want you to have all your dreams outside of the family. Surviving to see change then continue that change is a form of resistance. Survive this war so you can tell the tales to future generations. Stay safe. I will come back, by the grace of God."

Regina wrapped her arms around Flor. "Will you tell *her* you are leaving?"

Flor wanted to say goodbye, but it didn't really matter. Dorotea would ignore her, and her father was barely able to recognize where he was.

"I wrote her a letter for you to give her once I am gone. And don't you worry, your time is coming. My father won't notice with his mind so weak from his senility. I will give him a hug and a kiss, which he probably won't remember."

Flor left, not knowing what the future would hold except death, which could happen years from now or in a week. As she rode away, she turned to see her son Rafael scowling with disappointment and Regina crying with a smile on her face.

She looked up to her mother's window. A shadow appeared to recede, but it couldn't have been her mother because it was too tall. She blinked and faced the dusty road ahead.

Flor met Emiliano serving caldo she'd prepared for the camp. "Some glorious fight," she muttered to herself as she chopped vegetables and wiped sweat off her face from the heat of the boiling pot. The liquid bubbled as rapidly as her increasing frustration. This was not the fight she envisioned. But as a woman, you were first put in the bed, then in front of the pot.

Joining this fight was a way she thought she could be who she really was, a curious woman with fire that no longer had to be tempered. All those years in waiting meant to be useful, to fill her with purpose.

But Flor had nothing planned tonight other than cooking caldo, followed by washing up. Her caldo would fill Emiliano's belly, and her ideas about the future would fill his ears. She traveled with her cousin, Tomás, who felt it was his duty to shape the Mexico they wanted to live in for future generations, and to secure their family fortune they'd worked so hard to create. He was a big enough man, over six feet tall, whom no one questioned. And he didn't question Flor, because she'd agreed to pay him a small amount for allowing her to tag along.

The fire blazed high in the night with embers flying at the boots of a circle of men. She poured a bowl with an extra piece of salted pork and took off her apron. The other women in the camp helped her take the other filled bowls to the rest sitting next to their leader, Emiliano Zapata. He didn't wear his hat tonight, but she knew those intense dark eyes, thick mustache, and brown skin gleaming like newly oiled leather, small creases on the corners of his eyes from hours of riding in the sun.

"This is for you."

He gave her a nod and inhaled the aroma of the caldo. The other men stared at her as she continued to stand in front of them. One of them decided to speak to her. "You can go now, unless you are waiting for one of us to take you to bed."

The circle burst into laughter between bites and slurps.

Flor expected this. This was what you endured as a woman. You were at once a thing of ridicule and of desire. "I'm waiting to be heard. I have something to say. May I speak?"

Emiliano put his bowl on his lap. "Where is your husband?"

Flor had to be careful not to invite unwanted attention. "I have no husband. I'm with my cousin, Tomás. But if I wanted to chop vegetables, I could have done that in my own home."

"Then why are you here?" Emiliano asked.

Flor continued to stand tall. "Because this is my country too. This country, our land, and the future belong to my children. My husband is dead, but I am still here. We bring future generations into the world, and we should have some say in how that world looks. I fight for my family land and the future of my children. My father is too old to take up arms."

The circle went silent because of this female, unflinching, refusing to soften her words. Loose hair flew from her messy braids after a long day of riding. Emiliano didn't stop looking at her through the bonfire. "This is good caldo. And I agree with what you have said. I'm listening."

"So am I." Another man in the circle nodded and pointed to an open space. A few of the men grunted and whispered in irritation, but she ignored them, as did Emiliano. The man with a smooth, square face who invited her into the circle extended his hand. "Colonel Amelio Robles Ávila, and you are?"

Flor sat on the spot open in the circle. Her large skirt tangled between her legs as she tried to sit without revealing what was beneath. God, she hated those skirts. A few of the men broke into laughter. She finally found a comfortable enough position, not minding there was nothing on the ground for her to sit on. She needed nothing but the silence of these men. "Flor Castillo."

"We are really going to do this?" A man with food clinging to his mustache spat. Colonel Robles wasted no time. "Andrés, have you seen the way you ride? I know women who have better technique and can shoot a bottle twice the distance as you. Don't be a cabrón now."

Laughter broke out between the men. The silenced soldier snorted and turned back to his meal.

"All right, Flor, now is your chance."

After her speech on ideas of reform, only three remained in the circle. All the men wandered off after finishing their meal or shaking their head in disagreement. Flor kept her blinders on to this distraction. Her tone or volume never faltering. She had a private audience with Emiliano Zapata. That was enough. Those opportunities did not happen often when you lived in wartime: Death was more certain than the promise of living another week or a month.

Emiliano continued to stare at her through the fire without expression. Flor met his gaze, trying to not let her thoughts wander to how attractive she found him. It was more than attraction; it was almost like destiny unfolding in real time. Colonel Robles, on the other hand, could not contain his smile as he nodded.

Emiliano stood up to leave when Flor grabbed Amelio's waterskin to take a hefty drink. He looked at Flor before walking away. "Tomorrow you may ride with us and show your skills with a rifle. This is a war, after all. The opposite side will not sit and listen over soup. It's life and death out here. Sometimes worse for women."

Flor stood to nod her head in thanks.

Emiliano returned this with a warm, short smile. "I must rest now. We can discuss politics more over breakfast. Be sure you are not on kitchen duty. If someone has a problem, tell them to come to me."

Amelio stood next to Flor. "Come with me. I might have something to help you out."

Flor blushed and turned angry. "Sir, I will not go to your tent. If that is the only reason you let me speak . . ."

"You only have to stay in the opening of my tent. Nothing more. It is a gift. Believe me when I say you never forget the first time you wear your first pair of trousers."

Puzzled, Flor decided to follow. His tent was in the back of a cluster of tents and seemed safe, with men and women still milling around. "You can wait here if you want."

Flor stood beneath the opening while Amelio opened a leather bag, pulling out a pair of charro trousers. He held them to his waist inspecting the size before looking at Flor. "These should fit."

Flor took another step inside the tidy tent. "You want to give me your trousers?"

"Yes, it's better than that dress."

Flor looked down at her skirt, stained with oil in the front and mud caking the frayed hem. "If only you knew."

Amelio stepped forward. "You know there is a reason I wear these oversize shirts with double pockets. I do know where you are coming from. You will find these more comfortable on the road." He undid the two top buttons of his shirt. Flor could see bandages wrapped around his chest. In her eyes his kindness was enough to accept him as he was. As a Catholic she was always told to love others as you loved yourself. This was simple enough to apply to everyone.

"Thank you." She touched the soft brown fabric with elegant black stitching on the outside of the leg and took them from his hands.

He extended his hand to her. "Call me Amelio."

Did it matter when it began? Do volcanoes know when that first burst of heat pipes through its cold rock? The molten earth forever changes its shape. Emiliano and Flor became lovers.

When they lay in their tent, grateful to have survived another day, their fingertips never left each other's skin. The small hairs on their bodies bowed to each other in devotion and mutual admiration. The deep connection volleyed between them like embers from a bonfire lit at the beginning of time. How death and war could nurture this kind of love seemed impossible. One in a million. But it had happened.

Emiliano asked nothing of Flor but to stay alive. To allow him to be at her side the same way she showed up with a bowl of caldo and all her ideas. She could be who she was, wear what she wanted. Their days had no number. It could be one or a thousand. This was war. At least whatever days they had were spent in each other's company, creating a better life, a better Mexico for future generations. Together.

They did everything as equals in each other's eyes. In the cold of the night, they discussed the life they wanted to build beyond the tent world they slept in. Then they made love in silence, the light in their eyes reflecting the deep comfort their bodies provided each other in uncertain times. Flor orgasmed for the first time in her life as he focused all his will on giving her the gift of pleasure. They were two of those horses living as destiny had seen before their birth. She wanted to scream to God, thanking him for creating this force within her body, everyone's body. And knowing they loved every part of each other made it even better.

But it was also after one of these soul-stirring nights, she saw *it* for the first time. La Llorona.

Flor left Emiliano reading in the lamplight. It was a book she had finished and thought he might enjoy. He didn't hesitate to give it a try. Electricity passed from his hand when she gave it to him, to the look in his eyes when he thanked her for it. She wondered how any of this was possible.

Flor left the tent to fetch fresh water from the river. The cool air livened her dull senses from the warmth of lovemaking. The crescent moon smiled upon her in the sky. She felt it could be a good omen for their future.

As she continued to walk toward the water, she noticed not a sound of a single insect around her. She looked around until she spotted a figure at the river's edge dripping like a white candle in what looked like a wedding dress. Water pooled around her bare feet. She did not move.

No way this was someone from their camp. Flor felt terror like she had never felt before, even in this war, even in the many times she had seen death up close. Even though the scent lingered in your nose for days when that death was particularly gruesome.

La Llorona, she whispered to herself. Flor had never believed the stories of the woman in white, but here she stood. The figure continued to watch her, but this time it extended its arm and pointed a finger in Flor's direction. Flor looked around to see if anyone else stood nearby. But everyone was asleep.

She took two steps forward before stopping again. The face of the woman was not that of a woman. Flor's entire body quaked with dread. It was a patchwork demon made from putrefying human flesh, eyes scalding with white heat, and umbilical cords wrapped around its waist.

Flor looked to the sky as a cloud floated over the moon, taking away the only source of light. Then she looked back to see if it was still there. Nothing. She ran back to the tent without getting the water. Once inside, she could hear Emiliano snoring. It brought her back to reality. *You're a fighter. A soldadera! Don't make up stories about a ghost,* she told herself before settling next to her lover. When her eyes closed and she could feel the rise and fall of his chest, she forgot about the image until her mind began to dream. It started as a memory of when her mother told her about La Llorona, even though she had heard it from a friend years before, and the first day of her period at thirteen. This was one of the few times her mother had shown concern and caring. Dorotea sat her down, fidgeting with the gold band on her finger. "This means you are almost a woman. Your body is capable of having children, although you are a few years from that happening."

"Why do we bleed like this?"

"Because you are not with child. Your body creates a space inside of you for a baby to grow, then it releases what is inside if the part of a man and part of a woman to make a baby do not meet. It is a cycle, just like the seasons and the moon follow a cycle. Do not be afraid of releasing from your mind or body what is not needed. Your body is capable of many things and so is your soul. Never forget that. When we take in communion at church, we transmute the bread and wine into the body and blood of Christ. To make a new human being you take in that part of a man, your husband, to create. Sometimes trying to have a child works and other times it does not, and your body will release blood again."

"Is being a grown woman with children hard?"

"For some it is easier than others. Everyone's story is different. Take La Llorona. She killed her children and herself. What despair that must have been, but I don't doubt for a second there had to be more we don't know. It was too much for her to hold inside, and her only release was death."

"Can you transmute anything?"

Dorotea stared at her daughter, not knowing how to respond. "I don't know. I would like to think miracles are possible."

"Will you help me when I am older and maybe a mother?"

Dorotea stiffened. "I will do my best. Know I will always pray for you. I believe in the Odor of Sanctity. When you smell rose or flowers you will know you are protected. That is enough now. I'm very tired."

Her mother stood quickly and left the room before she could ask any more questions. The idea of transmutation had always fascinated Flor whenever she kneeled to take communion from that day forward.

The following morning, Flor's stomach lurched and churned. She left the tent for the water she had been too afraid to fetch the previous night. Seeing the river in the daylight made her feel silly, childish. She continued to walk, but the smell of the charred goat carcasses caused her to vomit where she stood. Food and saliva clung to her lip. Without it being her time to bleed that month, her body knew she carried Emiliano's child. Her belly had told her the news twice before. She looked toward the river where the phantom had stood the previous night. It pointed at her because it *knew*.

They barely escaped the ambush on horseback in a tornado of dirt and gunshots. Flor had no choice but to leave her Emiliano behind, because he was dead.

Dead at thirty-nine years of age.

She felt blessed to have fought side by side with him during this great revolution, to have shared his secrets, ideas, and bed. To find the love of your life, a true soul mate, is the finest of experiences. Now it was gone until they met again in the stars.

She would be dead too, and soon. The gunshot wound had pierced her somewhere in the abdomen as she tried to flee the trap. Blood soaked her skirt, and she wished she'd worn trousers so she could move faster. The other men decided she would be tolerated at their meetings only if she appeared more ladylike. But these skirts were always a burden, fight or no fight. Emiliano would tease her when she wore her charro trousers because it took his mind off war and back to the scent of her braided hair and brown eyes. He loved how he could see the movement of her curves when she walked. When she walked with Emiliano, no one dared to challenge her. Unfortunately, they still pinned her value on him valuing her opinion. And without the help of her dear friend Colonel Amelio, she might not have been able to rise through the ranks the way she had.

Despite the hardship, it was far better than being at home in an arranged marriage. She didn't begrudge those who enjoyed that life; however, it was not a natural fit for her. It felt even more unnatural because the man she was married to had expectations of what a marriage was, passed down from their family. But she'd only married that man her family had chosen because it had been a good match for the family business.

Emiliano, though, was part of her soul. And they'd fought in this war with the same fire in their heart.

She never had the opportunity to fall in love before being married. Emiliano, this visionary fighter who loved her independent spirit, was her first and only love. They met as two minds. A spirit forged from their mutual love of their country.

After the battle they rode hard and fast to a farm belonging to a family who sympathized with their cause. She lay in bed for hours now, sweat covering her body followed by chills on and off. She could hear her fellow fighters, including Amelio, whispering in the other room. They didn't think she would make it. Emiliano was dead, but the fight had to continue. And now she would lose their child, and possibly her life, from her gunshot wound. Flor's pelvis seized and quaked in excruciating pain.

Flor didn't want to die. Not yet. She wanted to see Mexico liberated. She wanted to see her children again. Be a grandmother. Not in a million years had she thought she would carry another child, and they had tried to be careful every time. And she'd agreed with Emiliano to have the child at her family home with her parents in safety. Too many things could go wrong in battle. Pregnancy and childbirth did not need more risks. She was meant to leave right after the fateful meeting.

But none of them had made it that far.

The candle next to her cot flickered toward the corner of the room. The flame swaying back and forth from a force she could not feel, with no windows or doors open. Flor imagined this was a trick of the eye as she possibly neared the end. All they could do was patch up her wound. Who knew what damage the bullet had done to her organs?

As she lay there, a silhouette in white stood in the darkness. Flor had to stop herself from jumping at the sight. She thought, *Is it her again? The ghost woman La Llorona from the river?*

Her eyes widened upon seeing two bright orbs set inside a skull emerge from the shadows. As it moved closer to the flame, she could see its loose flesh that resembled a dress because of the way it draped across its skeletal frame. Odd pieces of fabric and animal skin clung to its body. Strings of hair matted and wet like that of a dead animal sprouted from its skull. It lifted hands capped with arrowhead-shaped nails, the edges jagged and sharp.

"Give it to me before it dies!" it screeched as it pointed to her belly.

Flor squeezed her eyes open and shut, not believing the thing real. This could not be the end of her life. She tossed a glass of water across her feverish face.

But it was still there, pointing at her with its bladed hand. Would it slice her open with one sweep of its fingertip? She responded, "No. It is all I have left of him. You can't have us."

The creature hopped to the edge of the bed with bony feet digging into the blanket. It began to crawl on top of her, skin stretched and joints cracked with every movement. Bubbles of flesh appeared on its face, oozing rancid fluid. Its head flicked in desperation between her face and her belly that continued to twist, like a molcajete pulverizing her insides and the baby to a paste of flesh.

"Now, you stupid woman. It won't survive. I can feel it. It belongs to me. See."

It grabbed her left arm and flipped it. One fingernail traced the birthmark, its eyes and mouth taking in her fear. Without warning it punctured each individual brown spot on her skin. She tried to pull away but found herself unable to move. A bead of blood pooled to the surface of each puncture mark.

Flor didn't know if this was a hallucination or real, the devil come to take her to hell for killing men in this war. For celebrating victories after bloodshed. Yet the physical pain was very real. The creature released her arm before clawing at her dress like a dog digging in the dirt. Sweat drained from her scalp down her temples as Flor felt herself falling deeper into agony. With a strength she didn't know she had—and perhaps the invisible hands of her ancestors propping up her shoulders—and the image of her mother's altar in a small shed in their garden flashing in her mind, Flor lifted her torso as high as she could despite the pain. She released shortened screams between clenched teeth, grabbing the creature's neck to pull it closer to her. The creature thrashed, the light in its eyes going darker, like a solar eclipse, until Flor could feel a flood from between her legs. Both she and the creature looked down at the same time. She screamed at the sight before crumpling inside like layers of fabric.

"Find your father in heaven, little one. He has passed through death too," Flor whispered.

The creature ground its nubs for teeth seeing the spilled meal. "You did this. Wretched woman. Dead woman. Just like your mother."

When the creature said the word "mother," the thought of giving birth, period blood, transmutation, and release flashed in her mind with the large pop of a cannon. Flor pulled on the thing with the intention of destroying it by taking it inside of her own body. As she used all her strength to bring it closer to her, the stitches on the wound in her abdomen ripped open. She glanced down. It looked like a bloody mouth ready to consume whatever it was fed. Her shoulder sockets were on the verge of popping as she held on to the creature that thrashed in her grasp. There would be only one way to end this. Flor didn't know how she knew, but this had to be done, and she surrendered to what her body felt was right. She would transmute this creature into the blood of her womb if it wanted it so badly. Just like wine to the blood of Christ.

The creature struggled against the woman's strength pulling at its delicate skin. Her anguish was too powerful. Her anguish would swallow it whole. The creature screeched and broke away into the shadow of the corner of the room.

Flor fell back onto the bed after she lost her grip on the thing and it fled. Every muscle ached, and she could no longer move. It was one battle followed by another. But she survived both. Tears streamed from the corners of her eyes. She missed her older children in that moment.

It was probably better she'd lost this child, as much as it hurt to admit that. Her mother, who had always been distant, would most definitely not approve of her returning home with a bastard infant. And what would the rest of her family or the town have to say? The family business would have to weather the scandal. She'd left the children she already had to fight like a man then get impregnated by one, and not just any man, their leader. But her children were older, her firstborn son was nearly a man, and families were most likely already asking about her daughter's future marriage prospects. The knowledge that her son would enjoy more freedom than her daughter was not lost on Flor. It kept her up some nights because she didn't want to see the look in Regina's eyes that she had seen in the mirror on her own wedding day.

This memory slid from the corner of her eye like a drop of kerosene.

Flor looked at the two bandoliers on a chair facing her cot. She still had fight inside of her. The will to live and see her children burned again like a torch of holy flame. No demon from hell had enough breath to put it out. She would be the miracle. Her daughter would need her. Flor didn't want her daughter to end up like Dorotea. She would need a guide, a protector.

"Amelio. I need help. My stitches. I need to get home. My children need me. Amelio! I want to go to my family home."

Amelio rushed into the room but stopped short, seeing her

wounds and the blood spilling from between Flor's legs. "Your child is gone?"

Flor nodded, but upon hearing those words, hearing the reality spoken, she burst into sobs.

Amelio ran to her side. "Don't worry. You have two healthy grown children at home. I promise to get you back to them. The battle is not lost unless we give up."

"Thank you. You have been a good friend to me since that first day. Emiliano will have an angel by his side today. His child. Both of them will guide me back home. I don't want to waste any more time here. Please get me home."

"Then we better get started." Amelio began to clean and stitch Flor's wounds. He gathered fresh clothing and a basin of hot water to clean her lower body.

As Flor rode home, bouncing on the horse's back, she was in constant pain from her wound. Her uterus and lower back cramped the entire trip. But she was determined to see the faces of her children again.

When they reached the edge of her family property and she saw her home for the first time, she couldn't stop herself from crying. After seeing so much destruction, it was a relief her childhood home was still standing, just as it had been before she left, miraculously unscathed from the war. Amelio dismounted his horse first before helping Flor down. The patch of land she called home seemed so quiet compared to the camps and towns she had gotten used to. The air filled with only the sounds of insects and chirping birds.

"Amelio, it has been an honor to be next to you in battle. You will always have a home here and are welcome to whatever I have should you ever find yourself in need."

"We will continue the fight. And after this, maybe I will come for a visit."

"You better stay alive."

Flor winced through the pain to embrace Amelio, a man she loved like a brother.

"Are you sure you won't stay for a few days?"

"We have to keep the momentum going, perhaps get Emiliano's body back. Another time."

Flor was sad to see him go but understood. "Take care of yourself."

She watched Amelio ride off and promised to keep him in her prayers for all he had done for her. She prayed he would have a long, happy life just as he was, as Colonel Amelio Robles Ávila.

Her son and daughter had been waiting, not knowing if she would make it back or if any letter would make it into her hands with the war disrupting everything.

Regina ran to Flor, seeing her walk into the kitchen, and threw her arms around her mother. "We heard what happened to Emiliano. Are you all right?"

"Ouch. Not so tight. I'm fine, Regina. I'll need some time to recover."

"It's good you are back. Grandmother is not well, and she can't stop calling out for you in the night. Grandfather is still in his own world with his dementia." Rafael looked stern as he looked up from his newspaper. "My mother the soldadera has returned. I haven't heard the end of it from my friends."

Rafael returned to reading the paper that covered the war. Before she left to fight, Rafael had made it very clear he was not pleased to be left without his mother despite nearly being a grown man. She loved her son, but he was spoiled, a little king in need of assistance for the things only women could provide. The idea ingrained and reinforced daily was that his sole importance was to the business and to lead the family. Flor held back her lecture on how if Emiliano and the others didn't fight for his rights, Rafael would have nothing to build a future on. War was not playing dress-up. For their family, neither rich nor destitute, it was a very precarious time. If Rafael wanted so badly to be a big man, he had to put boyish ideas away.

"I will go to her now. Alone." As much as Flor wanted to sleep for days after her days of travel, she knew this was important. Flor limped to the staircase and held on to the banister. Every step slower than the previous one. She didn't know if this was the pain from the wound, or if she was avoiding the inevitable confrontation.

The room was bright and smelled of wildflowers and lavender oil. Dorotea wore a fresh white nightgown as she lay in bed. Her white iron headboard was in the shape of a bed of roses. She stared at the ceiling with a rosary and Bible in her hands. It had been nearly a year since Flor saw her mother last.

"Sit next to me, Flor."

Flor took a white wooden chair from the corner of the room next to the ceramic wash basin and pitcher. She sat close so her mother would not have to speak loudly.

"I am here. Regina said you have been calling for me. I've been at war."

Her mother's lips quivered like a child's. Tears fell from her eyes. "I know. You are alive. It worked. Now it is time for me to tell you everything. All your life I have tried to protect you from me, my bad thoughts. The unholiness that has plagued me."

"I thought you didn't want me."

Dorotea turned her head to face Flor. "Of course I wanted you. I didn't want you to have the curse." Her expression appeared as soft as the mattress and pillows she lay upon with the innocence of a baby.

"What curse?"

"I don't know where the curse came from or why. I just know I felt cursed seeing horrible things after your birth. I felt horrible things. The best I can explain it is as a terrible sadness even though I loved you so very much. Not knowing how to be close to your child when you are told you should seemed like a curse all on its own. There was no one I could tell these things to. In the midst of this turmoil there was also a shadow in white who spoke to me, trying to make these feelings worse. It whispered I should end my life and yours. That is why I often stayed away. Perhaps it would leave us alone. I still love you more than anything I could ever possess."

"What did this shadow really look like? A creature?"

Dorotea shook her head. "No. Just shadow and whispers."

Flor didn't want to worry her mother with her experience with the entity. Dorotea had already experienced her own pain, and Flor had managed to ward it off. Flor remained silent about her experience. Now that her mother was opening up, she had something else she wanted to express that had hurt her for so many years. "You loved my brother more. You married me off to a man I didn't love." Flor tried to withhold the bitterness in her tone, but it came out anyway.

Dorotea reached for Flor's hand.

"I'm sorry you think that. I'm sorry you went through life feeling like that. Regina feels your love. I have spent a lot of time thinking about my life in this bed. La Virgen in the corner whispers to me. I see her sometimes. But she is not wearing the robes, and her heart is not burning. She looks like the indigenous women wearing the clothing of the time before the Spanish arrived. Maybe she is an ancestor trying to speak to me. But she has to be La Virgen. I know it. Who else could she be? I don't know. She is so very beautiful and full of love. All she wants is to take back the curse. Since you were young I prayed to her to give you strength when you needed it. I fantasize it is my mother who died in childbirth along with a child who would have been my brother. On that day I cried all day. On Día de los Muertos I cry because I swear, I can feel their presence."

"Mama, sleep."

"I need you to forgive me. I need you to know without any doubt that I love you with everything inside of me now and after I am long gone. May my soul always be there to protect you and future generations of our bloodline. Tell Regina about the curse so she can arm herself. Although I do feel she is somehow protected, not being the firstborn."

"You really think it's a curse on us?"

Dorotea's face became alive, more vibrant than Flor had ever seen. Her cheeks were rosy pink. "Yes. La Virgen said so. She came to me after I began keeping an altar in the huts in the back of the house. I needed something. I had no one to speak to. I figured a ghost was better than a priest who dismissed me when I asked for help."

"I don't want to dismiss you, Mama. But I think you are tired and have been worried. I'm sorry I didn't tell you I was leaving."

"You don't need to apologize to me. Go to the altar. Take care of it. Call to our ancestors. Arm yourself with love and knowledge. The deep wisdom of intuition that is inside."

Flor remembered her nightmare fight with a demon, how it thrashed and fled as she pulled it closer to her. How she swore in her delirium that an unseen force had propped her body up to face the demon. "Why the girls and not the boys? Another trick from God?"

"It's just the way it happened. I've been praying for a way. Help from the ancestors and God. But things possessing power like the dark shadow telling me to harm myself do not relinquish it so easily. You have to take it. Take your power back and keep it inside of you."

"That is enough, Mama. I am here now, and we will spend every day together."

Flor left her mother staring at the corner of the room. She ventured downstairs into the back of the house, past two squat adobe storage rooms, to where the old fig tree stood. Flor had to dip her head to enter the cool space filled with spiderwebs and dust. Against the wall was the small wooden table littered with dried marigold petals and remnants of pillar candles melted to the bottom. There was also a comb, pieces of jewelry, a crocheted baby bootie. Flor smiled at the chipped wooden cradle that both her children had slept in. She had slept in that cradle.

But the child she just lost never would. Only in spirit.

This sight brought back the memory to her of every Day of the Innocents and Day of the Dead, when her mother would venture out with fresh flowers and food. No one was allowed to disturb her. Flor would watch her enter and exit, her mother like a ghost moving between worlds.

Flor gathered the small pieces of dried flowers from the little wooden table. And tucked beneath a statue of La Virgen was a folded piece of paper.

Hear my pleas. Taste my tears. Send help from the ancestors I never met to guide me through the darkness. To lift the white mantilla from the dead crying woman's face so I may send her away. Protect my children and their children. Show them the way.

It was her mother's handwriting.
"Mama?"

Regina's voice made Flor jump. "My love, you frightened me."

"Well, this place used to frighten me," Regina said.

"It shouldn't. I know she said stay away, because she thought you would disturb the altar, but I think we should spend more time here, listening to our ancestors."

"When I was little it just seemed like this dark, small place where Grandmother kept her secrets."

Flor took both of Regina's hands into hers. "I need to tell you something. And it is part of life so you must know. But I was carrying a child. The gunshot wound took it from me. So next Day of the Innocents we will pray for your sibling. And we will pray for ancestral knowledge to be guided to you."

Regina threw her arms around Flor. "I'm sorry. I'm guessing it was Emiliano's by the way you spoke about him in your letters. Come inside and rest. I'll be sure to freshen the ofrenda."

Flor gave the altar a final glance. She had brought back her bloody skirt for some reason unknown to her at the time. Now it was clear why she had done it. She would cut off the area where she had been shot, where her child departed this life, and keep it with the altar. Blood dies and dries, but the invisible particles of family are forever.

Three days later Dorotea lay in her bed feeling content with the time spent with Flor. They had spoken of their lives, and said all the things they had ever wanted to say to each other. They even shared joyful laughter. Dorotea only wished her husband, Alvaro, had fared better and they could be together like this. His senility was worse than ever before. Her daughter came home just in time. Everything needed always finds a way to make its way to us. Love, lovers, friends, miracles, and hope.

A long shadow fell across the room. The moonlight illuminated a tall figure. And from that figure came the sound of dripping water, and in a demonic raspy voice it said, "As agreed, I have
come to claim you after the safe return of your daughter. But I am
not happy. She had something I wanted. She tried to harm me.
You have been seeking help to thwart my desires. I will make this
painful for you." It took slow steps, using its nails to rip her sheets
and scratch the paint on the bed until it stood next to Dorotea.

Dorotea's eyes grew large. She saw the veil that appeared to be
stitched together with dried fish skin and human flesh. "You can
do whatever you want, demon. I have found a way to possibly
stop you from your constant torment. And I do not fear death
because I know part of me will remain to watch over them. And
every generation of us can pass on our knowledge and strength
after death. You can't touch us there. You are not as powerful as
you think. One day it will be the end of you."

Dorotea gave the creature a smug grin before breaking into
hysterical laughter.

"Die." It hissed before punching her in the gut. Dorotea
coughed without control, spurting out blood with the velocity
of water escaping a broken dam. The creature sucked the breath
from her body, causing her to cough with increasing violence.
Blood burst from her mouth into the creature's eyes and mouth
as she clutched her chest with one hand. The other tried to catch
hold of the flesh garment of the creature. On her last breath she
tore a chunk of its flesh from its waterlogged arm that felt like a
slug split in half.

It shrieked and gnashed its teeth before retreating from the
moonlight back into the shadow of the corner of the room.

Flor carried a tray with tea for her mother in the morning. She knocked expecting to hear her mother's voice, happier than it had ever sounded. When her mother didn't open her door or answer, Flor placed the tray on the floor and walked in.

Flor had seen dead bodies before, far more than one should see in a lifetime, but it was different to see her mother's body. Her lips were a pale shade of violet, and vacant open eyes stared at the ceiling. A large purple ring surrounded her mouth and eyes as if she had been punched. There was violence in the marks, and cruelty. The same cold cruelty she saw in the demon. She dropped to her knees and prayed between sobs. "Why did you have to leave me now? Please be at peace. Know we love you."

Her estranged mother she had only begun to understand. They'd only had three days. Three glorious days together that had felt like an entire lifetime. Even for these three days she held immeasurable gratitude, considering all the lives cut short in war. The people who never had the chance to make their peace. Children who would never meet a parent. No, she would not feel sorry for herself with the second chance she had been given. Death teaches so many lessons in the hardest of ways.

The room had the stillness of a crypt. She inhaled the scent that could only mean her mother was near: roses and lavender. It was why they named her Flor. Dorotea loved both flowers immensely because of their fragrance.

She smiled and lifted her face to the window, allowing the energy of the sun to kiss her on the forehead. The heat evaporated her tears before radiating throughout her body. Time stood still for Flor. In that moment she felt internal peace, and knowledge of the eternal presence of true love. Eternal because it passes on from one generation to the next. It is another form of generational wealth.

"Thank you, Mother." Basking in this light made her think of her father, Alvaro. Still a young man at seventy, yet he would only half understand what had happened if it was a good day for him. His lucid moments had declined quickly since she returned.

"Don't forget to visit Papa. Let him know you will greet him in peace." The scent blossomed again. Flor breathed in deeply to forever remember the lightness of it. As she moved to rise from the floor, rays of sunlight drew her eyes back to her mother.

The brightest rectangle guided her to her mother's hand that dangled off the side of the bed. She clutched something. Flor crawled over for a closer look. It appeared to be lace at first, but on further inspection Flor found it had the texture of skin and the scent of rotting fish. The sunlight remained strong and warm on Dorotea's hand. Flor tucked the odd thing into the pocket of her apron. She would place it on the altar with hopes an ancestor would have some divine guidance that would help her in the future. Flor hadn't managed to rip its flesh when it came for her; however, this did mean the creature was not invincible. Flor kissed her mother's hand before getting to her feet to tell the family and call the doctor.

The doctors declared it to be "natural causes," not wanting to waste time on reports or the authorities. This was not unusual for many women. Dorotea had been complaining for months of chest and abdominal pains.

Before the funeral, Flor looked through her mother's chest of clothing to find Dorotea's wedding dress for her wake. It was made of white lace and a mesh of delicate, intricate flowers. Flor held the dress to her face as she let out her anguished cries. She would bury her mother in this wedding dress even if the back had to be cut to fit her. How beautiful she would look when appearing in their dreams.

The funeral was small. Her father sat in the pew crying as he stared at the open casket, glazed eyes fixed on the flowers. He breathed deeply, which worried his sisters, but Flor knew perhaps he was taking in the scent of his wife who was sending a message to him alone. Flor almost wished he was in one of his states where he didn't quite know who anyone was. The pain in his old face pierced her heart like the stab of a brooch pin being placed directly into the heart. He looked as if he wanted to close his eyes and follow her to the place of dreams. This dream state he lived in now was too confusing most of the time.

Now that she was home, Flor made Rafael look after her father. He reluctantly took the role after Flor said he would receive nothing in the family business if he didn't contribute to the family first. Men could look after the vulnerable too. They had the capacity to give comfort without it reflecting poorly on them. Rafael must have taken this to heart, because as he held his grandfather's hand he was also crying.

Flor's two aunts on her father's side, Carmela and Luisa, had prepared food at the house earlier in the day, and so they would all return to the family home to remember Dorotea. But first, they had to see to the burial.

Flor and Regina stood in the rain holding hands. The rest of the funeral attendees had already run to the dry church or headed to the family home for lunch.

"Mama, I do not want to ever have children or marry. I want to fight like you," Regina said.

Flor squeezed her daughter's hand. "Darling, you can be whatever you want in my eyes. I want what you want for yourself. You have to know, there are many who will not let you. The disappointment will wear you down, and you might give in to those pressures. You might even tell yourself everyone is right except you. Please do not fall for it. I promise to do my best for you."

"I promise. As long as you promise not to force me into marriage. I know you and Papa did your best not really loving each other. The older I get, the more obvious it is I don't want that."

Flor had to catch her breath. She held Regina in her arms tightly. "I'm sorry you had to experience that. We did our best. Now I want you to always do your best to preserve the items I have added to the altar that is now in my mother's old room. Bloody buttons from the nightgown she wore on her deathbed, a piece of something I found in her hand, and a patch from my skirt with my blood and the spilled blood of your sibling. Every Día de los Muertos and Día de los Inocentes we will sit for the entire day and listen."

Regina gently broke from her mother's embrace. "Listen for what?"

Flor squeezed Regina's hand just as a gust of wind blew her mantilla past her face. The coldness made her shiver. She looked around them with the sensation of being watched. A thick, creeping fog had descended upon the cemetery. Her first reaction was to tighten her body into a ball, make herself smaller to reserve her warmth, because the fear of not having any sight of what lay ahead or getting lost in such a fog was overwhelming. As they left the cemetery for home, Flor wondered as she thought about the La Llorona creature, *How do you defeat a foe in the mind who feeds off the mind?* She looked at her daughter and held her hand. This gave her an inkling, and she felt moved to speak.

"We must listen to the women who came before us. We change the future by unloading the sorrow of the past. We sever the cord of generational curses. Some cords are meant to shrivel away to blackened dead flesh. They are our blood, but we are not them. We do not have to accept it. None of it."

The demon slinked into the shadows behind a tree in the cemetery, angry it didn't get its way. But this one had a daughter, who would one day bear a child. And even if this daughter did not, then the demon would wait. It had time, which gave it patience—unlike this species who always seemed to be worried about the lack of time. Who were always digging themselves into an emotional grave over the moment when time as they knew it would come to an end: death.

It would take out all its revenge on the girl and those who followed in her bloodline. Nothing would stand in its way again. The world which the demon came from had been destroyed by natural violent forces that gave it an all-consuming bitterness.

The creature only knew of the power of destruction and nothing of love.

Alejandra and Cathy

The children would be safe spending time with their father and grandparents for a long weekend. Alejandra sat in the Uber trying to not cry, knowing that she was about to risk it all. In that moment all she wanted to do was jump into bed with her children, beneath the covers, because the warmth and love between them were torches in the dark. Alejandra knew now that this love charged them through life until they arrived at their given time of death. And that connection between humans was like a spiderweb created from blood and spirit. The creature wanted to consume this love, destroy it as easily as you might a real spiderweb.

Never.

Alejandra closed her eyes and thought of the women in the cenote. She would call on them. Let their spirits charge her now in this battle for her soul.

"Not a lot of traffic. We should make good time to the airport. Music?"

"Uh, yes. Why not?"

As they pulled away from her home, the driver turned on the radio.

That unmistakable voice and beat. Just what she needed to hear. "Personal Jesus," by Depeche Mode. She thought of her older brother, Charlie, before he left home. He loved Depeche Mode. Later he confessed to having the biggest crush on Dave Gahan. Who didn't? Charlie had always kept in his locker at school the clothes he wanted to wear but that didn't meet the approval of their parents. The memories made her smile. He entrusted her with his secrets. After this, she would make an effort to get back in touch. Real touch. They were family even if they did not share blood. It was unfair to run away from all of them, but at the time it had been what she needed.

"Hey, never mind with the radio. I'm just going to listen to my headphones and close my eyes."

"Sure thing." The driver flipped the radio back off.

Alejandra pulled out her phone to play "Halo" by Depeche Mode. Every note and word pure poetry to her soul. She was ready to die for the transformative work she had been doing up to now to be complete.

When she arrived back in Texas, a sense of being *home* returned. Cathy waited for her in the car at the curbside pickup at the airport.

"I suppose you haven't changed your mind on the flight?"

"No. And I want to do this tonight. La Llorona has claimed her last souls. But first I need to do something, if you don't mind."

"No problem. What is it?"

"I found my father, at least I think I did. It is an off chance. No way to verify."

Cathy's smile faded. "I'm not ready. I will take you there, but I am not ready for that."

"I understand. You don't have to do anything."

"Where are we going?"

"It's a flower shop downtown."

Cathy's face now drifted elsewhere. "That sounds so familiar. I can't remember . . . but it is worth a try."

A car honked twice behind them. "Shit. I better go."

Alejandra stood in front of the flower shop, Rosas. In her hand she held the photo she had found in the box of albums with the same signage. Thanks to Google Maps, she'd found the sign and its exact location. From her car she watched a man who looked about sixty years old sit on a stool behind a counter playing solitaire on a computer. Not a single customer went in or out. Her stomach felt like a thorny bramble was rustling inside. Could this be her father? This man looked like a hippie, with his long gray ponytail and beads on one wrist. He wore a long rosary around his neck and Birkenstocks with socks. She had to confront her fear of meeting the man who could be her father.

A little bell rang when she opened the door. He looked at her and paused. His eyes softened with recognition when they fixed on her face.

She too felt this undeniable familiarity as they matched each other's gaze. "Are you Rogelio?"

He nodded. "You my daughter with Cathy? I remember those eyes."

Alejandra nodded, not knowing how to react or what to say

first. For such a long time she'd felt the need to manage her words and emotions with other people, especially men. The work she had been doing with Melanie had helped to untie those knots while healing the buried wounds. This was a chance for her to trust herself as her authentic self while being open to receiving and giving love to this complete stranger who had given her life. "My name is Alejandra, and I am your daughter."

Tears she didn't bother to control rolled from her eyes.

He gave her a big smile and upturned his palm to another stool behind the counter. "Well, sit down. What do you want to know?"

"I want to know everything, eventually. But right now, tell me what you think I should know."

He nodded and grabbed the rosary with one hand. Before speaking he studied her face, looked into her eyes. Alejandra matched his gaze, not feeling insecure or afraid. What could she possibly have to fear now, after all that had occurred?

"I was just a young dumb kid. Not that it's an excuse to run without a fight, but my mother left me with my dad when I was maybe five or six. Didn't come back or say a word. I would have been all right if they just separated or divorced. He sent us to stay with family in Guadalajara for a few years so he could settle himself. I guess all the wondering about my mom and moving messed me up. Years later I found out she had more kids with another man. That is when she came back into my life. That messed me up even more. I love women. I mean, them and the Mary Jane have always been my weakness. Couldn't trust them, though. When Cathy said she was pregnant, I freaked and ran away. Not that it's Cathy's fault, but she seemed pretty adamant about not wanting to be a mother right then. I don't blame her."

Alejandra couldn't help but forgive him and feel compassion. He too suffered under a different kind of curse.

"I'm sorry. I hope you had a good life . . . have a good life."

She didn't want to lie or hide any longer to anyone, so she told him the truth. "I'm grateful to be alive. I didn't always want to be." His lips quivered and eyes filled with tears before he hung his head and began to sob like one of her children. She went behind the counter and placed her arm around his shoulders. "I forgive you. And I wish you the best. You have Cathy to thank for me finding you. She gave me your old records."

He looked up with tear-streaked cheeks. "She did? Music is how I bonded with Cathy."

In that moment she felt a piece of her soul float back to her: not a piece taken from anywhere or anyone else, but her own living flesh put back in place. She would be made whole again.

They swapped information to keep in touch. His face brightened when she told him he was a grandfather to three children. His eyes filled once more with tears when she showed him the photo. "I should probably tell you that you have a sister named Natalie. I finally found the guts at forty-five to settle down and be a husband and father. Bernice, Natalie's mother, was a fling to start, but Bernice and I are still going strong. Can I tell Natalie about you? Maybe give her your number?"

Alejandra could feel the tears in her eyes and her body respond with uncontrollable tremors inside. She had a biological sister named Natalie. Her mind could never have conceived of this reality. It made her think of how much more intricate life is beyond the senses and bubbles we live in. Forget about multiple universes being "out there," they existed right here on Earth. Her idea of her family tree had grown another branch in an instant.

"Of course you can tell her to contact me. And you are free to message or call whenever. I want to take it slow, though."

He gave her a warm smile. "I can do that. I'm not going anywhere. I've run so much in my life that now it seems I am running out of time. It's not my intention to waste it."

Alejandra didn't know if she should give him a hug or shake his hand because he was a stranger; however, expressing her love felt right in that moment. She wrapped her arms around her father, and he embraced her back.

"Thank you for finding me," he whispered with his voice cracking.

"We will be in touch. I have to go now." She pulled away and headed to the door.

Before she left, he called back out to her. "And Cathy? How is she? Would she want to talk?"

"She isn't ready. Might not ever be ready. You will know in time. By the way, what is the story with this place, Rosas?"

"When I was a kid it was a bakery. My brother and I always ran here when we had pocket money. When I was discharged from the military with no job I came back to reminisce, maybe grab something sweet. It was no longer a bakery, but there was a Help Wanted sign in the window. I took a chance to walk through that door. Been here ever since."

Alejandra walked out feeling free. She walked to the nearby historic hotel, the Redwood Inn, where Cathy said she'd be waiting for her at the bar. When she stepped inside, a sense of déjà vu overcame her. There was something about the oiled scent of the wood that made her feel far away. It was so different from the usual scents of her home, like washing detergent and a full garbage bin. The deep hues of the fabric on plush loveseats and wingback chairs emitted dust filled with yearning and despair.

Cathy sat at the bar drinking a Coke while reading a magazine, *The Lancet*. Alejandra walked slowly, taking in every sensation and thought. She placed her hand on Cathy's shoulder.

"He was there. I can't believe this one-in-a-million chance, my father was at the shop called Rosas. It's a florist now."

Cathy gave her a warm smile. "I am so very happy for you. This is important for you. Did he look well?"

"I think so. He asked about you. I told him it was your decision to ever contact him."

Cathy nodded. "That is the past. Besides, there is a cute pediatric nurse I might ask out for coffee."

Alejandra raised her eyebrows before giving her mother a grin. "Do you feel anything here?"

Cathy's mouth opened. "Oh my God, yes. As soon as I walked in. Déjà vu. I am ready to go if you are."

Alejandra nodded as she scanned the room, still feeling a sense of familiarity. There was also something else.

Cathy's apartment looked exactly how Alejandra imagined it. All her accolades and accomplishments on one wall next to the photos of all their extended family. The furniture was cream-colored—after all, she had no pets or children. There were no crumbs on the floor or counter. A bowl full of fresh fruit sat next to a Nespresso machine in a kitchen that looked hardly used.

Cathy did say she hated cooking. Alejandra enjoyed cooking when it was for her and Matthew. The kids ate what kids ate. She missed them already, something she hadn't felt in a very long time. And she longed to hold them again without worry.

"Let me show you to your bedroom." Alejandra followed Cathy to a small spare room decorated in powder blue and seaside scenes from South Padre Island. The water in one of the photos looked so calm. At some point she would take the children there. Just her and Cathy and the children.

It saddened her that Matthew was not part of her mental picture. Perhaps they had only been meant to be for a while, their time together coming to a natural end as she blossomed, released her true fragrance. She couldn't be who he wanted her to be any longer.

The woman on those first dates was long gone. And so was the frightened mother with so much pain in her heart she wanted to end her own life. Alejandra wanted to live to be the woman she chose to be.

Hot water filled the bathtub. Alejandra lit candles with saints even though she still didn't really believe the saints were anything like the images depicted on the candles. She believed that something beyond existed, just not like *that*.

Melanie had given Alejandra a list of herbs to place in the bathtub, and had promised to pray for her and do a fire limpia on her behalf. Each of the three women had a role to play in Alejandra's plan, but this was for Alejandra to do on her own, with the help of the power in her bloodline. Her plan had as much risk as reward: Ridding the world of this thing would be a great feat for anyone. But Alejandra would do anything to stop her daughter from experiencing the pain she had endured, the constant feeling of self-doubt and defeat, like rotten eggs that saturated everything with their stench as they decayed.

Alejandra stepped into the tub and lay down. Her hands touched the light stretch marks and loose skin across her belly. Her son always grabbed it and asked why it was so soft and thick: her "jelly belly," he called it. She would say playfully, "I made the perfect home just for you because I loved you so much." In that same bath he asked where he came from.

"Heaven," she would say.

"Were you there too?"

"I was, and as soon as I saw you, I knew you were mine. This also happened with your sister. Then the heavens wanted to give you to me with a beautiful bow, so we were attached with a long cord. It fed you and kept you close to me while you grew big."

He stopped and looked deep in thought. "When we die, will we be together again?"

"Of course. We will always be together and bound by our love. We have the same eyes and blood. Even though that cord was cut when you came to this world, it was replaced with another one. This way we can always find each other in any time or any place. You never have to fear." He giggled and kissed her on the cheek. Since the day he was born he had bright eyes reflecting the power of stars, of creation.

This memory gave her the courage to continue. In her mind she pictured her altar at home next to the family photos. With a deep breath she reached to the floor of the bathroom for a vial of each of her children's blood, dumping them one by one into the water. The red creating eddies of pink in the water like little guppies swimming around her body. Cathy had managed to contact a local nurse to take the children's blood and air-ship the vials to her home for this ritual generations in the making. A ritual of courage, faith, and sacrifice.

Alejandra reached over the side of the tub to the floor again, for a knife with a mother-of-pearl handle. Just like Cathy showed her, she slit the inside of her left wrist deep enough to release blood but not enough to put her at immediate risk. Red and pink continued to color the water like splaying strands of hair, then taking the shape of clawed fingers. She felt weak, the pain of the cut on her arm worse than she imagined. It was supposed to be just enough blood to lure the demon but hopefully not enough to kill her.

Alejandra leaned back in the tub, hoping it would be enough. She placed the knife on the soap holder next to her. Steam from the hot water rose to the top of the room, fogging the mirror. It reminded her of the dream of La Llorona floating on the ocean. Despite the heat that made sweat bead on her top lip, a chill ran through the length of her body. She stared at the bottles of shampoo to distract herself from the heaviness of death. *I hope you are all there. The women from my bloodline. Ancestors long dead. Give me your strength. I can't change the past. Help me to give our future generations something better. I float in this pool of water just like you. May it turn to oil so I might cleanse us of this curse. Give my body and blood the power to purify.*

Alejandra slowly moved to sit upright. Even though she'd turned the tap off, more thick steam rose from the water. The water between her legs moved. The blood began to separate then gathered in a whirlpool, spiraling and bubbling. In the center of the whirlpool of blood a black spot like an oil slick appeared. And the form of a head rose between her knees.

A forehead covered with slimy, iridescent skin emerged. Deep crimson drool dripped from its open mouth, revealing thick gums with razor nubs for teeth. It was the same face that had hovered above her son's bed, had haunted her dreams and her home. It released ghastly laughter that smelled like the head of a newborn. How could a smell that evoked such purity come from something so insidious? How much innocence had it devoured?

But it would not devour her. Alejandra would end its reign of death.

"Where are they? Where are the rest of them? And you are dying too slowly," it hissed.

Alejandra sat upright, leaning into the creature to look into its burning, starlike eyes. She was face-to-face with the nightmare that had plagued her all her life without her knowing it. The ugliness did not frighten her. It was the ugliness she felt for herself.

The worst level of hell to be held captive. Alejandra felt sorry for the thing because it could never experience the true beauty of existence. That was its curse. It would hunger and never feel satiated, living in a constant state of hatred of what it lacked.

"Where are they? They are here," it growled as it bared its teeth. Hands trembled like it was experiencing withdrawal. Roving eyes desperate for what it wanted. Real pain when it didn't get it.

The demon hissed; its cracked, pus-filled lips curled as it spoke. "I'm going to drain you here then rip your children to shreds. Humans have no power except the power to destroy themselves and all they love. I have seen it time and time again."

In her mind, Alejandra prayed, pulling at the power inside of her, imagined the water warming from her inner heat and the heat from her ancestors' energy. *Ancestors, I call on you. The time has arrived for you to rise. To cleanse and purify with water and fire. Purge the world once and for all of this insipid creature of destruction.*

The demon rose farther out of the water, exposing its torso dressed in what looked like a gown of lace made from human flesh, fish carcasses, and varying fabrics. Heavy sagging breasts weeping bloody tears wobbled as the creature moved. "You have no special powers, and you are no witch. Stop this game!" Its hands trembled in rapid movements. The white eyes eclipsed to a darker shade of gray.

The demon's flesh made Alejandra think of the women in her dreams, their different clothing and skin from different times in history. A piece of their past remaining alive. It grabbed her left arm with its nails sinking into Alejandra's flesh, leaving sharp pinpricks on top of her birthmark. Alejandra reached for the knife while ignoring the flesh and nerves in her forearms ripping, fought past the pain that would have caused her to faint any other time. The demon snatched her other wrist as she took hold of the blade. It attempted to manipulate her tendons and muscles so she would cut herself.

Alejandra tried to resist its strength even though she was beginning to feel physically weak. The blood loss was taking its toll as the creature tore deeper into her other arm. She had just enough energy to grab the creature's wrist and twist it away from its attack on her flesh.

Alejandra's screams echoed in the small room as she used all the oxygen her lungs could hold. She didn't care if her lungs collapsed, they would be filled with the white smoke from the flames of her ancestors. The heat still burned strong within her body. The creature fixed its horrid gaze on Alejandra's eyes. She didn't look away or shudder as she focused her intention on surviving this fight until it was destroyed. Water spilled onto the floor as she fought to free herself from the creature and her body hit the sides of the tub. She wrestled for the lives of her children, screaming into the void of the bathroom, never turning away from the heat of the creature's white eyes. She could hear Cathy at the door trying to get in, calling her name. It wasn't locked. The demon gave her a sinister glare with a shrieking laughter. "See, you both are pathetic and weak compared to me!"

Alejandra knew it was now. Within her chest and belly, she rolled the panic and fear into a fist. There remained something left inside: her love. Her love that had once sunk to the bottom of the pit of her pain and loneliness, that had weeviled its way out of sight year after year since she was a child.

It gave Alejandra a second rush of strength to plunge the knife into her lower belly.

She would give the beast exactly what it wanted. And that would be the creature's demise before realizing what was happening to it. This was the only way.

"You want my seeds! Take them!" She gritted her teeth to contain the pain. Squeezed her eyes to maintain focus as more blood left her body.

The demon swayed, intoxicated with the waterfall of blood flowing into the water. With greedy urgency, it dove into her wounded belly. "So many. I will have them all." It gurgled inside of her. It ripped her ovaries and uterus with its teeth and claws, relishing the feeling of her organs in its hands as Alejandra screamed out to now release her anguish, let it brighten the room like fireworks. She gripped the side of the bathtub, tears streaming from the corners of her eyes.

Her chest convulsed as she sobbed in joyful ecstasy. Nearing death was the purest moment she had ever experienced. She appreciated the overflowing cornucopia of abundance bestowed upon her. The sheer gratitude blinded her. Pale yellow feathers in the brown hands of her ancestors took away the pain. "Thank you. Thank you for making me a mother. Thank you for making me *their* mother. I accept love. My love. I am and they are all I need to complete me." Another cannonade of pure power exploded in her mind.

A woman wearing charro trousers with two bandoliers across her chest and two braids at the sides of her neck nodded before pushing the demon farther inside Alejandra from behind. Alejandra met the woman's eyes. It was the woman from the photograph and her dream, Flor. She knew what she had to do.

Alejandra clawed at the demon's upper back to pull it closer to her. With the strength of a force she could not conceive of, like something that lives beyond the atmosphere of Earth or the perceived world, Alejandra found a way.

There is always a way in the dark.

She used her soul as a wooden match. Invisible fingertips touched her skin. In the mirror opposite her, a brown woman without eyes wore a white skirt and huipil. Another, looking like a 1950s Pachuca with the same nose as her birth mother, watched Alejandra with smeared black mascara and red lipstick. She stretched out her arms to Alejandra. Through waning vision she could see more brown women all dripping wet from watery graves with sorrow-filled tears, all dressed from different eras. "Ancestors," she cried out. In the back there stood a woman in a white wedding gown with a lace veil over her head, chanting a prayer. Alejandra could not see her face to know who it was. They gathered around the bathtub, then stretched out their hands to push the demon deeper into Alejandra's lower abdomen. She braced her open legs against the sides of the bathtub. Her breathing kept her alert. By some miracle the blood loss had not knocked her out. The demon still relished gnawing and twisting in her uterus. Despite the agonizing pain, she continued to pull until there was nothing left of the demon in the bathtub. Her ancestors kept their hands outstretched. Their voices whispered prayers as they gave thanks for her courage in putting an end to the demon.

Alejandra's mother screamed outside the bathroom, banging on the door and rattling the doorknob. "I'm calling an ambulance now."

Alejandra had no physical strength left to pull herself out of the crimson-filled tub as she bled out from the belly and forearm. The ghosts of women hovered over her; the one wearing the charro trousers floated toward the door. Alejandra leaned back feeling contented, even if this was the end. She had declared her true love for herself and for the divine gift of her children. She tried to conjure the voices of her children in her mind, wishing for their sweetness to be the last sound in her ears instead of water draining. Her vision clouded.

Alejandra didn't know how much time had passed before she saw Cathy's face near hers, crying and holding her hand while whispering her love. Their arms linked together, forming a cord. She could feel Cathy's energy surging into her. Alejandra thought of the births of her children that her mother had missed. Is this how it would have been if she had been there to help Alejandra through the contractions? Give her advice? Longing for this connection, this love that was so present, overwhelmed Alejandra. All she wanted to do was live. To cry. To love. That was the last thing she remembered before her eyes closed.

Alejandra stared at her phone knowing she had to call Matthew. The low-level anxiety she felt in his presence returned. How would he react? She didn't want to be scolded or interrogated. If she could find the courage to fight a monster, then she could call the one person who should be on her team. She pressed the icon for "home" and waited for him to pick up. He answered straight-away.

Without any pleasantries, she told him she was in the hospital after attempting suicide.

He paused before speaking. "Why didn't you tell me it was this bad?" Matthew kept his voice down because he knew that, despite the door being closed, children could barge into the bedroom at any moment. And his parents were still there. He wouldn't want to explain to them that anything was less than perfect.

It was easier to tell Matthew she tried to kill herself than the truth about the demon. She didn't trust him. She didn't trust him to believe in her, to be there for her, to love her as she was.

"I'll try to be home more. Just tell me what you need to get better. The kids can't stop asking for you."

"What are you telling them?"

"I told them you were not well and needed the doctors to take a look. I also mentioned Cathy is taking care of you. Mothers need their mothers."

It almost felt like this was love, and Alejandra wanted to feel that he genuinely loved her. On a level she knew he did care for her. She would always be the one who gave him children. But the woman he fell in love with was no more. That was the same woman who fell in love with him. You can't love a ghost.

Her old identity no longer existed. She needed time to heal from this rebirth, to allow herself to continue to grow into this new way of being. Of living with her eyes open for the first time, with her heart open to the world's beauty instead of its pain. She wanted to discover it on her terms, without fearing what others, including Matthew, thought.

"Do you want to live? Do you want this life?"

She wanted to live. It remained to be seen if she wanted a life with him. "Let's start by getting me home. I miss the kids."

"I guess we will have a big discussion when you get back."

He hung up the phone, and she was not sorry to let him go.

The next call was to Melanie, who had been texting Cathy for three days into Alejandra's week-long stay in the hospital. Cathy hadn't responded, wanted to let Melanie hear the full story from Alejandra. She respected her daughter's privacy. Alejandra sent a quick message to Melanie letting her know she had been taken to the hospital for stitches. She would tell her the full story in one of their sessions, but she wanted to send her gratitude. Melanie answered after two rings.

"Melanie, it's over. We did it. I can't thank you enough for your guidance. For everything."

"Are you all right? When I didn't hear back, I was worried. And I did nothing. It was the work you put into our sessions and at home. Your love. Your idea. Congratulate yourself."

"I haven't seen the women again or had the dreams. Maybe it was the drugs they gave me to sleep."

"They must be at peace, knowing their final task is done. But you are still alive and have so much life to live. So much love to give yourself and others."

"When I'm better, we can resume our sessions."

"I will be here. We can begin when you are ready."

"Thank you." Alejandra hung up the phone feeling more positive about the future than she had in a long time, maybe ever.

She spent another week in Texas before she was at low risk for a short flight. In that week she met more of her extended family and thought about what she wanted to do with the rest of her life. To organize her thoughts, she jotted down her ideas, dreams, and stray images in her mind in a journal Cathy gave her. Cathy attended to her every need, but not in an overbearing way. It was easy, like two friends who enjoy each other's company. It was better than any painkiller a doctor could prescribe for healing. In the end, they didn't say goodbye, instead they hugged and said, "Speak to you soon."

When she walked through the door with Matthew, all three children ran to her. Mary, their babysitter, ran out from the kitchen to round them back up. Alejandra hugged them as tightly as she could despite residual pain. When she winced, Matthew pulled Will away gently. "All right, kids, go back to Mary. Let your mom rest." She wanted to have them near, but also knew she needed more recovery. It was good to see Matthew possessed some concern for her. Their split could be amicable or a living hell. They had the power to create the reality beyond hurt emotions. Maybe leaving him would be the catalyst for him to take more responsibility for parenting.

Catrina stood behind, fear in her eyes. Her tense posture with her hands clasped in front of her told Alejandra that Catrina knew something of the evil that had occurred. Her voice was wispy as she looked into her mother's eyes. "Please, tell me. I need to know. I had a nightmare you were drowning."

Alejandra could not treat her like a child. She had been touched by this very real adult horror. "What do you think happened?"

She looked around to see if anyone was close enough to hear. Elodia and Will were in the kitchen making cookies. "You killed it. I think you drowned it before it could drown you."

Alejandra took Catrina's head to her chest. "That is exactly right. Smart girl. It will never bother you again. Just promise me one thing."

"What's that, Mom?"

"You will never look around and lower your voice when you speak."

Catrina squeezed her harder. "I'm proud of you, Mom. I'm so lucky to have you."

A flow of warmth covered the crown of Alejandra's head. Her scalp felt electrified as it traveled down her neck and settled in her chest. The beating of her heart pumping what it meant to be alive. She had experienced love without the stain of thought or expectation. Alejandra believed those words and savored them. "I'm proud of you, Catrina."

"For what? I didn't do anything."

"Just you being you."

La Llorona: The Woman

1616

It was too much and too little at the same time: The pain felt like a cyclone of powerlessness and despair.

And Rosa decided to end her children's lives because they would be filled with the same pain.

The unholy trinity of pain made her do it: The guilt of not wanting children. The belief that this was her only source of worth or power. And her envy of men who could do whatever they pleased with very few consequences. It made her want to destroy them all.

Below the surface of Rosa's flawless skin was a putrefying rage for not having the ability to change the way of the world. The anger at the constant feeling of never being enough even for herself made her not want to exist. What was the point of any of it?

There was only one way out: Death.

Rosa was married at sixteen to an older man in his thirties named Matias who her parents thought would take care of her.

He owned a small plot of land and a few horses. Most of his money was inherited as he was the only heir to a once wealthy ranching family. With each year a piece of land had been sold off. Their relationship consisted of him demanding sex without caring whether she said yes or no, then running to the local tavern to drink with the few other rancher friends he still had. As the wealth dwindled, so did the friendships with those who retained their land. He had more enemies than friends.

He left one evening and never came back, something she didn't regret until she saw the hefty tax bills and debts her husband had built. A month later his body was found in a pond not far from their home. She and her daughters would lose everything. Another marriage would be the only solution. What else was there?

Two girls, two innocent girls who would bear the curse they had no control over. Neither their bodies nor their minds were their own. She didn't see any way forward for any of them in this life. She knew what she was doing was beyond wrong, that she would burn in hell forever. She would receive the worst of punishments and believed she deserved it.

How insidious it was that she had to betray the trust her daughters had in her. But she could think of no other way to save them. Now her daughters would never suffer abuse or have to sell themselves. Ever. Even animals in the wild sometimes eat their young. This world was a cruel one with no hope, no one to give her hope.

The god of the church hung before her in silence. The priests called the woman who washed his feet a whore. So very little love from a place supposedly built on it. With tears in her eyes, she remembered the conversation she had with a friend that made her come to this agonizing conclusion. They discussed the one suitor who approached her two months after her husband's death. He owned the adjoining property. He was unmarried in his forties with no children. There was something about him she didn't like. His gaze lingered on the curves of her body. She was used to that. But he also carried that same leer to her daughters. The worst part was that most of the debt left by her husband was to this man. He would essentially own them.

"You have to marry that man. How will you survive as a widow without someone by your side?"

"I don't trust the way I see him looking at me—at my girls."

"What else can you do? Just go along with it. That is how we survive."

It was then that she made the decision to end it all forever. The limited options they had in life made her imagine the worst outcomes for her daughters. The despair of knowing her daughters would most likely live a life like hers seemed too insurmountable. That despair stood before her like a mountain that could not be climbed with her bare feet.

So she took them out for the day.

"We are going swimming."

Four-year-old Morelia and ten-year-old Celia skipped with joy along the dirt path, wildflowers in their hands. The sun was warm and reflected in their eyes and hair. "But we can't swim."

She caught her breath and tears at the beautiful sight. Her heart broke with the brittleness of a dry leaf beneath her steps. "I will show you. On the count of three we jump and fall into the hands of the angels; their wings of pure love like my love for you will take us to our destiny."

"We love you, Mother, don't we, Celia?"

The ten-year-old girl nodded with her eyes full of fear as she gazed at the fast water. "I don't want to. Can we leave now? Please?"

She couldn't break now. They would know. Celia knew by the

look on her face. The fear. "Hold hands, my daughters. Ready. One. Two. Three. I promise it will all be okay."

Little Morelia moved first, then they all jumped into the fast-moving river.

"Mama!" Celia cried out after the initial splash as she was pulled back up by the current. The ten-year-old girl saw her four-year-old sister from the corner of her eye coming close to her, spurting water from her mouth. By some miracle, she grabbed hold of her hand. Their bodies crashed together as they bobbed in the water. Celia's suddenly stopped with Morelia right next to her. They were caught in an overturned tree fallen from the side of the riverbank. Celia used all her strength, almost superhuman, to help her sister hold on to a branch with one hand with her other holding on herself. She used her body to shield Morelia from the oncoming water. They both watched as their mother passed by facedown. Her hair and white dress splayed. Then she was gone beneath the dark water.

"I want Mama!" cried little Morelia.

The two girls clung to the tree as the cold water soaked them, their skirts heavy and weighing them down. Celia looked to the sky and the few wisps of cloud floating across perfect cornflower blue. One looked like a feather or an angel's wings. Was this what her mother spoke of?

"God in heaven! Alejandro, come quick. Now!" a woman screamed next to them.

"Where are your parents?" She looked around the river then behind her. A man dressed like a farmhand ran toward them.

Celia's teeth chattered as she spoke. "They are dead."

The woman's eyes filled with tears as the man lifted both girls out of the water. Celia burst into tears when they touched ground again. Morelia instinctively wrapped her arm around her sister.

"What happened? You are safe now. I too lost my parents at a young age. My husband was taken from me in an unexpected accident. I'm so sorry they are gone. But I can't help to think seeing you . . . I want for nothing in my life except angels. And now you have been cast from the heavens in the most tragic of circumstances."

Celia continued to comfort Morelia, rubbing her little arm. Part of her felt suspicious of the strangers, yet she didn't want to think about what would have happened if they had not been passing by. Maybe her mother was right, and they had the angels with them. "Who are you?"

"I own this land. Nothing owns me, thanks to having my own little militia. My name is Adana. I would very much like to care for you unless you have other family."

Celia looked at her wet dress, the small puddle of mud created by water. "No. There is no other family."

"I'm still cold." Little Morelia left her sister's side to snuggle into the woman's side. Adana wrapped her arms around the child, covering her little body. "Why don't we move directly into the sun." She lifted Morelia off her feet and walked a few feet. "There. Is that better?" Morelia nodded in the crook of her neck. Instinctively, Adana rocked her back and forth. "Alejandro, we will be going to town. We must get fresh clothes for these children and whatever else they may need."

Adana touched the side of Celia's face, looking deep into the eyes of someone much older than her years and who now unfortunately felt the scarring of life.

"If you will allow me, I would very much like to take care of you both. We can make other arrangements if you have a change of heart."

Celia could only nod. "We don't have many choices."

Adana knelt next to Celia, wanting her to really hear what

she was about to say because it had been said to her and changed the course of her life.

"There are many times in life we feel there are no choices. Sometimes that is true. But I feel perhaps the true answers to the choices we must make find our way to us. Sometimes it is right away and at times it takes patience. Look at today. I have been asking for years for little angels to bless my life. You have been waiting for minutes to escape that lethal water. We were brought to each other at exactly the right moment. I had no choice or say that I could never conceive. But I choose to give you a good life with many choices if you choose me."

"I want to go with Adana. She smells and feels good, like Mama did."

Celia looked to the sky. In the air flew a quetzal, its wings glittering beneath the sun like a spirit. A sign, perhaps.

"We will come with you. Thank you."

"I think when my life is over, I will owe all my thanks to you."

The three walked to the wagon where Alejandro waited to take them to town then back to the large hacienda where Adana lived with a host of animals.

Morelia and Celia never forgot their mother on Día de los Muertos. They gave her thanks and love when they both swore they could feel her close. Her warmth before the sadness she didn't know how to overcome. Adana indeed gave them a good life through a thorough education, safety on the farm. The sun never ceased to shine on any of their lives until their natural deaths.

Three days later Rosa's body was found along with two corn husk dolls and ribbons in the pocket of her dress. Word about the body spread fast through the village. Those who knew her also knew she had two daughters who were not found in the river or at home. The assumption without investigation was that they drowned with their mother and some animal must have carried the bodies away. And so the gossip began.

I didn't know her personally. Did you know her? Where are her children? A woman of her age surely had children. I heard she had children. She had two dolls still in her cold, dead hands. Someone told me when they pulled her body from the river, her mouth was wide open, like she was suspended in a scream. A no-man's-land of susto. Pain. Both her eyes were gone and eaten by the fish. River water poured out of the sockets. Dirty, horrid tears. She must not have had a man, only a woman without a husband would do such a thing. No sense.

Well, she will most definitely be punished for her deeds. Yes, wander the Earth looking for them. Never able to rest. La Llorona crying for her children.

The creature stalked in the shadows. It heard the story of this woman who attempted to take the lives of her children and herself. What a wonderful disguise to frighten them. How they conjured nightmares out of thin air. So potent were these images and tales. They thrived on the fear. Killed themselves with it. It would come and go as this La Llorona because their small minds would easily surrender to it rather than surrender to themselves.

Rather than face the fact they are their worst nightmares.

Epilogue

While her wound healed, and unable to move with the frenetic energy of caring for the children and the home, she took her time with every task. Alejandra finally and purposefully made sure to be kind to herself. The children took every opportunity to help out and Alejandra, in turn, took every chance in the day to give them her affection.

One night after the children were in bed, Matthew approached her with a glass of wine. She shook her head. This had to be a sober conversation. "I'm glad you are feeling better. You seem happier. But I feel like you're avoiding me. I'm still your husband, aren't I?"

Everything she wanted to say to Matthew came out in that conversation, even the truths that hurt. Bruised egos heal; scarred souls are not so easily repaired. He promised to listen, and he did.

"I want out of this marriage," she said after everything was finally in the open.

It didn't come as a surprise to either of them.

He didn't beg for her to reconsider or try to ask why; he seemed more disgusted than hurt as he went into his study.

It was another weight off her soul. She could feel her heart expand a little more knowing she wouldn't have to live with his judgment. Life was too short. Her children would not be children forever. She could now better spend that time cherishing them and herself. Alejandra felt like pieces of cloud were descending into her body, filling her empty limbs with their divine ether, settling into her anatomy. It was a sensation of impending wholeness. Alejandra knew what it felt like to be brought back from the dead. There was also the heaviness of knowing the beginning of this new chapter meant the closing of another.

Five weeks after the incident in the bathtub, Alejandra knew something wasn't right. She and Matthew were attending the mini ceremonies and a concert that made up the last-day-of-school festivities. Little Elodia didn't want to sit still. She ran off at every opportunity, squealing in childish play, discovering her world, doing what children are meant to do. Fighting the urge to internalize the angry stares took more energy than running after a toddler. Alejandra only had the opportunity to see parts of Will's and Catrina's graduations. She reminded herself that this was okay. Matthew recorded both; she would watch them later.

They were still cordial as they began the process of separating themselves, if not friendly. By the time the four of them made it home, all she wanted to do was sleep. Exhaustion weighed heavy in her body, making every step more difficult than the last. She could feel her shoulders begin to sag along with her eyelids. Her bag fell off her shoulder onto the floor as soon as she walked through the front door. All three children ran past her to get snacks from the kitchen. Matthew remained in the car on a work call.

Seizing cramps made her lower abdomen feel like it would burst wide open. She swayed mercilessly in the middle of the foyer, nausea overwhelming her. She grabbed hold of the credenza to brace for another wave of pain before making her way to the bathroom on the second floor of the house. Alejandra pulled down her jeans and underwear to find her thighs covered in blood. Legs devoid of strength collapsed onto the toilet, the cramps stronger, more like contractions. She gritted her teeth, feeling something move inside of her until a slimy thick liquid slid from her vagina. Her thighs trembled, her knees nearly knocking together. Sweat rolled from her armpits and back. The crease beneath her breasts was slick with sweat.

Just as this placenta-like clot left her body, all her energy returned. She wanted to look down but was too afraid. There could only be one explanation. The creature had found a way back. She closed her eyes to find the women of her bloodline. For a moment her faith wavered; what if it was right and she didn't have the power to destroy it? No. Failure was not acceptable.

The ancestors were gone, this had to come from her—alone. Slowly she parted her thighs and opened her eyes. Her breathing quivered from her nostrils with her heart beating too fast to count. Floating in the round body of toilet water, a ceramic cenote, clotted blood the size of a fist giggled and gurgled. The bloody mass throbbed, croaked obscenities. One sharp flint barb emerged from the side. An eye snapped open in the center. It radiated gamma ray hatred. Alejandra jumped off the toilet in fright as the thing seemed alive—wanting to live again.

The demon had been metastasizing inside of her body, eating

her eggs slowly. It stared back at her in the flesh. Alejandra's anger swelled followed by the satisfaction of seeing the curse so helpless. It was within her grasp. *In her grasp.*

She reached into the toilet, grabbing the one-eyed clot. She brought it close to her face and looked deep into its one pathetic eye. Nothing. Not even the spirit of the heavens and all its stardust glory could be seen. Nothing good remained from its origin. "Your time is over. Go in peace, never to return." Alejandra squeezed the mass until her knuckles went white. In her mind she said a prayer for it, for her ancestors, for her children, and for herself. A slow fizzing noise resembling a scream screeched from the clot the longer she held it.

"You are nothing to me," she whispered. Blood and tissue oozed from between her fingers until she heard a loud pop. It broke. The heaviness of sorrow, all the resentment she still held in the marrow of her being lifted, and she felt light. Alejandra let go of the remnants in her hands and flushed it down the toilet. Not a trace was left when the whirlpool of water settled. She washed her hands of blood until only the light fragrance of the soap remained. Her heartbeat returned to normal.

She allowed herself to cry one last time over the sink, a tribute to La Llorona, one of the many misunderstood women roaming the Earth, stuck between worlds, passing on curses they may or may not understand. And, as she'd found out when she met her birth father, men have their own toxic curses. The ripples of unresolved pain dissolved like invisible stitches. How many of these demons wandered the earth causing pain and death, feeding on the fragility of humans? How had any of it begun? Was it the only one or were there many more?

In that moment, the question she asked herself nearly every day since she could remember was answered. Why was she even born? It crossed her mind the times she listened to Soundgar-

den at school in the quad without a friend and in the stolen moments she cried in the shower when her period was at her worst.

She had been born to kill this demon. Someone had to end
the cycle. A sense of calm filled her from the pit of her uterus to
the crown of her head. Break the curses. Feed your soul.

In the bathroom she also answered another question. She
knew what she wanted to do, and it involved Melanie. Alejandra
ran downstairs to her phone to send her a message.

Hi, Melanie. I have an odd question. I know you will answer
honestly. Will you teach me the ways of the curandera? If there
are more out there feeding on other people, I want to help. I
want to give others some of this light because it is bursting from
me. I also plan on writing about my experience.

Melanie typed back straightaway.

I would be honored to do this. The more we share our light, the
brighter this world can become. However, I can no longer be
your therapist if we do this. Why don't you come by tomorrow
and we can discuss the details?

Alejandra could not contain the sense of something falling
into place at the right time.

In the glass door leading to the backyard Alejandra caught
her reflection.

*No one has ever seen you. Not your family, friends, lovers, even
your children. For the longest time I didn't. I see you now. I see you
like no one else because we are one and the same and forever will
be. And I adore you.*

She had become a medicine for herself, and her story could
be the medicine for others.

READ ON FOR A PREVIEW OF
V. CASTRO'S NEW NOVEL

Immortal Pleasures

An ancient Aztec vampire roams the modern world in search of vengeance and love in this seductive dark fantasy from the author of *The Haunting of Alejandra*.

Chapter One

It's my last night in Dublin before I head to the south coast. Ireland was the first stop on my way to London because of its landscape, particularly its grass—that dreamy electric green, surrounded by dark cold waters and even colder winds.

That landscape had called to me while I was flipping through an airline magazine during one of my business class flights across South America. The advertisement had showed a green pasture that ended with a cliff dropping to leaping waves in the shape of giant conch shells. I had to see that grass with my own eyes, feel it beneath my feet.

You see, my name is Malinalli, which means grass in my native Nahuatl language. The glossy photo ignited my soul with wonder, and I knew I had to overcome my irrational fear of exploring this part of the world, Europe. It was a European who changed my given name Malinalli to La Malinche and Doña Marina. Neither did I choose, nor could I refuse as a human. At least as a vampire I could take back my name. Small steps.

But you may wonder why a Nahua vampire from the sixteenth century like me would harbor a fear of anything after being an apex predator for so very long. After all, my blood is powerful and intoxicating—it comes from a vampire made by one of the very first vampires. However, like the demolished temple Tenochtitlán, my heart still bore the scars of history.

Before this trip was even an idea, my concentration on work had been waning. I kept finding myself slipping into daydreams of distant places. My heart would sink to depths of emotion I could not allow myself to wade in. In train stations and airports, I used to walk with a smug swagger past couples if I saw an obviously out-of-sync partnership, and past families if I saw screaming children throwing themselves at the feet of exhausted parents. *Ain't no one holding me down or holding me back,* I'd think. But recently I'd also think soon after: *Ain't no one waiting for me either.* Walk enough crowded terminals alone, your hand swinging aimlessly by your side, and it starts to feel dead. And mine had hung empty for centuries. I could care less about the offspring. As a vampire, my bearing a child was not an option. But lately I'd wanted to feel an arm around my waist. A companionship that lasted longer than a night would be nice.

Two days after the idea of traveling to Ireland first struck me, I received an out-of-the-blue opportunity to purchase rare Mexican artifacts from a dealer in Ireland. I am a collector, buyer, and seller of antiquities from all over the world; however, my specialty is Mexico and South and Central America. As a blood huntress it was a natural fit.

Since 1972, I had made my living tracking rare objects, although I began my search for these objects long before I'd ever earned a cent. My career had begun not as a career but as a sort of spiteful secret mission to reclaim our culture's lost treasures one object at a time from the colonizers. The more I learned about my new vampire life and all its strengths, the more I thought about my purpose in life. My work has given me purpose beyond servitude or mere survival. I could create some good for myself and others.

The artifacts are two skulls I first encountered when I was still human. When I read the email and saw the photos of the skulls, the excitement in my work that I'd lost came back, and I nearly jumped out of my skin. My instinct told me that these were the very same treasures I had been hunting for since I began my journey in acquiring antiquities. One skull is carved from pure, clear quartz. The other is an embellished mosaic of turquoise and obsidian set in a human skull with most of the teeth still intact. Judging from the photo, the gold that once plated the human skull had been scraped from the bone.

The skulls had once belonged to someone I loved dearly. Her name was Chantico. She was like a mother to me when I first became a vampire. She helped me find the will to live for myself.

I had been searching for centuries for these skulls with no luck, and I'd been on the brink of giving up on ever finding them. It wasn't until the birth of the internet that my journey began to gain a little momentum, though every path had led to a dead end until now. However, life can be as unpredictable as the height of waves crashing on a shore; now, at long last, the skulls were within my reach. The universe presented me the perfect opportunity to act on my desire to reclaim these treasures.

So I simply had to fly across the Atlantic to purchase those skulls and keep them safe. The catch was the skulls were now in London with a private collector. But this purchase was too important to leave to chance, to buy on the evidence of digital photographs alone, even if the photos I'd been emailed appeared legitimate. My usual London-based antiquities broker, Horatio Hutchings, a trustworthy man in the business, assured me it was not a scam. However, he did not possess the same skill that I did in detecting forged objects—and I had seen my fair share in my many centuries of existence. To reclaim the skulls—and with them, a part of my soul—I had to take the trip. And that trip would be first-class all the way, including the best hotels. Everything paid by the business I had built from scratch and the antiquities I'd acquired over time. I deserved to have everything I wanted in this life. Divine timing can be a stubborn bitch, but when she comes through, she delivers divine rewards.

And so, eager to finally possess the skulls and with a nagging desire to travel, I created a four-week itinerary to explore Ireland and England at the same time. Spain would be the next place I'd visit—where perhaps I could finally lay my anger at its colonizers to rest—and finally Vienna, Austria, to see the Penancho, a rare surviving Aztec headdress, bright green and feathered, that didn't belong halfway around the world from its country of origin, in a museum for people who could not fully appreciate its true importance. Indeed, part of my mission has been to reach out to museums around the world and broker deals to give back stolen items to their original cultures. The treasures can then go on tour or on loan to museums in other lands; however, sole ownership belongs to the people who created them. That particular headdress had long been on my radar. I figured that my kind emails to the museum were not doing enough, and that my power of persuasion in the flesh could serve me better. After years of practice, vampires can use their energy to influence the emotions of humans. We can't force them to do something, just steer them toward what we want from them. I was not opposed to using my vampire magnetism to get what I wanted, and I wanted this headdress back in Mexico City.

In my human life, as a translator, I'd watched villages and temples be sacked by the conquistadors. The terror and sorrow at one's powerlessness to stop the destruction of one's home were something no one should experience or witness. And with the treasures of our past stolen, our children would grow up without anything to remind them of their history or story. The children of Europe had no tie to this object and could only see it at best as a unique piece of history of a people they could not fully understand, but more than likely, as just a nice artifact with pretty feathers from a bird they had never seen before. But the headdress had the potential to instill pride and awe in my people if returned to its rightful place in Mexico. And that is exactly what I was going to do. The Hapsburg Archduke Ferdinand II was long dead—what would he care if an item he acquired out of imperialist greed was taken back?

And as soon as I landed on the distant cool shores of Ireland, I knew I'd made the right choice. Even the sight of the drizzle on the small window as we landed excited me. An undercurrent of expectation made my body alert to every sensation and sight. The climate in Ireland differs greatly from my home. Although it was summer in Ireland, there was always a damp chill in the evening air. What a change from the heat I'm accustomed to! This was exactly why I'd made the decision to cross the pond to explore the Old World. My trip would be a gust of change to rid myself of my inner demons—and perhaps introduce me to a few new ones along the way, just for laughs.

All this to reclaim the freedom once stolen from me back when I was a mortal. Imagine going from "Will this be the day I die as a slave?" to becoming the very embodiment of death. And now I wanted to appease the restlessness that had settled over me the last few years. I am worth millions, but as life has shown me, cash only goes so far in creating a fulfilling life.

And so on this trip I felt open to the unexpected. Perhaps destiny had even brought me across the pond for a reason beyond the skulls. Part of me wanted to believe that Chantico watched me from wherever her spirit hovered and sent me a blessing of joy.

V. CASTRO is a two-time Bram Stoker Award–nominated Mexican American writer from San Antonio, Texas, now living in the United Kingdom. As a full-time mother she dedicates her time to her family and to writing Latinx narratives in horror, erotic horror, and science fiction. Her most recent releases include *Aliens: Vasquez, Mestiza Blood, The Queen of the Cicadas, Goddess of Filth,* and *The Haunting of Alejandra.*

www.vcastrostories.com
Twitter: @vlatinalondon
Instagram: @vlatinalondon
TikTok: @vcastrobooks
Find V. Castro on Goodreads and Amazon

ABOUT THE TYPE

This book was set in Minion, a 1990 Adobe Originals typeface by Robert Slimbach (b. 1956). Minion is inspired by classical, old-style typefaces of the late Renaissance, a period of elegant, beautiful, and highly readable type designs. Created primarily for text setting, Minion combines the aesthetic and functional qualities that make text type highly readable with the versatility of digital technology.

DISCOVER MORE FROM
DEL REY &
RANDOM HOUSE WORLDS!

READ EXCERPTS
from hot new titles.

STAY UP-TO-DATE
on your favorite authors.

FIND OUT about exclusive
giveaways and sweepstakes.

CONNECT WITH US ONLINE!
⊙ f 𝕏 @DelReyBooks

DelReyBooks.com
RandomHouseWorlds.com